FIRE

POINT

A NOVEL BY

JOHN SMOLENS

FIRE

POINT

Michigan State University Press | *East Lansing*

♾ The paper used in this publication meets the minimum requirements of
ANSI/NISO Z39.48-1992 (R 1997) (Permanence of Paper).

 Michigan State University Press
East Lansing, Michigan 48823-5245

Printed and bound in the United States of America.

26 25 24 23 22 21 20 19 18 17   1 2 3 4 5 6 7 8 9 10

Originally published by Crown/Random House, Inc., 2004

Permission to use the poem "North," from *The Shape of the Journey*, granted by
Jim Harrison.

LIBRARY OF CONGRESS CATALOGING-IN-PUBLICATION DATA
Names: Smolens, John, author.

Title: Fire point : a novel / by John Smolens.
Description: East Lansing : Michigan State University Press, [2017]
Identifiers: LCCN 2016034152| ISBN 9781611862423 (pbk. : alk. paper) | ISBN
  9781609175245 (pdf) | ISBN 9781628952940 (epub) | ISBN 9781628962949
  (kindle)
Subjects: LCSH: Dwellings—Conservation and restoration—Fiction. | Rejection
  (Psychology)—Fiction. | Superior, Lake, Region—Fiction. |
  Michigan—Fiction. | Revenge—Fiction. | Psychological fiction. | GSAFD:
  Suspense fiction. | Love stories.
Classification: LCC PS3569.M646 F57 2017 | DDC 813/.54—dc23
LC record available at https://lccn.loc.gov/2016034152

Cover design by David Drummond, Salamander Design, www.salamanderhill.com.

Cover image is a detail from a photo of a bonfire on the shores of Lake Superior in
Northern Michigan and is used under license from Jason Patrick Ross/Shutterstock.
com.

g green press INITIATIVE Michigan State University Press is a member of the Green Press Initiative and is
committed to developing and encouraging ecologically responsible publishing
practices. For more information about the Green Press Initiative and the use of recycled
paper in book publishing, please visit www.greenpressinitiative.org.

Visit Michigan State University Press at *www.msupress.org*

To Peter, Elizabeth, and Michael

Having fulfilled

my obligations

my heart moves lightly

to this downward dance.

————

JIM HARRISON

"NORTH"

Fire point: The lowest temperature at which a volatile liquid, after its vapors have been ignited, will give off vapors at a rate sufficient to sustain combustion.

PART I

1

IF HE HAD A RELIGION, it was that things in this world ought to be plumb, level, and square. He was forty-four and had lived his entire life in Whitefish Harbor, in Michigan's Upper Peninsula, a village on a hilly node of land that juts into Lake Superior. His full name was Joseph Pearl Blankenship Jr. To distinguish him from his father, a Canadian ore boat crewman who was washed overboard during a squall in November 1956, his mother always called him Pearly. Her maiden name was Janet Hanninen. Her mother was Ojibwa; her father, a Finnish miner. She died violently, too, in the spring of 1974. While driving home from Marquette in a blizzard, a cement truck veered into her lane and hit her Ford Fairlane head-on. Pearly was only comforted by the fact that the impact was so great, there was no time for her brain to register pain as her body was thrust into the backseat by the car's engine; however, he was certain that there had been a moment—the notorious split second—when she was horrified by the sight of the oncoming truck.

Sometimes Pearly believed he could see them both, his mother, crushed and bloodied beyond recognition, and his father, bloated and adrift in the deep, cold waters of Lake Superior. He was convinced that they still resided where they had died. His father was in the better place. After his death his mother became a taciturn, bitter woman, and, not surprisingly, a drinker. Pearly hoped that if his father could find refuge at the bottom of his beloved Lake Superior, his mother, at the very least, might be allowed her tumbler of whiskey, her chaser of beer. Because of the way his parents had died, he suspected that he, too, would die violently.

He knew what people thought of him and, to put it politely, he didn't care. He was a loner, but then it had always been a Yooper's privilege to be left in peace. If he hadn't lived in his dead mother's house, he'd have had difficulty keeping a roof over his head. His jobs were mostly seasonal; long spells during the winter months you'd find him mid-afternoon in the Hiawatha Diner or, more likely, the Portage, one of the bars along Ottawa Street. If there was a problem, something that might involve the police, the first name that came to mind was Pearly. Yet some, particularly older folks, also knew that he frequented the public library. And to be fair, he was a good house carpenter. If he repaired a roof, it wouldn't leak; if he hung a door, it wouldn't stick. If he had a philosophy, it was that things in this world ought to be plumb, level, and square, but seldom are.

2

HANNAH LECLAIRE CLIMBED the steep path carved in the bluff overlooking Lake Superior. She was nineteen, her legs were strong again, and she liked to walk, even on such overcast afternoons, when the damp east wind could make April seem colder than January. From below she could hear the pounding of the breakers on the rocks. She reached the top of the bluff, walked through woods toward the old house, and paused at the edge of the backyard. The property was in miserable condition: cracked and split clapboards with peeling white paint, broken windowpanes, mullions in need of glazing, black shutters sagging of their own weight.

Something was different this time. Hannah noticed that the back door was ajar, and she waded through chest-high weeds toward the house. She squeezed through the door sideways and entered a dim kitchen. Plaster crackled beneath her boots as she moved through the rooms on the first floor. There was a powerful smell—the scent of animal decay—which caused her to hold her wool scarf over her nose and mouth. She tried going out the front door, but it wouldn't open, so she decided to return to the kitchen. Halfway down the front hall she stopped and let out a gasp as a man stepped out from the shadows beneath the staircase.

"That stink is really something," he said. There was the slightest gleam and she realized she was looking at the roundness of the man's skull.

"What is it?" she asked.

"Dead cats." He took another step toward her—he was tall and lean, his head was shaved, and a trim mustache seemed to give his face definition. He might have been ten years older than she was, and he kept his hands visible as if to show that he wasn't dangerous.

"Whose cats?" she said.

"Vivian Pence's—the last of the family line," he said. "Seems she had a house full of cats, I suspect." His eyes were pale blue and he was wearing an old overcoat, dark wool, knee-length, with the collar turned up.

"What are you doing here?"

"That's just what I've been asking myself," he said. "You've been here before?"

She hesitated. "I walk here a lot. The back door—I never noticed that it was open before." He smiled, which she took to mean that he was responsible. "The house is condemned," she said. "They're going to tear it down."

"Who is?"

"The town, or maybe it was the county—there was a piece in the paper." She raised her eyes to the hall ceiling. Large sections of plaster were missing, exposing wood lath beneath. "It's sad. Something should be done."

"Someone would have to buy it, then invest a lot of time," he said. "And money."

"I remember coming here on Halloween. All the kids were afraid of the old woman—Vivian Pence. So naturally we wanted to come up here and see inside. That was ten years ago. The last time I was in this house I was nine."

"What were you when you were nine?"

"A gypsy, I think."

"That makes you, what, nineteen? I thought you were older."

Hannah wanted to explain—she wanted to say that she should have graduated from high school last year, with the class of '95. But she didn't, and he nodded his head once—it seemed like an old-fashioned gesture of courtesy—and walked into the kitchen and out the back door.

She suddenly felt weak and sat on the bottom step of the staircase. Her heart was beating fast, and for a moment she could only stare at a knot in the worn tread. Raising her head, she watched as the man passed by the window above the stairs. Quickly, she went out through the kitchen door and up the overgrown driveway. He was climbing into a gray car, something vintage but well maintained, something European. He rolled down the window and said, "A lift in to the village?"

She hesitated.

"I understand," he said.

She walked across the gravel and got in the car; it had bucket seats, black leather that smelled rich and creaked beneath her. When he turned on the ignition, the engine rumbled deeply. She watched his hand work the stick shift—the knob looked like it was made from ivory.

"What is this? Looks like it belongs in a black-and-white movie."

"It's a Mercedes."

He put the car in gear and drove halfway down the hill, where he pulled over to the side of the road. "Ever drive a standard?" For some reason the question seemed incredibly personal. Before she could answer, he said, "Care to learn? Not here on the hill, but in the parking lot by the harbor—that would be perfect. No traffic. Not until you get the hang of it, working the clutch and stick."

She could see that his skull was covered with fine black stubble. His eyes were direct yet acquiescent. "How old are you?" she asked.

"Old enough to give a driving lesson."

"Are you thirty?"

"I will be next winter. Why?"

"I should get home. It'll be dark soon."

"All right. Perhaps another time."

———————

MARTIN REED'S MOTHER was from Whitefish Harbor, so since he was a boy he had been coming north from Chicago to visit relatives. When he was eleven his mother died of cancer, his aunt Alice quit her job with an insurance agency and moved into the house in Winnetka. She had never married and had no children. Like Martin's father, she believed in work and she approached raising her nephew as though it were a job. She cooked, cleaned the house, did the laundry. Her fierce efficiency nearly concealed her tenderness for Martin.

During his visits to the U.P. he often listened to aunts and uncles at night in the kitchen. They'd talk about the mines, about ships on Lake Superior, and always about the weather. Compared to Winnetka, Illinois, the U.P. seemed a heroic, even mythical place. He used to walk or ride his bike all over this little peninsula and he knew every inlet in Petit Marais, which meant "small marsh" and was the shallow water that embraced the west side of Whitefish Harbor.

Now that Alice had died, his mother's other sister, Aunt Jane, was the last of the U.P. clan. Her health was so poor that she couldn't travel from her condominium in Florida; she couldn't even manage the flight up to Chicago for Alice's funeral. The ceremony was small because most of Alice's friends had already died. The day after she was buried, Martin learned from her lawyer that she'd left him $40,000. But there were stipulations, which didn't surprise him because Alice had always been a great believer in stipulations: She placed them on the food he ate, the time he had to be home, where he could go, what he could do. Once, while she was in the kitchen folding laundry, she said, "If you get anything from me, it'll be an appreciation that in life there are always stipulations." Her stipulation now, in death, was that Martin could use the money only when he married or bought a house. This made perfect sense, coming from a woman who had never done either.

LATE AFTERNOONS MARTIN took to waiting for Hannah to return from school. He would park on one of the side streets above Frenchman's Channel, the deep bay to the east of the harbor, and watch for the school bus to come out to the village. He usually had Cokes in the car that he'd bought at the Hiawatha Diner. At first all Hannah knew about him was that he was from Chicago. She really didn't want to know much more about him, because that would only invite questions about her own past.

They would drive to the parking lot above the harbor, which at this time of year was usually as empty as it was long. Hannah would sit in the driver's seat, working the gears, and she couldn't believe how splendid it felt. She only ground the gears occasionally, but he was very patient, even when she stalled out. "Let's go somewhere," she said during the third lesson.

"Think you're ready?" he asked, and she nodded. "All right, take Shore Road and we'll go all the way around the peninsula."

She liked working the clutch and shifting as the car went in and out of curves in the narrow road.

After a couple of miles, Martin said, "Pull into this road and stop in the second driveway on the left." When they were parked in the drive, he opened his door. "Come on in for a minute. I've got Cokes, then we'll get you back to the village."

"You live here?"

"Belongs to my aunt Jane. Come on—I want you to meet someone." He walked away, and after a moment she got out of the car.

The cabin was small, but next to the kitchenette there was a sliding glass door with a view across Petit Marais toward wooded hills. He got her a Coke from the refrigerator, a bottle of beer for himself. A large gray cat sat at the edge of the sink and he stroked the back of its head.

"This is Gracie," he said. "I want to ask you a favor. One of my other aunts, Alice, died recently and I have to go down to Chicago to deal with some legal matters. I was wondering if you'd check on the place for me while I'm gone. Gracie will need food and water, and I know she'd like the company."

"When will you be back?"

"Four, five days."

She sipped her Coke and stared out the sliding glass door. The deck was badly weathered, except for several new boards in the floor, which were pale as flesh. "Did you replace those?"

"Yes." For the first time since she'd known him he seemed uncertain, even awkward. "I could pay you ten dollars a day."

"That's not necessary."

"It'd only be fair."

Hannah suspected there was more to this trip than a visit to a lawyer, but she didn't want to ask. A job. A girlfriend. Maybe even a wife. "I'll be glad to take care of Gracie, but not for pay. I like cats."

EACH AFTERNOON HANNAH walked from the bus stop in the village out to Martin's cabin. Though it was a couple of miles, she liked the walk. Occasionally boys from school would slow down in their cars and offer her a ride, but she turned them down. The cabin was her secret; walking there, Hannah imagined she was someone else, someone—an adult—with a mysterious past, not a high-school senior. Because she should have graduated the year before, her classmates this year pretty much left her alone. Some boys, however, watched her, looking for encouragement. They knew about her, and their eyes were often crude.

At the cabin Gracie would climb in Hannah's lap when she sat in the leather reading chair. The cat liked to be stroked behind the ears and down the spine. She would purr as her claws worked into Hannah's skirt, sometimes hooking into her thighs. On the bookshelf next to the chair was a stack of old histories of Lake Superior and the Upper Peninsula, several with marked passages that referred to Vivian Pence's house. In the hallway Martin had moved a door to one of the bedrooms and there was a section of wall that was covered with new Sheetrock, taped and joined but still unpainted. He was tidy—she could see where he'd swept sawdust off the floor, and his tools were neatly stored in boxes and white plastic buckets. What she liked most were his calculations and measurements, the tiny, precise figures written on scraps of wood, some of which were down to "1/16 shy."

Friday was one of the first warm days of the year, and when she arrived at the cabin, Hannah looked in the refrigerator and found that there were no more Cokes. She opened one of the beers. It had been over a year, and she drank this beer down fast as she watched Gracie eat. She drank another beer, this one slowly, while standing at the screen in the open sliding glass door. Sunlight filled the cottage, making her drowsy. She finished the beer, went into the bedroom, lay down, and fell asleep with the cat.

She dreamed again that her feet were painfully caught in the stirrups, and the doctor kept telling her to hold still. When she awoke suddenly, she was aware of Gracie's absence. Raising her head, she saw Martin, standing in the doorway. He wore sunglasses. She started to get up but then realized that she was soaked with sweat and was chilled.

"Stay put," he said. He took the blanket from the rocking chair, came to the bed, and spread it over her. "You were having a nightmare, I guess."

"I had to leave school last year." Her voice was shaking and she was afraid that she would start to cry. "God, why can't I get *past* this?"

"You will." He took off his sunglasses. His eyes were different. There was something in them she hadn't seen before. They weren't crude, but there was a longing, and she could see that he was embarrassed by it. "How about if I made you some tea?" But he didn't move.

She took her arm out from beneath the blanket and reached for his hand. He held it tightly, then knelt on the floor and laid his head on her lap. She ran her other hand over his scalp as she sobbed.

They slept, both fully clothed; he remained outside the blanket. When Hannah awoke she could recall no dream, and Gracie was curled up between their knees.

"Feeling better?" he whispered.

"Yes. Why are you—what are those history books for?"

"Research," he said. "I'm thinking of buying Vivian Pence's place."

"You're staying, then," she said. "I didn't think you would."

"I wasn't sure either. That's part of why I went to Chicago. To see if there was something to go back to."

"A job. Carpentry, something like that?"

"I was working for a guy who builds condos. I wouldn't exactly call it carpentry."

"And there was a girl?"

"Turned out that was the easy part." He smiled and she believed him. "While you were sleeping, you said . . ." He touched her face with his hand. "What happened to the boy?"

"Joined the army," she said.

Though she turned her head away, his hand remained on her cheek.

HANNAH'S MOTHER, Suzanne, was a nurse at Marquette General Hospital and she was planning to attend a conference in Detroit the following weekend. Hannah and Martin agreed that after school on Friday she would go home and pack a small suitcase. That evening Martin pulled his car up in front of the house. When she got in the front seat, he said, "You know, we could go somewhere for the weekend."

"Oh, sure—someplace exotic, like Green Bay. Or maybe Duluth?"

Though it was nearly dark, he was wearing his sunglasses. He wore them often since she had said they made him look cool. "No, the thought of you staying with me till Sunday is—it's been driving me nuts all week."

"Me, too." She laughed, then put her arm around his shoulders and kissed his neck.

"We'll be able to have breakfast together," he said. "How do you like your eggs?"

"In bed."

In bed Hannah told Martin about how since eighth grade, when she'd begun to develop hips and breasts, boys had paid attention to her. They looked at her eagerly, and she knew that her body was a source of jokes, of remarks. Girls also took notice. In the shower after gym class sometimes girls would glance at her as though in awe. They'd make jokes, too, but more often, particularly once they were in high school, they'd warn her to keep away from the boys they liked.

The boy's name was Sean Colby. He played football, he was funny in class, he hung out with the neatest group of guys in school. She started going with him and quickly found herself in a crowd of kids who seemed to drink and smoke dope all the time. The following summer, when she discovered she was pregnant, she actually thought that it was a good thing. She imagined herself quitting school—which she had come to dislike intensely—and going off to college with her new husband. Colleges and universities had family housing, and she imagined them living there, raising the baby while Sean studied something like marketing or pre-law—not criminal justice, because he had made it clear he had no interest ending up a small-town cop like his father. When she told Sean her period was late, he was stunned, but he said something about how it could be worked out. That's what he said: *We could work it out.* But when it was certain that she was pregnant, everything changed. She wouldn't see him for days, and when she did he was distant, uncertain. Finally, he told her his parents were furious, and his father had decided that Sean needed to get straightened out.

"So he enlisted," Martin said.

"He's in the Mediterranean—Italy, I think."

"Your mother, what'd she do?"

"She arranged to have it taken care of. Sean's parents paid for it. Last time I saw Officer Colby, he and his wife were sitting at our kitchen table writing a check to my mother." Hannah stared at the ceiling for a long moment. The room was lit only by candles, and shadows danced on the walls. "There were complications, and I missed so much school I had to repeat senior year."

"You're an outcast," he said.

"They hardly speak to me, except for some boy who wants to get his hands on me. Some of them tape anonymous notes with drawings to my locker. It's a small town and now I'm the town slut." She sat against the headboard, pulling the blankets up over her shoulders. "This is the first time—first time I've dated since then."

"When you graduate, what would you like to do—leave the U.P.?"

"I don't know."

"College?"

"Haven't applied."

"What happened to your father?"

"He left when I was two. Mom just says he found a job out west."

"You're not interested in college?"

"I'm not interested in school, right now. I know a lot of people my age leave the U.P. after graduating, but I've been here all my life, and the fact is I like it. Even though I'm an outcast, as you say. . . ."

"What's the matter? Tell me."

"Now we have histories."

"They're unavoidable," he said. "What do you want, Hannah?"

"I don't know. I just know I *don't* want to end up like my mother—tired and raising a kid on my own. That's why I agreed to it."

3

PLACES LIKE WHITEFISH HARBOR send kids like Sean Colby out into the world after high school. They go to college, they enlist in the service. The local newspaper prints their photographs and reports their accomplishments, degrees, scholarships, or promotions in rank. Then they take jobs, in Chicago, Detroit, Minneapolis; they marry; they return less and less each year as family and obligations engulf them. The world had, in effect, accepted them, and family and friends back home felt proud and perhaps a little envious.

But Sean Colby went out, and then returned suddenly—it was as though he'd been rejected, sent back by the world due to some flaw or defect. Just ten months after he went off to boot camp, he flew into Green Bay, Wisconsin, and took the bus north to the Upper Penin-sula. Hung over, Sean slept during most of the five-hour trip, only occasionally opening his eyes to see where he was—Iron Mountain, Ishpeming, Negaunee—and each time he was confronted by the face of a boy hovering above the seat in front of him. The kid was four, or maybe he was six; Sean was just nineteen himself and wasn't very good at determining the age of children.

When the bus finally arrived in Marquette, Sean sat up and saw that the boy's brown eyes were still gazing at the pins on his uniform. "Would you like one of these?" he asked.

The boy's mouth hung open, and when he inhaled there was the sound of snot clogging nasal passages. He nodded his head.

"Why don't you pick one?"

Reluctantly, the boy lifted his hand off the back of the seat and pressed a finger against Sean's chest.

"This pin? You like this one? It means I was a sharpshooter." He removed the pin from his uniform. The boy's mother turned around and looked over her seat at him. She was in her mid-twenties, overweight, and had limp blond hair. "You mind if he has this?" Sean asked.

"You can do that, just give him one of those medals off your uniform, eh?"

It had been a while since he'd heard a Yooper accent. "I'd be happy to give it to him," he said. "Okay?"

"You betcha," she said.

Sean carefully fastened the pin to the front of the boy's Packers T-shirt. "I won't be needing it anymore."

"Jason. What do you say to the soldier?" Snot ran out of the boy's right nostril. "Jason?" the mother said.

The kid lowered his eyes and muttered, "Thank you."

Sean said, "You're welcome, Jason."

The boy looked up as though he'd been rewarded. Then his mother got up and began to gather their bags. The boy was staring down at his pin, the snot now streaming over his upper lip. Sean took a handkerchief from his pocket and watched the woman. When she bent over to pick up something, he swiped the boy's face with the handkerchief. The kid was taken by surprise and his eyes were suddenly confused and alarmed—they began to tear up. Sean leaned forward, putting his face within inches of the boy's, and whispered, "You keep those boogers out of *sight*."

He sat back quickly and smiled as the woman straightened up, loaded with bags on both arms. She thanked Sean and then guided the boy up the aisle toward the front of the bus.

Sean waited as the other passengers got off. Across the parking lot he could see his mother's Ford. He knew she was sitting there behind the wheel, staring at the bus, sucking on one of her menthols. She would have come alone, while his father stayed at home—and she'd make some excuse, probably about his being tired from work. Then she'd try to touch him and say, "Sean, it's good to have you home, no matter what." She'd have to throw in something like "no matter what." It wasn't possible to just be happy to see him. With his mother everything was a burden, and she'd have to declare it immediately so that it was there between them, where she could use it.

BY EARLY MAY Martin usually let Hannah drive the Mercedes. They were on the stretch of Shore Road that ran above Petit Marais—even with the windows opened, he could still smell the French fries they'd eaten in the car. As they rounded a bend in the road, a police car came into view, parked on the side of the road by a stand of pines. She downshifted and took the next curve slowly, but soon the cruiser appeared in the side-view mirror, blue lights flashing. She pulled over to the side of the road and the cruiser stopped behind them.

She looked in the rearview mirror and said, "I knew it. It's Colby."

"It's all right." Martin dug the car registration out of the glove compartment.

Officer Colby walked up to the car, leaned down to her open window, pushing his reflector sunglasses back against the bridge of his nose. His face was wide and blunt, and his shave was so close that his cheeks had a faint sheen. "Hannah, this isn't your car." Then, reaching across for the registration, he said to Martin, "Of course not. And you are . . . her uncle?"

"I'm sorry," she said, removing her license from her wallet and holding it up to Colby. "I might have taken that corner a little fast."

"You should know these roads don't get any straighter because you're driving a Mercedes-Benz." Colby glanced at the registration for a moment as though it were an insult to his intelligence. "Martin Reed. Twenty-nine. Chicago, Illinois. Aren't you up here on vacation a bit early?"

"I just moved up here."

"I wonder what would bring you here in the off-season?" Colby sniffed and almost smiled. "The French fries?"

Martin didn't answer.

The officer's expression didn't change. "You say you're living here? Mind if I ask where, since it's not indicated on your registration?"

"Not at all," Martin said. "Jane Kendall's, on Blue Heron Road. She's my aunt."

Colby nodded as he took the license from Hannah's fingers. He straightened up and walked back to his cruiser.

Martin said, "The 'uncle' bit was a nice touch."

She looked like she was about to cry and he took her hand, which was trembling. They sat without talking for several minutes, then she put both hands on the wheel as Colby approached the car again. He leaned down and handed her a slip. "I'm only giving you a warning, Hannah." Then, speaking across to Martin, he said, "You get a Michigan license and registration if you plan on staying up here, Mr. Reed, and I'd suggest you be careful about letting teenaged girls drive this fine old car."

ALL SMALL TOWNS need a Frank Colby, because all small towns have a Pearly Blankenship. Colby explained this to Pearly early one morning when he was nineteen years old. Needless to say, Pearly had had a few. Colby had stopped him shortly after he'd put a twenty-two-pound walleye on Judge Emmett Anderson's front porch. It was 1971 and the judge had recently given stiff fines and probation sentences to several dozen people in Marquette County. They had all been found guilty of possession of marijuana, based on the testimony of a bearded guy who called himself Rainbow and had been hanging around Whitefish Harbor all summer. Pearly spotted Rainbow for a narc and avoided him, so he didn't get hauled before the judge.

Colby was certain Pearly had put the fish on the judge's porch but couldn't prove it. It was tough to get fingerprints off a fish. For the next twenty-five years, most anything that went wrong, any of the frequent petty crimes—a "hijacked" sailboat (discovered adrift to the east, off the mouth of the Two-Hearted River), cut fishnets, headstones overturned in the graveyard, the flagpole stolen from in front of the town hall—Colby ascribed to Pearly Blankenship. Pearly wished he could take credit for some of these transgressions, which were the work of kids who were terminally bored in a town with an off-season that lasts nine and a half months. In truth, Pearly could only claim responsibility for the walleye and the flagpole. An oak mast, it had stood in front of town hall since the last days of the square-riggers. He took it down with his chainsaw but could not have transported it to safe hiding without the assistance of the DeJohn bothers, Peter and Michael, and their fishing trawler, *Elizabeth Anne*. Some suspected that this act of larceny had political connotations, considering that it occurred in April 1975, when the Americans pulled out of Saigon.

"I've always been curious," Frank Colby said to Pearly, years later. "What did you do with that flagpole?"

"What flagpole?"

It was one of the many times Colby had hauled him into the station, a snowy night in February, sometime after two A.M. Because of the weather, Colby decided not to drive Pearly over to the county jail in Marquette. Instead Colby would "invite" him to spend the night at the station, where he could sleep it off in the back room. Colby had been working on something, a report, and he looked up from his typewriter, his eyes bored, noncommittal. Pearly knew this was intended to conceal his anger.

"What is it with you, Pearly?"

"What do you mean?"

"Is this it? Is this going to be your *life*?"

"I feel I'm necessary."

"Really? How so?"

"All small towns need a Pearly Blankenship, to make a Frank Colby necessary."

"Is that a fact?"

"Must be," Pearly said. "You told me so."

"I did?"

"I'll never forget it."

"Thanks for reminding me."

"It's your little nugget of wisdom and you deserve all the credit for it."

Colby busied himself by typing a few words, then stopped. "I'm serious. Does anything matter to you?"

"Frank, are we going to engage in a philosophical discussion?"

Colby took his hands off the keys of the typewriter and leaned back in the swivel chair. "Why not? Weather's awful. We got all night."

"True," Pearly said. "Neither of us is going anywhere."

Colby seemed faintly disgusted.

"Since I'm here by 'invitation,' what's to stop me from walking out the door?"

"Nothing," Colby said. "Not a thing."

"But just try it and we drive to Marquette, despite the weather."

"You know, you're not like some of the others."

"Like what others?"

"Like, say, the DeJohn brothers."

"How are they?"

"Slightly brighter than the fish they catch." He raised a hand before Pearly could launch into a defense of the DeJohns. "I was talking with Ena Stanton outside the library the other day and your name came up. She said that except for old Mary Latvala, nobody checks out more books at the library than you do."

Pearly smiled.

"I say something funny?"

"No. I like to read. Is that a crime?"

"You have the moral and civic responsibility of—" Colby paused here and a small crease developed in his otherwise high, smooth fore-head. Despite his fading beer buzz, Pearly was suddenly shot through with anticipation. "Of a beachcomber," Colby said finally. He watched Pearly for a moment and then added, "You look disappointed."

"I was hoping for a fresher metaphor."

"Well, I don't have the time to read as much as you do."

"I see. You know, I worked today. Spent over eight hours strip-ping shingles off a roof over in Au Train." Colby seemed unim-pressed. Then he asked, "What's wrong with a beachcomber? Don't they have a civil purpose? They walk the beach picking up refuse left by others. They turn in empty bottles and cans for the deposit, and as a result our beaches are cleaner."

"They're bums," Colby said.

"Bums."

Colby leaned forward and it was clear that he was about to con-clude this little seminar. "They're bottom-feeders and you're one small step above the beachcomber. You may get up and go to work in the morning hung over, but you have no real purpose in life. You just want to be—" And again he paused a moment. "You just want to be free and clear."

"Something wrong with that?"

"In theory? No. But it's just humanly impossible. Now follow me."

They got out of their chairs and Colby led Pearly down the hall to a tiny back room. Pearly had been there before. It was primarily used for storage, and there were cartons of paper products—toilet paper, coffee filters, paper towels—stacked almost to the ceiling.

Pearly sat down on the long wooden bench that stood against the back wall. "You know, my mother would have said that this room isn't big enough to sling a cat."

WHEN SEAN AWOKE he couldn't believe he was in his own bed. His room was in the basement and he could hear his mother overhead in the kitchen. She had the television on, as always, tuned to a morning talk show.

Sean got out of bed, put on an old high-school T-shirt and a pair of sweatpants, then went upstairs to the kitchen. She cooked him blueberry pancakes, his favorite. The smell of the batter on the griddle was diminished by the haze of menthol smoke. When his mother put the plate of pancakes on the table, she retreated to the counter, where she kept her coffee mug and cigarettes. Her first name, June, was printed in red letters on the pink mug. Keeping a thin shoulder toward him, she raised the cigarette to her mouth and her cheek went hollow as she inhaled fiercely. He'd forgotten how she tended to hold the elbow of her cigarette hand in the palm of her other hand.

"You have plans for today?" she asked.

He was relieved. This meant that they weren't going to talk about his early discharge yet. Not last night, not this morning. Everybody was going to pretend it wasn't there.

"Absolutely none." He poured maple syrup on his pancakes. "Feels pretty good, to have no plans. I tell you, the army can organize your day."

Her hair was shorter and it seemed to have lost what little color it had—now it was just a faint rust tone, which made her skin seem withered and pasty. "Well, he wants you to stop by the station around lunchtime."

"What?"

"Just go see what your father wants."

"I need wheels."

"You'll have to use my car, but I need it by one because I have errands to do."

His mother turned and gazed hard at him. He lowered his head to the job of cutting his pancakes. "Well, I really need my *own* wheels," he said. "I got a little saved up, so I'm going to stop by Arnie's and see what he's got for sale. I was thinking one of those downsize trucks."

She crushed out her cigarette. "You'll need a job if you're going to go buying a truck. So you go see your father."

"That what this is all about? Dad's going to get me a job?"

She picked up her cigarettes, then seemed to think better of lighting another one so soon. "I'll tell you one thing, Sean. I don't know the whole story, but it's fortunate that they gave you an honorable discharge. Otherwise he couldn't help you."

He was surprised that she had mentioned it at all. But then he realized that this was how she was different from his father. They would all ignore something, until his father would suddenly explode over it. But his mother would slowly, methodically chip away at it as though she were working on a piece of marble with a hammer and chisel.

"There's nothing in my record," he said. "They cut a deal. Because of this other guy—he's from Minnesota but his old man's got some kind of connections in Washington. They let us out on a medical discharge, so nobody came out looking bad in this, including the army. And that's what's most important. The one thing the army's really afraid of is newspapers, CNN, and all that stuff."

"What's that supposed to mean?" his mother asked.

"The army's like everything else: It's how it *looks*, not how it *is*."

With resignation she began to work a cigarette out of the pack.

"This job," he said. "Let me guess: summer cop."

"Something wrong with that?"

"I'm not sure I'm ready to put on another uniform."

Now his mother came to the kitchen table and placed her hands on the back of the chair across from him. "You go *down* there, Sean, and you *talk* to him."

"I'll be standing out there in the village in July, writing parking tickets and—"

"*Don't.*" She raised her bony hand and slapped the top of the table. "Don't *start* that. *Hear?*"

———

POLICE CHIEF BUZZ GAGNON leaned back behind his desk and rubbed his enormous belly. His blue shirt was so taut it might have been a balloon. "Bet you're a little disoriented," he said, "just getting back from Italy, huh?"

"Everything's in English," Sean said. "Street signs, everything. Amazing."

Buzz dropped his head back and laughed, revealing gold in his molars. Then he looked at Sean's father and actually winked. "Those Italian girls, Sean, they as hot as they look in the movies?"

"You betcha," Sean said, kissing his fingertips. "*Belle donne de Italia.*"

"Sophia Loren," Buzz nearly shouted. "I think the first time I had a tingling in my pecker was when I saw her in a movie. That's back when films were in black and white, Sean, long time ago." Suddenly he rested his forearms on his desk. "But it was that Gina Lollobrigida that really got to me. I don't know what it was about her, but she just looked, you know, *ready.*"

Sean glanced at his father, who was sort of smiling. It was the porcelain smile his father reserved for the captain, kind of up hard at the corners of the mouth, which brought out a little dimple in his chin.

"I'll tell you the truth," Gagnon whispered in total earnest. "When they were putting me under for my double bypass last year? You think your life flashes before your eyes—your wife, your kids, your dog, whatever." He shook his head solemnly. "All the way down to zero I was seeing Gina. She was wearing this low-cut dress, kinda snug at the hips? Cripes, I thought, I deserve to die!" Laughing, he leaned back again, causing his chair to creak dangerously. His face and his bald dome turned crimson so quickly that Sean wondered if the man was going to have another heart attack right there. When he caught his breath, he looked at Sean's father and said, "Sure, Frank, let's put him on days to start."

Sean's father stood up immediately. "Fine," he said, heading for the captain's door. He took Sean by the upper arm and began to usher him out of the room.

"So tell me," Buzz said, just as Sean had his hand on the doorknob. "You were in for, what, about a year? Discharged a little early?"

" 'Fraid so," Sean's father said. He nodded toward the file folder he'd placed on the desk. "It's all there, Buzz. Medical reports, everything."

"You didn't catch something over there?" Buzz asked.

Sean waited, expecting his father to say something. The moment hung there, but the captain smiled right through it. "Nah," Sean said finally. "Nothing the army doctors couldn't fix."

Gagnon clapped his hands together once and laughed again.

Sean's father smiled, too, and it was at that moment that Sean wanted to say something in the worst way, something that would break through the bullshit. But his father reached past him, yanked open the door, and gave his shoulder a little push.

4

THERE WERE EIGHT VEHICLES for sale at Superior Gas & Lube. Arnie Frick was up-front about all of them. He and Sean had graduated from high school together, and with Arnie nothing seemed to have changed, except he'd moved out of his parents' house and now lived in the apartment above the gas station. And he'd grown a brown mustache that curled right into his mouth.

"Most of these are junk," Arnie said as they crossed the lot. Overhead a row of red, white, and blue plastic flags snapped in the wind. "The Bronco needs brakes and ball joints, the clutch in the Ford pickup won't last to the end of the year. This Subaru's in good shape, if you like that sort of thing." He stopped at the end of the row, in front of a white Chevy pickup. Sean took a walk around it. The faded bumper sticker on the tailgate read GUN CONTROL MEANS USING BOTH HANDS. "It's clean," Arnie said. "This one's really clean."

They got in the cab, Sean behind the wheel. He turned the key and it started right up. Sounded smooth. He put it in gear, popped the clutch, and laid a little rubber as he turned out into Ottawa Street. They drove toward Petit Marais. Arnie took out a pack of Marlboros and removed a tightly rolled joint. His hands were grimy from working on engines.

"Don't light that up in here," Sean said. "I buy this, my dad'll smell it right off."

Arnie tucked the joint back in the pack of cigarettes. "Jack wants twenty-five hundred for it, but I know he'll take two. You got that?"

Sean didn't answer. They were out of high school now and Arnie called his old man Jack. Sean had never even thought of calling his father by his first name. He downshifted as they went into a tight curve, then floored it on the straight. He ran it up to seventy-five and fifth gear, then eased up. "What's wrong with it?"

"Nothing. *I'd* buy it if I had the dough. It could use tires maybe. We can work them into the deal."

"Put some big ones on there?" Sean asked.

"Yeah, it'll really look cool." Arnie turned on the radio. "Good speakers, too." Hendrix's "All Along the Watchtower" was on. He turned it up until the end of the song, then lowered the volume. "So how are those Italian girls?"

"Unbelievable."

"Yeah, really?"

"Do anything you want."

"*Any*thing?"

"Long as you pay for it."

Arnie stared out the windshield, deep in thought. "Not a lot of girls from our class still around. 'Cept a few that got kids. Some of them are even married."

Sean wanted to ask about Hannah, but he let it go.

MARTIN AND PEARLY walked around the house while a fine mist drifted in off Lake Superior. They were related, second or third cousins through their mothers. The last time Pearly had seen Martin was at least a dozen years ago at a family gathering in Whitefish Harbor. Martin was a Chicago relative and usually they were easy to lose track of, but not Martin; he'd come to stay, and had bought the old Pence house. And he wanted Pearly's opinion.

Pearly flicked his cigarette into the weeds and followed his cousin through the back door. In the kitchen he raised his head and took a long, deep breath—he might have been savoring a fine wine. He exhaled slowly. "Moldy wallpaper, powder post beetle, dry rot, and dead animals."

"Aunt Jane says you're the last of a breed of carpenter, the kind that works with a twelve-point handsaw, a block plane, and a folding rule."

"I didn't think she cared for me."

"So what do you think about this place?"

"Might be wise to torch it and start from scratch."

"I don't want to do that."

"Good. You're a fool, but good. Maybe it runs in the family?"

"Guess so."

"You're gonna need help."

"You offering?" Martin said. "I don't know that I can afford you."

"I got to tell you something. Aunt Jane called me from Florida. She wants me to send the bills for my labor down to her."

"She does? Why?"

Pearly shrugged. "Maybe we really are a family of fools? Between the mortgage and the materials, you're going to eat up that inheritance quick. With the two of us working you might have a chance to fix this place up."

"I want to have an apartment on each floor," Martin said. "I'll live here on the first floor and rent the second and third."

"What you need first is something to get rid of the cats, and that smell."

"I aired the place out yesterday, but it could be weeks before it'll be inhabitable."

They went to the front door, which was swollen in its jambs. Together they yanked it open, and cool, damp lake air drifted into the hallway.

Pearly walked down the brick steps and crossed the front yard to the sidewalk. "Secret potion," he said, leaning into the bed of his Datsun truck. Amid the toolboxes were two white plastic bottles of Clorox. "It'll take several doses over a few days, but once this stuff soaks into those old floorboards, you'll be able to breathe in that house again. And whatever cats are still alive in there will clear out pronto." He handed Martin one bottle, then grabbed the other. Starting toward the house, he said, "Don't worry, I kept the receipt."

In the front hall Pearly removed the cap from the bottle and walked down toward the kitchen, sprinkling Clorox on the floor. Martin did the same, working his way into the living room.

"This is not work to be done on an empty stomach," Pearly said.

"Absolutely."

"You still like cudighi?"

"*Cudighi!*" Martin's voice echoed through the rooms. "The U.P.'s the only place I've ever had it—the only place anybody's ever *heard* of it—and it was always one of the main reasons for coming here to Aunt Jane's. They still make them at the Hiawatha Diner, don't they?"

"Best Italian sausage this side of Ishpeming," Pearly said, and Martin laughed. "You just bought this house so you can spring for the cudighi sandwiches."

HANNAH GOT OFF the school bus and walked uphill from the village. It was drizzling and she had the hood of her rain slicker up over her hair. By the end of the first block she realized the vehicle approaching from behind was not stopping, was not turning, but was just crawling along behind her. She glanced over her shoulder once, looking past the edge of the yellow hood; it was a white pickup, ten yards back. She looked forward and kept climbing the hill. There was one group of boys who cruised Whitefish Harbor in a van, but she didn't recognize this white truck. When she walked faster it kept pace.

The houses above the village were old, some with clapboard, asbestos, or aluminum siding, many with their front doors opening right onto the buckled concrete sidewalk. When Hannah reached the end of the block, she paused, and the truck stopped behind her. She turned around but was unable to see through the reflection of the windshield, the wipers slapping back and forth.

The truck began to move forward, a front tire rubbing against the curb, and through the rain-streaked window she could see Sean sitting behind the wheel. At first she thought he was in a military uniform, but then she realized that it was a policeman's hat he was wearing. He rolled down the window a few inches and said, "It's really starting to come down. Want a lift home?"

It was beginning to pour. "What are you *doing* here?"

"Well, technically, I'm on duty for another half hour or so, but with this weather there's not a lot of parking tickets for a summer cop to write. It's too early in the season—tourists won't show up till after Memorial Day." With his hair shaved close to his head, he looked innocent, even pure. His jaw seemed beefier, but his mouth still did this little thing at the corners that always suggested that he was sharing a private joke with her. "Come on," he said. "You're getting drenched."

This was true; her slicker was worthless and she was beginning to shiver. She went around the front of the truck and got in the cab. "You're supposed to be somewhere in Italy, aren't you?" She pushed the hood back and wiped wet hair off her face.

"Came home early." Sean let out the clutch and the truck moved slowly up the hill.

"Why?"

He smiled. "Missed this weather, so I got discharged." He was heavier and there was something about the way his shoulders and arms moved under his pale blue shirt that suggested he'd been working out, perhaps lifting weights. "So now I'm what I never wanted to be: my father's son." His laugh was strange, eerie, and she thought of the sound some dogs make when they're startled—a high-pitched yip. "But after the army my mother's cooking seems better than it used to be," he added. "So it sort of evens out, you know?"

Hannah's fingers gripped the door handle. The rain was now pounding on the roof of the cab. "How did you get discharged early?" she asked.

"*What?*" He nearly had to shout.

"You were discharged *early.* You arrange that *yourself?* Or your parents do *that* for you, too?"

"*Look,* I'm *home,*" he said. "I was *in* nearly a *year* and now I'm *back.*" He pulled over under a maple tree a block from her house. Beneath the canopy of leaves the rain wasn't as loud on the roof. "I know—" he began, but then stopped. He wasn't shouting now. He leaned toward her and spoke softly. "I know last year was hard for you, and I wish—I'm sorry about what happened. I really am. It's just that I . . ." His lower lip was actually quivering, and it was for real. His eyes were misting up. "What do you want me to *say,* Hannah? *Tell* me."

She yanked the door handle, hurting her finger. The door opened and she climbed out. As she started walking quickly away from the truck, she looked down and saw that she'd broken the fingernail on her middle finger and it was bleeding. She crossed the street and when she was out from under the tree the rain pounded on her skull. She didn't bother with the hood but just broke into a run toward her house.

5

"I SAW HER," Sean said to Arnie.

They were at the Portage. Sally was working the bar and she probably knew they were underage, but she left them alone as long as they behaved and stayed near the back door.

Sean waited but Arnie didn't say anything.

"She was walking home in the rain. She looked real good."

"Christ," Arnie said.

"What?"

"You stupid or what? You fool around with her, she gets knocked up, the parents get all involved, and you end up in boot camp. Besides . . ." Arnie sucked foam off his mustache, then said, "Besides, she's seeing some guy."

"What guy?"

"Dunno. He's older. Hear he's from Chicago. They come into the station for gas sometimes. He has this old Mercedes that he lets her drive. I hear he's bought that old house they were going to knock down. His name's Martin something."

"How much older?"

"Thirty, maybe. Hard to tell 'cause he's got this shaved-head thing going for him."

The next day Sean drove by the house. An old Mercedes and Pearly Blankenship's rusty Datsun were parked out front. The sound of a hammer and the whine of a power saw came from inside the house. Piles of rubble and scrap wood filled the yard. Sean drove by several days in a row. He never saw anyone. He just heard them at work.

It was easier to see Hannah. He knew her routine. In the morning she walked from her house, down through the village to the school bus stop. And about three-thirty in the afternoon she got off the bus and walked home. He remembered how much she liked to walk. The first thing he had noticed about her was her stride when she came into study hall late. She handed Mr. Talbot a hall pass, then walked up the second aisle to her desk. From the back of the room Sean could see that every boy in the room had looked up to watch her. It was a warm fall afternoon, Indian summer, and she was wearing a white blouse and a long orange-and-yellow skirt. The skirt was an Indian-type thing that wrapped snuggly around her hips, which moved with ease beneath the fabric. Some girls developed hips and breasts quickly and they walked awkwardly, as though they didn't know how to control everything. But Hannah strode gracefully to her seat, and when she sat down it seemed to be a relief to the boys in the room.

Late one afternoon, when he was driving back to the police station at the end of his shift, he saw her on the beach at Petit Marais. She was about fifty yards ahead of him, but he recognized her walk immediately. She carried a burlap sack over one shoulder and leaned forward to balance its weight on her back. He knew she was collecting stones, which she sold to Althea Briggs, the old woman who ran a secondhand shop in the village. He got out of the cruiser and followed, staying up on the road, where he was concealed by bushes and trees. After about a half-mile she headed up the beach and crossed the road. She went up a short drive and into the front door of a small cabin. He had no doubt that this was where Martin from Chicago lived.

So he started driving by both the old house and the cabin.

He just wanted a look at the guy.

One night he saw the Mercedes parked in the small lot beside the pharmacy. He walked over to the car. In Italy a Mercedes was a sign of prestige; here it was just an oddity, a sign of someone wanting to be different. Sean looked around the lot, which was empty except for a couple of other cars. He went to the back of the Mercedes and kicked the right taillight. There was the sound of glass falling on the pavement as he walked away.

MARTIN SELDOM SAW Hannah on school nights, and when he did it was more or less on the sly. She said she didn't want to "advertise it"—she was already the subject of enough rumor and speculation. She was also wary of her mother finding out she was seeing a man ten years her senior. So he agreed that she would contact him and arrange their meetings, and often it became a game for them. His phone would ring and she'd say something like "Petit Marais Point at nine-thirty" or "The far end of the harbor parking lot at eleven." Sometimes she wanted to just talk and hold hands, tell him about her day. Other times she made it clear immediately that they were meeting for a quickie because she didn't have a lot of time. It was part of the game, urgent and clandestine. She had one stipulation: They could not make love in his car. Spring is slow to come to Lake Superior, but on the occasional warm evenings in May they'd take a blanket and find a place on the beach. Usually they went back to his aunt's cabin. There was something frantic and desperate in her approach to sex. She seemed determined to achieve an orgasm followed by total exhaustion. It was self-negating, a purgative, as though only during those moments of release could she completely expel all knowledge, all recollection of who or what she was—afterward she once said, "For a minute there was just *this*."

———

ONE FRIDAY AFTERNOON Hannah went to Martin's house after school to help. She particularly liked demolition. She wore a mask and leather work gloves, a blue bandanna wrapped around her skull. Her black T-shirt read *U2* in white letters. For over an hour she tore out plaster and lath with a crowbar and sledge, loaded it into the wheelbarrow, and took it out to the pickup. When they were through for the day, they sat out on the front steps drinking beer. After Pearly packed up his truck and left, Martin opened the last two beers.

"Your mother working at the hospital tonight?" he asked.

"Three to eleven," Hannah said.

"She know yet?"

"About us? I haven't, you know, told her outright that I've been seeing you, but the other day she said something about how I wasn't hiding in my room as much."

"You do that at home? Hide?"

"Since last year I've spent a lot of time staring at the ceiling above my bed. I don't know—I just get turned inside out. Ripping out walls and ceilings is therapeutic."

"Think it might be better if you told her before she, you know, finds out?"

Hannah wanted to tell Martin about Sean, that he had returned to Whitefish Harbor. But she couldn't because it might seem that Sean still meant something to her. It shouldn't matter whether Sean was back or not. It shouldn't make any difference to them at all. But she knew it did. "Martin, you want to meet my mother?"

"How do you think she'd take it?"

"After last year, I don't know," Hannah said, and then she smiled. "She's forty-two. Maybe she'd want to date you herself."

"She ever see men?"

"Mom? Not in years. She works at the hospital, comes home, eats, reads in bed, sleeps, goes back to work. It's been years since she's gone out—says she's too exhausted."

"My guess is she finds out on her own, it's not going to sit well."

"I like the fact that nobody knows," Hannah said. "It's our secret."

"She's going to find out eventually."

"Does it have to be tonight? Mom won't be home until late, so it's just us."

"No. I like it this way, too. We can go public when you want."

"My mom is not the problem."

She knew Martin was staring at her. "Is there a problem?"

"Not exactly." She looked at him. "Not between us."

"Good," he said.

PEARLY MADE HIS usual rounds, concluding at the Portage a little before last call. The bartender Sally was in her late thirties and she had strawberry curls and a nose that veered slightly to the left. On nights that her teenaged son Jason stayed with her ex-husband in Newberry she sometimes took Pearly home with her. For which he was indeed grateful.

MARTIN DROPPED HANNAH off at the end of her street a little after ten. On the way back through the village, he noticed the patrol car fall in behind him. He was well within the speed limit, but the cruiser followed for about a mile. When the blue flashing lights came on, Martin pulled over to the side of the road and rolled down his window.

It wasn't Officer Colby who approached the car, but a young policeman.

"Problem, Officer?" Martin handed him his license and registration.

"I usually have to ask for these. You've been pulled over before?"

It was hard to see the officer's face in the dark, and his flashlight at times struck Martin right in the eyes. "I've had some experience, yes."

"I'll have to check to see what kind of record you have."

"Is that the reason you pulled me over?"

The officer leaned down to the window. "You wouldn't be challenging me?"

"No. Just asking the nature of this—"

"It's the nature of your taillight. Which is broken."

"It is? I didn't know that."

"Because otherwise you wouldn't drive this vehicle at night, would you?"

"No, I wouldn't." Martin turned his head away from the flashlight and looked out the windshield.

After a moment, the officer said, "If you'll wait here. *Please.*"

Martin watched him in the rearview mirror as he returned to the patrol car. Even his walk was pissed off. The flashing blue lights gave his movements a strobelike jerkiness, as though he were in an old movie. When he got in the patrol car, the interior light shone down on his face. For perhaps five minutes he sat in the cruiser, his head lowered, and he hardly moved.

Finally he got out and came back to the Mercedes. Handing the license, registration, and a slip of paper to Martin, he said, "I'm giving you a warning this time. You have ten days to repair that taillight."

Martin looked down at the slip of paper. It was difficult to read by the car's interior light, but he saw the officer's name: *S. Colby.* He looked up, trying to see the face above the flashlight beam. "You Sean Colby?"

"I am."

"Now I understand."

"You do? *What* do you understand?"

"I thought you were overseas in the army, Sean."

"I guess you did."

Martin leaned toward the open window, trying to get a better look at his face, but Colby had already turned and begun to walk back to the patrol car.

———

HANNAH LAY IN HER BED, staring at the ceiling. She wanted to fall asleep before her mother returned from her shift at the hospital, but she was wide awake. Other nights at the cabin with Martin had been so perfect that they seemed unreal. She believed that a kind of grace had enveloped them. But tonight was different; the more they tried in bed, the more difficult it became, until they finally gave up. They went out into the kitchen and he made an omelette with mushrooms, onion, and cheese. The red wine was sharp on her tongue. His bathrobe wasn't warm enough, so finally she went back into the bedroom and put on her clothes. They hardly spoke while they ate.

She couldn't get over the fact that Sean was back, couldn't stop thinking about him. After he had gone into the army, slowly she was able to put him aside—that was the way she thought about it, *aside*—and as the months passed she came to realize that there were more and more days when she didn't even think about him. So she came to understand that when she first started going with him, she had become obsessed. It seemed both easy and harmless at first, and it was such a high-school thing. Sean came on so calm, so cool. With Sean, it was all how things looked. The way they met in the halls between classes. The way they drove around in his mother's Ford. Sitting close to him in the car was a sign of possession. Their favorite place was the dirt road that ran up into the woods above Petit Marais; the two-track was overgrown, so the grass ticked against the chassis.

The first time her period was late, she was frightened, and she swore that if the blood would come, she would make sure it wouldn't happen again. But when it finally came, she didn't, and eventually there was the month when she lay night after night on her bed, trying to will her blood to flow. But this time it didn't. She removed tampons from the carton anyway, just so her mother—who she knew kept track of such things—saw that their supply in the bathroom cabinet was diminishing. Eventually, that deception no longer worked, and the morning she was vomiting into the toilet, her mother stood outside the bathroom door and said, "You're late, aren't you." The dreaded word *late*. But it was her nurse's voice, calm, direct, officious. Then there was a catch in her throat as she said, "Honey, I knew it. You *always* leave some blood on the underside of the seat." Hannah reached up, unlocked the door, and her mother came in; she was wearing her nurse's uniform, white pants and a yellow print blouse. Her face was stern, determined, with bright blue eyes and short blond hair. She no longer bothered with makeup. The model of efficiency. She soaked a washcloth in cold water, and as she wiped her daughter's face, she said, "Hannah, you don't have to hide this, not from me." They put their arms around each other then, sobbing.

Hannah heard her mother's car pull into the driveway. For the next few minutes she listened to the routine she knew by heart: Her mother came into the house, put ice in a glass, and poured herself a drink, always Scotch except in the heat of the summer when she'd have a beer; then she sat in the living room and leafed through a magazine or newspaper. The turning of pages in the middle of the night—it was the loneliest sound imaginable. Hannah feared that sound more than anything. After another shift at the hospital, her mother was waiting for the one thing she still craved in life: sleep.

6

SEAN WAS GETTING OFF his morning coffee break when he came out of the Hiawatha Diner and saw Hannah standing across the street by his patrol car. He thought it was funny how some people reacted to his uniform. They would look away quickly, trying to pretend that they didn't see a cop—as though that would keep him from noticing them. Sometimes a driver, who was well within the speed limit, would slam on the breaks. Others tended to raise a hand to shield their faces so they might not be identified. But not Hannah. She was leaning against the parking meter, her arms folded, and when she saw him she did not look away.

He crossed Ottawa Street and said, "Hi."

"What do you think you're doing, pulling Martin over?" She was wearing jeans and a hooded sweatshirt.

"I didn't know it was him."

"*Bullshit.*"

"He had a busted taillight."

"Yeah, and how did he get *that*?"

She took her weight off the parking meter and started walking quickly up the sidewalk. Sean stood there, holding a warm Styrofoam cup of coffee in one hand; then he placed the cup on the roof of his patrol car and followed her. At the end of the block, she turned in the alley that went down to the harbor. Conscious of the fact that he was in uniform, Sean walked quickly but tried not to look anxious or desperate to catch up.

When he reached the end of the alley, he was relieved to see her standing on the beach, surrounded by a cluster of rowboats, turned upside down. He stopped next to her and for a moment they both stared out at the harbor. "Listen, I didn't give him a ticket," Sean said. "Just a warning."

"*Why* would you do that? Why would you *break* his taillight?"

"Did I *say* I broke it?" She turned toward him; he shrugged. "All right. I just wanted a look at him."

This simple admission seemed to undermine her anger. She sat on the nearest rowboat and pushed the hood off her head. A slight breeze coming off the lake blew fine strands of hair across her face, which she ignored.

Sean propped one foot on the stern. "I'd heard he was older and I wanted to see for myself. Christ, Hannah, I'll bet he's ten years older than you."

"What difference does that make?"

"It's not just age. I mean, *look* at him, Hannah. He's, what, from Chicago? What's he *doing* up here?"

"His mother was from here. Maybe he *likes* it here, Sean."

"Well, there you *go*. That's *fine*. And he drives a Mercedes and has bought that old house. But do you think he's going to *stay* here? He going to settle here?"

"What's your point?"

"My *point* is it won't last. Whatever it is between you two, it'll never—"

She stood up. "Who are you to say?"

"It's so obvious—you should at least admit it."

Her hands were jammed in the front pocket of her sweatshirt; he glanced down at her breasts for a moment, then looked out at the water. "Listen," he said, "I miss you—I really do. I'm glad to be back and I was hoping that we could—"

"I *know* what you miss, Sean."

"We had bad luck. We weren't careful and we got caught. But remember what it was like before all that?" To his surprise, there was a softening in her eyes, her mouth. "I behaved badly," he said. "I know that. I was scared. Afraid of the whole thing. What my parents would do, what people would say. I lost sight of the most important thing: us." Her eyes were welling up, glinting in the sunlight reflecting off the water. "I wish I had—"

"Had what, Sean?"

He took off his cap and studied the inside, where his name was written on a card in a plastic sleeve. "I wish I had just said we have it and we raise it. I wish we were married now."

"Do you?"

"I do." He continued to stare at the cap.

Hannah began walking up the beach, but then she stopped. She stood with her back to him and he wondered if he should go to her. But he waited. A rising puff of wind lifted her hair off her right shoulder. She lowered her head and turned around. He'd never seen her face like this: stone.

"I don't believe you, Sean." She said it carefully, evenly, as though for the record. "I don't believe you at all. You did what you did. What you say you wish you'd done doesn't matter. You have no *idea* how this has affected me. At school. All over town. My mother, too. So don't tell me otherwise. Your folks sent you away to the army, but I guess you screwed that up, too."

"I lost a year in that shit," he said.

"You're talking to me about a year? It's a piece of *time,* Sean. I'm talking about something else, something very different. The way people see me now—it'll never change, it's this—I don't know, this *thing,* this perception set in their minds. And you know what? I don't care. *I—don't—care.*"

"You think it's been easy for me?"

"I don't know what to think, but I know you're not any different than before. I wish you were—I really do. But you're not. And now you think you can spoil what I've got—that's what's really behind this. That's why you busted his taillight. Well, you can't," she said. "Do you understand me? You *can't.*"

She walked up the beach. Because of the sand, she almost appeared to be marching.

He thought, I can't? We'll just see about that.

Then he said it aloud, for the record. "We'll see about that."

But she had reached the alley between the two buildings that faced Ottawa Street, too far away to hear him.

MARTIN HAD GONE to Superior Gas & Lube and talked to Arnie Frick. They didn't carry Mercedes parts, of course, but Arnie had found a place in Marquette that did, and he called the next day when the taillight cover was delivered. A few minutes after Martin arrived, Sean Colby showed up in a white truck; he got out and came over to the Mercedes.

"This wouldn't be just a coincidence?" Martin said. He was kneeling on the pavement, a Phillips-head screwdriver in his hand. He glanced past Colby, to Arnie, who was standing in the door of the garage.

"I want to talk to you." Colby wasn't in uniform, but wore a T-shirt and jeans. He looked like he worked out regularly.

"Fine." Martin began to screw the plastic cover onto the taillight.

"It's about Hannah."

"I gather that."

"It's not right, you and her."

"There a law? You going to give me another warning?"

"No more warnings."

"I see. Just tickets?"

"I don't know what she told you about me, but it's not like that."

"Like what? What's it like?"

"She's told you a lot of . . . stuff. About what happened between us."

Without looking away from the taillight, Martin said, "What Hannah tells me is, well, it's between us, right? I'm not concerned about what happened between the two of you. It's in the past. She recognizes that, I think. Don't you?"

Colby's face turned soft with disbelief.

"The fact is she never even mentioned that you were back," Martin said. "What do you conclude from that?"

"Conclude?"

"Maybe she just didn't think it was that important."

"What, are you giving me a lecture?"

"Not at all." Martin tightened the last screw in the taillight cover.

"Then what would you call it?"

Martin got to his feet and tucked the screwdriver in his back pocket. "I would call it an assessment. An assessment of the present situation."

"Is that what this is," Colby said, his voice high and nearly breaking, "a situation?"

"It doesn't have to be, Sean." Martin could see that using his first name didn't work; something hardened in his stare. "I don't want a 'situation,' nor does Hannah." He went to the driver's-side door. Before getting in the car, he saw that Colby was staring down at the new taillight cover—and he looked like he was considering which foot to kick it with.

"Hey, Sean," Arnie said from the door of the garage. "*Sean.*" Colby seemed to come out of a trance. "Let it go," Arnie said. "Come on. Let it go."

Martin got in the car and started the engine. As he pulled out of the lot, he could see Colby in the side-view mirror. He was just standing there.

———

THE NEXT COUPLE of nights Sean drove by Martin's house, always in the evening, a little before sunset, just to see their progress. At that point the house had been gutted, the old plaster and lath thrown out the windows and loaded in Pearly's truck. The tall weeds had been cut down, so the house stood tall on its clean, bare lot.

He hadn't seen Arnie since that day at the station, so at night he mostly drove around by himself. One night he drove by Martin's house around midnight. He was beered up and he felt light, quick, and alert. He knew of a two-track that ran into the woods at the bend in the road, so he parked his truck in there and then walked the shoulder of Shore Road down to the house. He went into the backyard, shinnied up a drainpipe, and climbed into an open second-story window. He could barely see, but after a minute his eyes adjusted to the dark. Interior walls had been torn out, and new partitions of Sheetrock re-divided the rooms. Some windows had been closed in with plywood, while new openings had been cut where none existed before.

He walked through the house as though he were looking for something. At one point he took a long beer piss on the floor. Then he found a pile of old velvet drapes in a closet and heaped them in the center of the room. He found some newspaper and separated the pages, balling them up and spreading them in a circle around the drapes. Taking a book of matches from his jeans, he was about to strike one when he thought he heard footsteps down in the front yard.

Quietly he moved to the nearest window, overlooking the road, but couldn't see or hear anyone. He remained still for at least a minute. Then he heard them. They were walking around to the back of the house. A pane of glass broke down on the first floor, the window slid open, and they climbed inside. They moved across the floor beneath him—whispering voices. Kids, looking for a place to drink beer, maybe smoke a joint, a place a little bit scary.

He walked to the back of the house and climbed out to the drainpipe. When he was on the ground he went around to the front door.

He could hear their shuffling footsteps in the dark, the echo of their voices in the large, empty rooms. There was the sound of an empty tin can rolling across the floor. And laughter.

He banged his fist on the front door. The kids scrambled for the back of the house, bumping into things, their suppressed cries full of panic. Then he ran down the road and disappeared into the darkness of the woods.

HANNAH DID ERRANDS for her mother and on the way home she stopped for gas at Superior Gas & Lube. Arnie was changing a tire, so once she started the gas pump, she went to the open garage door. "Hey," she said.

"Hey." Arnie didn't look away from the tire, which he had just mounted on the rear wheel of a car on the lift. He put one of the lug nuts on with an air gun, the rapid, stuttering blast of noise reverberating through the garage.

She walked around behind Arnie, but he turned his head so that his face was still away from her. Hannah had always liked Arnie; after all that had happened last year, he never acted any differently toward her. They had been in the same homeroom every year in high school and he always sat behind her. He made fun of everybody and he was good at it. "Arnie?"

"What?"

He put the air-gun socket on the next lug nut and pulled the trigger. She closed her eyes until the garage was quiet again. Then from the other bay there was the clang and echo of a steel bar that Arnie's father dropped on the concrete floor.

"What's up?" she asked.

"Not much." Still, he didn't look away from the tire.

Hannah returned to her mother's car and topped up the tank, then went into the office. No one was there. She stood at the counter for a minute, staring at the rows of cigarettes and candy. She listened as Arnie continued to screw down the lug nuts on the tire. Finally, between blasts of the air gun, she said, "I'm about to drive off without paying."

After a moment, she heard his work boots scuff the concrete floor as he walked in from the garage. His family owned the business; since eighth grade Arnie had maintained that he didn't have to worry too much about school because eventually he would manage the garage. He came around the counter and pushed some buttons on the machine that read the gas pumps. "Eighteen-fifty," he said.

She picked up a Kit Kat bar and slapped it on the counter.

"Nineteen-ten."

She picked up another candy bar, a Mounds, and slapped it on the counter.

"Nineteen-seventy." He still wouldn't turn and look at her.

She took a twenty from the pocket of her jeans. "What can you get for thirty cents around here?" She slapped the twenty hard on the counter. "A date with Fast Marsha Frohmeyer?"

Arnie lowered his head, as though he'd given in to something. "Not even that." Turning around, he added, "She upped her rates to fifty cents." Then he lifted his head so she could see his eyes beneath his grimy Red Wings cap. The skin around his left eye was black and blue.

"*Jesus*, Arnie," she whispered. "Where'd you get that shiner?"

He picked up the twenty and punched keys on the cash register— it was an old machine, had been in the office as long as Hannah could remember—and a tiny bell sounded as the drawer slid open. He fished a quarter and a nickel from the wooden coin slots.

Hannah leaned toward the counter. "Sean?" He slapped the change on the counter. "Is *that* it? Sean did that?"

Arnie slammed the drawer shut and walked back out to the garage.

7

PEARLY WATCHED HIS COUSIN for some sign of anger, but Martin just stood with his hands on his hips as he looked down at the red velvet curtains surrounded by crumpled-up newspaper.

"It's like some pagan ritual," Pearly said.

"Vandals would have lit it."

"It wasn't vandals? You know who did this?"

"It's more than a warning, it's a threat," Martin said. "I just don't understand why he didn't light it."

"Who?"

"Sean Colby." Martin went to the nearest window and rested a haunch on the sill.

Pearly lifted a curtain with the toe of his work boot. "This is because of Hannah, isn't it?"

"Maybe I should talk with Sean's old man?"

Pearly lit a cigarette. His hesitation was enough.

"Bad idea?"

Pearly squinted at him through smoke. "Hannah and Sean— that's a pretty tender subject for Frank and June. Funny, when I saw Sean walking around the village playing policeman, I wondered what he was doing back here so soon." He began to gather up the curtains and took them across the room to a large trash barrel. "Maybe they discharge you now if you're homesick?"

"Or if you miss your old girlfriend. I'm not ruling it out."

"What? Talking to his old man?"

Martin folded his arms tightly.

"Look," Pearly said, "before you go running to his father, I should—" But then he stopped and laughed. It was inconceivable: Pearly Blankenship trying to reason with Frank Colby.

SEAN WENT TO the Portage and Arnie was standing at the far end of the bar watching the Cubs-Padres game. There were mostly locals in the bar, people who assumed Sean and Arnie were of legal age, or people who didn't care if they weren't. Sean ordered a pitcher, and then walked down to the end of the bar. Arnie wouldn't look away from the television.

"I'm here to kiss and make up."

Arnie took a sip of his draft beer and wiped foam off his mustache.

"I brought a peace offering." He refilled Arnie's mug.

"Sally," Arnie said. "Could I have another draft? This one's gone flat."

Sally poured Arnie's beer out in the sink and drew him another. She placed the mug on the bar and said, "You two behave, or it's the back door."

They both nodded, and she went down the bar collecting glasses.

"Your eye's looking better," Sean said.

Arnie picked up his new mug of beer and took a long drink. He still kept his attention on the Cubs game up on the television.

"Well, what we going to do, Arnie, to settle this up? You tell me."

"Buying me a beer ain't it."

"All right."

"You got Hannah on the brain, that's your problem," Arnie said. "You did in high school and you've come back from the army with it. It's not healthy, it's not normal, what you got."

"I didn't come here to talk about Hannah, I—"

"It's like you got this disease there's no cure for. And now this other guy's doing her and you get all bent out of shape, and what do you do? You get pissed off at him, then you walk over to me and pop me a sucker punch? *What the fuck?*" Arnie picked up his mug and finished his beer.

Sean refilled Arnie's mug from his pitcher. "Easy, now. This isn't a payoff, it's just that you look a little worked up."

Arnie didn't do anything—a good sign.

"We had this situation in boot camp," Sean said. "Two guys didn't get along, and one guy took a cheap shot at the other guy. Our DI gets wind of this and he wakes us up one morning at like two A.M., marches all of us outside our barracks in our shorts—and it's fucking pouring—and he stands the two guys in the middle of all of us and says to the guy who was on the wrong end of the cheap shot, 'Hit him.' You don't refuse your DI, so this guy pops the other guy good. The DI says to do it again. He does it again. Then the DI says, 'You two men are square now. You are best friends. You are brothers. If necessary, you will die for each other.'" Sean finished his beer. "And he was right. From then on they were like brothers."

Arnie thought about this for a while. Sean waited. He knew that Arnie understood a day's work, didn't take any grief from anyone, and had an unwavering sense of fairness.

Finally, without taking his eyes off the television, Arnie said, "I'm not going to pop you a couple of times to make things even."

"We could go out back like Sally asked," Sean said. "Get it over with and come back inside before this beer gets warm."

"Nah. Cubs are coming to bat."

"What then? You tell me."

"The element of surprise. That's what your DI couldn't replace. The first was a sucker punch and the guy didn't know it was coming. *I* didn't know it was coming. I go out back now and nail you one, you got all the time to get ready for it."

"So that's what you want?" Sean asked. "Element of surprise?"

"It'd only be fair."

"All right. Whenever, wherever you want it."

"Fine." Arnie drained his mug of beer. "But it ain't gonna make us brothers."

"You know I would die for you," Sean said.

"I'd rather you buy another pitcher."

ABOUT AN HOUR LATER Martin walked into the Portage. The place was busy. He saw Sean and Arnie at the far end of the bar, so he stayed near the front door and ordered a beer. It didn't matter. Sean saw him, picked up his mug, and shouldered his way through the crowd. He moved like a guy accustomed to having people get out of his way. Arnie remained at the other end of the bar, watching the ball game up on the television. The Cubs had a rally going.

When Sean reached Martin, he said, "Like your new taillight?"

"It works."

"Glad to hear." Sean's voice had a pleasant bounce to it, as though they were old friends who hadn't seen each other in a while.

"This an official visit?"

Sean put his beer on the bar and tugged at the collar of his T-shirt. "Off duty."

"Just being neighborly?"

"Concerned for public safety. You need to take precautions."

"Maybe I'll order a spare taillight, just in case?"

"Now you're getting it," Sean said.

"And maybe I could talk to someone on the force about my neighborhood."

Sean appeared pleased. "You mean that old house you bought?"

"Right. Little stupid acts of vandalism. You know, kids with nothing better to do."

"Imagine that."

"Who would I talk to, your father? He handle that sort of thing?"

Sean's face went tight for a moment, but then he grinned. "He handles everything."

"That's good to know," Martin said. "Of course, it's nothing serious so far, and I don't want to get someone in trouble over a little thing."

Something was rearranged in Sean's face. His eyes seemed to shut down and it was almost as though the bones had shifted beneath his cheeks. For a moment he appeared unable to speak. But then he said, quietly, "That would change nothing."

Martin said, "I hope it would solve—"

"Wrong. It would solve nothing."

"I see." Martin looked out the window at Ottawa Street. In the dark reflection of the glass, he could see Sean, staring at him, not moving at all. His stillness seemed a preparation, a gathering of forces. Martin believed he knew what was coming. It was beyond talk, beyond any kind of reason, and he turned to face Sean, squaring his shoulders in self-defense.

Then a fist—Arnie's fist—came from the right and struck Sean's jaw. Sean's knees buckled. His forearms rested on the bar and he could barely keep his head up. Despite the noise in the bar, everyone in the place seemed to immediately recognize this sound, this slap of flesh on flesh, for what it was, and there was a sudden quiet in the room. Only the baseball commentators spoke, their voices languid and reflective as they waited for a relief pitcher to finish his warm-up.

Arnie said to Martin, "Now you get out of here." When Martin didn't move, he added, "You want one, too?" Arnie's eyes were steady, fierce. "I said *you* get out of here so I can watch the damn *ball game*."

HANNAH STILL OFTEN dreamed of blood. Blood and embryos. The summer she began her periods she saw pictures in a magazine article that portrayed the various stages of an embryo's development.

It described some of the methods used before the law was changed in 1972. Abortions were performed in "back alleys," and doctors were often not doctors at all, but butchers, tailors, seamstresses. There was a photograph of several crude instruments on a white metal table, a small knife, a spoon, scissors, a hot water bottle, a plastic tube, a wire coat hanger twisted out of shape. The caption read *Tools of the Trade.* Another photograph depicted a small room at the back of a shop in New Orleans. The shelves were stacked with bolts of cloth, and the woman, whose face was blurred to protect her identity, wore a turban, as though to emphasize her powers of magic and witchcraft. Her arms were folded over her abundant breasts in a manner that suggested she was both defiant and weary. The caption read: *Necessary evil—killer of babies or savior of women's lives?* Hannah kept the magazine hidden in her room for years. As she got older she realized that it was as though the article had been written in code. No one made love; the word *love* was never used. Only once, at the very end, the article mentioned intercourse. The word made Hannah think there was a secret river flowing inside her, a river of blood.

In high school she knew girls who had put all sorts of things inside themselves. Their fingers, a hot dog, elongated plastic toys, a test tube stolen from chemistry class. Girls bragged about letting boys put their fingers, tongues, and cocks inside them. Tongues were best; cocks the least predictable. Boys often came abruptly, sometimes before they got inside; they got it on girls' skin, which had to be cleaned up with Kleenex. It left damp, cold spots on their clothes.

The other side of *come* was *late*. It was usually whispered. *I'm late!* But then in a day or so there would be a look of relief, and everything would be fine, everything forgotten. Being late was cool. But not for Hannah. She was too late.

ONE IN THE MORNING, Sean sat in his pickup on the two-track off Shore Road. The woods were pitch dark. He'd been sitting there for perhaps ten minutes, working on the pint of Scotch Arnie had bought after they left the Portage. They didn't leave, they were thrown out. Sally rushed down the bar, pointing at the front door, and Arnie took Sean by the upper arm and walked him outside. On the sidewalk, the air was cool, and Arnie said, "Okay, brother, now we're even."

Sean's window was rolled down and he could hear peepers, millions of them, it seemed, screaming away. Or perhaps they made that sound by rubbing their legs together—he couldn't remember. He was certain it was a mating thing. Somehow all that noise was intended to get a female's attention. He wondered if they were the ones that got eaten while they were having sex—the female devouring the male's head while he's still pumping away. No, that was the praying mantis.

When he finished the last of his Scotch, he got out and stood next to the truck while taking a long piss. He realized he was barefoot but he couldn't remember removing his sneakers. It was too much trouble to look in the truck for them, and there was a fine mist, warm and slick on his face. Arnie had said, "You got Hannah on the brain." It might have been more accurate to say that she'd eaten his brain. A portion of it anyway. But then, Arnie didn't really know Hannah. So he didn't know anything.

Sean began walking away from the truck, along the two-track out of the woods. Part of him knew he should just drive home, but when he reached the road, he walked around the bend on the pavement. There was nothing ahead but the road curving into the darkness. When he was in boot camp he met guys who had wives and girlfriends back home, and some had kids. It was usually part of a plan; they would enlist, and then once they were stationed, their wives and kids would join them. A couple of times while drunk, Sean had said he had a girl at home, who had a kid, a boy, and they were going to join him, too, after boot camp. It made being there not seem so stupid. It was part of a plan. But it wasn't his plan, it was his father's. It was a matter of getting him straightened out, and of course there was no girlfriend, no kid. It had all been a mistake—not getting her pregnant, but not saying he would stick with her, get married, if she wanted. That's what he should have told his father, though he knew it would have infuriated him. Eventually his mother would have understood, and she would have brought his father around. They would have said, "You two kids made a mistake and now you're going to live with the consequences"—something like that. But what they wouldn't have said was he had defied his father and finally broken free. Hannah would have been the one to tell him that that's what had really happened, that's what *had* to happen. Instead, he was in boot camp, making up lies about a family back home that didn't exist.

The road straightened out and Sean was standing in front of Martin's house. He walked around to the back of the house, shinnied up the drainpipe, and climbed in the window on the second floor. He knew his way around now, and he walked through each room, one hand touching the walls in the dark. The floorboards felt rough beneath his bare feet. There was a familiar smell, something he associated with the laundry room at home. Bleach.

In one room he found a pile of scrap wood and a newspaper. He had matches in the front pocket of his jeans, and it didn't take more than a couple of minutes to get the fire going. He watched it until the flames licked the new Sheetrock ceiling. Burning wood popped and crackled. When the heat was too much, he ran down the front stairs, but in the hall he stepped on something sharp—glass, he thought—and fell. He lay on the floor, holding his feet, warm blood covering his hands. The pain was a revelation.

HANNAH HEARD THE garage door open, squeaks and chains, and metal rollers in greased tracks, an awful sound that always alerted her that her mother was about to pull her car into the driveway. This week she was on day shifts at the hospital; it was better when she was on night shifts and they saw less of each other. It was even better when their dog, Sugar, was still alive because she could detect the sound of the car's engine well before it turned into the driveway. Often Sugar gave Hannah enough time to pour the rest of the beer down the sink and get in the bathroom to brush her teeth, or to simply flee, run out the back door and disappear until she knew her mother had gone to bed.

But as the car pulled into the garage, Hannah went into the living room, sat on the couch, and clicked on the television. Her mother banged through the kitchen door, wielding a plastic bag of groceries in one hand, her big leather purse in the other; she spilled these on the kitchen table and came into the living room, yanking off her jacket. "You eat yet?"

"Hello, yourself." Hannah looked back at the television. "No, I'm going out in a while."

Her mother returned to the kitchen. Hannah listened as she took a glass down from the cabinet, got ice from the freezer, put it in the glass, then poured the Scotch. Knowing that her mother's back was to the door, Hannah turned and looked past the lamp shade. Her mother was wearing the nurse's uniform Hannah had given her last Christmas. White pants and green top with sailboats on it. "I was at the fish market," her mother said as she began to turn and come across the kitchen again.

Hannah looked quickly back toward the television, which was tuned to CNN. "I'm not hungry, really," Hannah said.

Her mother came into the living room and sat in her chair, putting her feet up on the hassock. "I was at the fish market," she said in her slow, precise voice, then paused to sip her drink. This was one of her signs of anger, repeating something she had just said. It was a strategy intended to force Hannah to sit up and pay attention. It said, *Don't change the subject.* She placed her glass of Scotch on the coaster, then said, "And I ran into Margaret Lusic." She was in her mother's bridge group. Her daughter had gone to college in upstate New York last fall—one of the good ones, Syracuse or Cornell.

"And she told you all about how well Jennifer is doing at—"

"We didn't talk about Jennifer."

Hannah had to look away from the television now. Her mother was staring right at her. There was no getting around those eyes. "Margaret said she was driving down toward Petit Marais last week—Friday, she thought—and saw you coming out of a cabin over there, and she asked if you were working there, baby-sitting or whatever. And then—" She paused and picked up her drink. She liked to put the beginning of something out there and then let it hang until Hannah couldn't stand it any longer. And finally Hannah would say something like "Then what?" Her mother, more often than not, wouldn't know what she had intended to say. It was just another strategy. The problem was, understanding these strategies didn't help. Hannah had often explained to her mother exactly what she was doing, and how aggravating it was, but it didn't matter. Her mother continued to do it—and it still worked. "And then," her mother said, "Margaret saw you another time, in a car, with a man. He was bald, she thought, and the car was, I don't know, foreign?"

Hannah was tempted to get up off the couch, waving her arms as she stomped out of the room complaining loudly, perhaps even yelling. For several years she did that often, but since the abortion it just didn't work anymore. Now she also wanted to stay seated and struggle through this with her mother. It wasn't just mother and daughter living together in this house now, it was two women, and when Hannah understood that, she realized that it gave her something new, like an ally. When she could remain calm and rational, it sometimes pushed her mother back, if only a little. Sometimes her mother would get angry and want to drop the whole thing, but eventually Hannah managed to at least get her point across.

Hannah turned off the television. "So?"

"So who is it?" her mother said. "This bald man?"

"He's not *bald*." Hannah tried to make it light, even funny, but didn't quite get there.

"He's not?"

"No, he shaves his head. Though I suppose he does that because he's going bald—which, when you think about it, is a rather remarkable solution. You're afraid of losing your hair, so you shave it all off!" Hannah now looked at her mother, whose mouth was open slightly. "I guess that means that it's not *being* bald that bothers men, it's the idea of *going* bald." She grinned. "It's the transition between hair and no hair. That's what embarrasses them."

Her mother nodded her head slowly as she reached for her glass. "Well." Sip. "Does this man with no hair—" Sip. "With some kind of foreign car—" Sip. "Does he have a *name*?"

"Martin." Sometimes being complete worked best. "Martin Reed."

Her mother put down her glass. She was nearly done with the first one. "He a classmate?"

"No."

"He's not in school?"

"No."

Now her mother looked absolutely stupid.

"Martin's—well, he's almost thirty. That's what you want to know, right? He's not a classmate. You don't know his mother. He's ten years older than me. He's taught me how to drive a stick shift in that old foreign car, which is a Mercedes-Benz. It's a really neat car." Hannah stood up. "Let me make you another one."

She crossed the room, picked up the glass from the table, and went into the kitchen. She took her time preparing the drink. This, too, was new. Sometimes she would wait on her mother. When she was little, all those bowls of cereal, pancakes, lunches and dinners; now her mother's legs were sore and tired, and the least Hannah could do was mix the second drink.

8

MARTIN AND PEARLY raked debris into piles, which they loaded into wheelbarrows and dumped into the back of the Datsun. They rarely spoke, and seldom looked toward the road, where cars streamed by—someone else's misfortune is always interesting. Half the roof was gone, but the front exterior was unharmed except for the charred clapboards above the window.

Around noon a police cruiser stopped in front of the house. Pearly dropped a piece of wood and its blackness came off on his hands. As he rubbed the gritty stuff between his thumb and forefinger, he watched Buzz Gagnon and Frank Colby climb out of the car.

Martin stabbed his shovel into the ground and came over and stood next to Pearly. When he reached them, Buzz stopped and put both hands on his hips. Colby remained a few paces behind, his arms folded, on guard.

Buzz looked at Martin as though he were trying to recall something. "I understand you're related to Jane Kendall?"

"That's right," Martin said.

"So," Gagnon said, looking at Pearly, "that makes you relatives."

Pearly nodded.

"And this is just a nice family enterprise you two have going here," Buzz said.

Colby pressed his sunglasses to the bridge of his nose. Like Pearly, he was primarily a spectator in this, the second. His face had no more expression than the fender on the police car.

Buzz asked, "Got any ideas why someone would torch the place?" When Martin didn't answer right away, Buzz said, "Don't hold back on me, son."

"I didn't start this fire."

"That wasn't my question. You know anyone who would?"

Martin hesitated, then shook his head.

"I see."

"Could have been some kids just goofing around," Pearly said.

"Maybe," Buzz said. "You can never rule out the random, sheer stupidity of vandalism." He squinted up at the house. "I don't believe this was done by just kids, but somebody with a reason. If there was a reason, it invariably means someone's pissed off. It means they have the inability to articulate their anger any other way."

"That's an interesting way to put it," Martin said.

"It's based on more than a few years of experience."

"I'm not doubting you, Captain."

"Didn't think you were. You know anybody like that, Martin?"

"No." Then Martin added, "I can tell you who's pissed off. *I* am."

"I can see that." Gagnon shrugged. "But no wife? Ex?"

"No," Martin said.

"Somebody you owe money?" Buzz said. "Girlfriend you dumped?"

"*No,*" Martin said.

"I see." Buzz shifted his weight. "I gotta ask you where you were last night."

"After work I went out," Martin said. "A few beers in the usual places, that's all."

"You didn't meet anyone?"

"Just briefly," Martin said. "Early in the evening . . ."

Buzz almost smiled and said slowly, "Who was she?"

Pearly glanced over at Colby. With those reflector sunglasses it was impossible to see his eyes.

"She got a name?" Gagnon asked. "Care to whisper it in my ear?"

Martin considered this, but then said, "Hannah LeClaire."

Colby's mouth opened slightly.

Buzz glanced at him, then back at Martin. "It's a sour feeling, isn't it? A fire like this in such an old place."

"You might say that," Martin said.

"I doubt you're the sort who'd have your own place torched for the insurance," Gagnon said. "On the other hand, it can't be ruled out. But then if that's the case, you'd better get your money back, because this place is far from burned to the ground. To torch a house this size, you got to know what you're doing. This fire wasn't started by any damned professional. And I think you know who did it." He waited a moment, then said, "All right, that's the way you want it." He began to work his way around the debris toward the street, but halfway to the car he stopped. "The county fire inspector said something about blood, fresh blood, on the floor in the front hall. You wouldn't know anything about *that*?"

"No, I wouldn't," Martin said.

Pearly shook his head.

Buzz continued on toward the cruiser.

Colby didn't move, as though he wanted to give the captain a head start. His arms were still folded, but his shoulders seemed less imposing and authoritative. For a moment Pearly was certain Colby was going to say something, but then he walked back to the car.

SUNDAY AFTERNOON SEAN was sitting on the rock jetty, working on his third quart of beer in a paper bag. Something about the lake put things in perspective. It brought you out of yourself. Sean watched the boats moored in the harbor and tried not to think about his feet, which were killing him.

Fortunately, when he'd gotten up that morning, his mother was at church and his father was on duty. Sean had managed to avoid seeing either one of them since Friday night. The problem was he could barely walk. The soles of both feet were cut and the gauze pads he'd put on them were stiff with dried blood. Sitting on the edge of the bathtub, he washed his feet, carefully peeling away the old gauze; then after drying them with paper towels, which he flushed down the toilet, he applied new gauze pads. He rinsed out the tub, making sure there was no sign of blood. It took several minutes to pull on his Nikes, and he left the laces untied. When he stood up, it was better— he was able to walk, carefully, out to the driveway and get in his truck.

Now he was thinking about getting another quart of beer and maybe finding out what Arnie was doing—tonight he could call and tell his parents he was staying at Arnie's apartment above Superior Gas & Lube. He climbed down off the rocks and began hobbling back to his truck.

At first he heard the crackle of tires on gravel behind him and he thought nothing of it. But then he looked over his shoulder and saw that it was a patrol car. His father pulled up alongside, about five yards away.

Sean stopped walking. "What?"

"What?" his father said evenly. "I'll tell you *what*." Though he was in uniform, he wasn't wearing his hat because he was sitting in the car. His face was slick with sweat and his sunglasses reflected two tiny suns. "Gagnon is starting to smell that something's up here." He raised a bottle of Fanta orange to his mouth and took a long drink.

Sean kept looking straight at the sunglasses. He knew those glasses were intended to intimidate; to avoid them would give his father the advantage he wanted.

"But look at your feet," his father said. "You can hardly walk on them. It was just a question of somebody dumb enough to go in that house at night in bare feet."

Sean grinned as he raised the bottle to his mouth. He drank some beer, and then said loudly, "So what're you going to *do*?"

"Do?"

"Yeah, call the police? You going to take me *in*?"

His father nodded his head. Then his head became very still. "I didn't mention anything to Buzz."

"That's because you're chicken." His father's face settled into something he'd seldom seen. Sean realized that a quart of beer ago he would have handled this differently, but now he couldn't and it seemed that there was no place to go but straight at it. "You know I'm right," he said. "Isn't that what those glasses are really about? You're chicken." He laughed and took another swig of beer. "When I was ten, twelve you could slap me around. A year ago you thought you could straighten me out by sending me off to boot camp. Well, I'll tell you something, mister: *You* can't do a thing to me!" Sean began walking again. Slowly.

He'd only taken a couple of steps when his father said, "Looks like you've already done enough." Sean turned and looked back at his father, who tipped his bottle of Fanta up to his mouth. Then he sort of smiled.

Sean was standing a few feet in front of the patrol car. He threw the quart bottle wrapped in the paper bag at the front grill. It broke the left headlight.

His father got out, came up to the front of the car, and looked down at the pavement. His movement, everything about him, was slow, compacted. He leaned over, hands on knees, and stared at the ground. Glass—both brown-bottle glass and the clear, bright kernels of glass from the lamp, which glinted brightly in the sun—littered the gravel.

"You got to admit it was a pretty good throw," Sean said. His father turned his head toward him, but he seemed to be looking past him. "I didn't think you could break a headlight with a beer bottle. Must have hit it just right."

"Oh, my *word*." A woman's voice came from behind Sean. Turning, he saw an elderly couple, Mr. and Mrs. Eichhorn. They stood not ten yards away, holding their ancient bicycle built for two, which they rode all around the harbor on summer days.

"Officer Colby," Mr. Eichhorn said. "That's willful destruction of public property." Though it was a warm day, he wore a blue dress shirt with a red, white, and blue bow tie. Beneath his wide-brimmed straw hat his gaunt face was supported by an ugly series of tendons straining beneath the loose skin on his neck.

"Oh, Jesus," Sean said quietly.

Mrs. Eichhorn was as tall and scrawny as her husband. Sean recalled that once during a high-school assembly she had spoken to the students about the virtues of good hygiene and a balanced diet. "We're going to report this," she said, "if you don't do anything about it. We see enough of this sort of behavior on the part of tourists."

Sean looked at his father, who appeared to be considering his options. Something about the set of his mouth suggested that he was at a loss. Finally he said to Sean, "All right. Get in the car."

"*What?*"

"You heard me." His father came over and took a firm hold of his right elbow. "I said get in the car." He walked Sean around to the passenger side of the cruiser and opened the rear door. As Sean got in, his father placed his hand on the top of his head.

9

ALTHEA BRIGGS MADE LAMPS with clear glass bases filled with beach stones, which she sold to tourists. She paid Hannah twenty-five dollars per sack of smooth, colorful stones. Sunday evening Martin went with her down to the beach at Frenchman's Channel. He carried the sack over his shoulder and followed her barefoot through the shallows. Occasionally she would stop, bend over, and reach down into the water, and she'd hand those stones that passed a brief inspection back to him to deposit in the sack. She was wearing cutoffs that were so short the bottoms of the white front pockets were visible against her thighs.

"I need to ask you something," he said.

She kept moving forward, staring down into the clear water ahead of her feet. "What's that?"

"Why didn't you tell me that Sean had come back?"

She picked up a stone, looked at it a moment, then dropped it in the water.

"I mean, you knew he was back, didn't you?"

She walked on, stooped over. "Guess it didn't seem important." They worked their way around a small point, where she found several more keepers. Finally she said, "If I had known he was going to be this way, I guess I would have said something." She handed him a stone, gray with perfect smooth holes in it. "Sean is the past." She moved on. After a minute, she said, "Are you mad? At me?"

"Do I seem mad?"

"I don't know. You seem . . . different."

"Well, maybe I am," Martin said. "This fire at the house, it's made me think."

"So what have you come up with?"

"Two things."

"Two things?"

"That house is one of them. You know, I've never really owned anything before, other than that old car. This house is different. I don't know how to describe it. It's a place that had been condemned. It's a piece of history. It represents something—the way people live. If it's not going to be knocked down, then it should be done right, so that people can live in it. It was a good house, and it can be again in the future. That house *is* the future."

"I think so, too." She had a stone in her hand. "What's the other thing?"

"Don't you know?"

Hannah leaned over and swished the stone in the water, then handed it to him. "That's the last one," she said.

He put the stone in the sack. She didn't wait for him, but walked up onto the beach and sat in dry sand. He followed and sat next to her.

"My mother knows now," she said. "I think I've lost sight of her in recent years—all she does is work, it seems. There's not a lot she doesn't know."

"How about if I meet her?"

Hannah leaned back on her elbows and stared out at the sunset on the lake. "In a few weeks I graduate."

"And after you graduate?"

"I don't know." She lay back on the sand, resting her head on one palm.

He took her other hand in his. Her fingers were rough from handling stones. "Have you ever lived anywhere but here?"

She shook her head. There was a crescent of sand on one cheek, which he brushed off with his free hand. "This is the first really hot day of the year. My mother used to tell me about how she gave birth to me during a heat wave. She came down here to the lake every day with a folding lawn chair. She told me that one day she stood up, squatted in the water, and a minute later brought me out, dripping wet. I really believed that until I was maybe in fourth grade."

"You ever think of leaving the U.P.?"

"Not really. Look—it's May and the days are getting longer. Why would I want to leave? Do you?"

"I keep thinking I'm going to get up one morning and find myself back in my old life. There won't be any house to work on, there won't be you. I'll be building condos in Chicago. Since the fire, I think I'm really beginning to see this house. What it could be."

"What could it be?"

"Ours." He lay down next to her, one hand on her hip, the curve there as smooth as the stones in the sack. "How does this sound?" he said. "When we get the house to a certain point—with the roof done, and the plumbing and electricity fixed—how would it be if we moved in? There's the kitchen and several rooms on the first floor—we could fix them up and live there while we finish the rest of the house."

She kissed him, and her arms came up around his neck. They held each other in the growing dark.

PEARLY SOUGHT HIS OWN COOL, watery haven. He drove a couple of miles west on Route 28 toward Marquette, parked on the side of the road, and walked barefoot down a path through the woods to a creek that fed into Lake Superior. He had a six-pack of Labatt under one arm, and as he waded up the creek the silt bottom dropped away until he was waist-deep. Pearly's spot was the third bend, where the current had built up a ledge of sand. He pulled off his shorts and T-shirt, tossed them up on the bank, and sat on the ledge. The water was up to his Adam's apple. He cracked the first beer and put the remainder of the six-pack by his feet.

A few minutes later he heard the sound of pushed water. Someone was walking upstream. Sally came around the bend, wearing a soggy yellow print dress.

"I was coming back from Marquette when I saw your truck, so I followed you," she said. "God, it was fun to be sneaky." She waded closer and looked down through the water. "Well, isn't this a pretty picture?"

Pearly felt like a boy caught doing something naughty. He slid his butt off the sand ledge and went underwater. Cold water seemed to compress his head. Through the murk he could see her legs beneath the swirl of her dress. He groped around the creek bottom, found the remaining cans of beer, yanked one off its plastic ring, and came up for air. "This might improve the picture." He sat on the ledge again.

Sally reached both arms down into the water and with one graceful motion raised her dress up over her head. She tossed the dress up onto the bank and sat next to him on the ledge. He handed her the can of beer.

THE *WHITEFISH HARBOR HERALD*, referred to by locals as the Fish Wrap, was published once a week. By Wednesday night Sean knew everyone had seen the front-page story about Frank Colby arresting his own son. The incident was described in detail, with supporting quotes from Lawrence and Mildred Eichhorn. Sean had been charged with drunk and disorderly conduct and destruction of public property, and Captain Buzz Gagnon had been quoted as saying that Sean would be suspended indefinitely from duty without pay. Frank Colby, the article added, had declined to comment, while Sean's lawyer, Owen Nault II, said that his client was confident that the matter would be handled fairly and justly by the Marquette County District Court. The newspaper had a photograph of his father in uniform, and the photograph of Sean had been taken during boot camp—his head was shaved to the nub. He looked like a clean-cut kid. He certainly didn't look like trouble.

"Nothing's gone right for you since you got that girl in trouble," his mother said. She was making a meat loaf in the kitchen, and she nearly spat the words out, which was always the case when Hannah was mentioned.

Since Sunday Sean stuck pretty close to home, allowing his feet to heal, and spent a lot of time down in his room, particularly when his father was home. "I screwed up, Ma, but this isn't like the end of the world. Mr. Nault says—"

"Never mind Mr. Nault. He'll be costing your father plenty, believe you me." She put both hands in the bowl, which contained a lump consisting of several pounds of ground sirloin, bread crumbs, chopped onion, A-1 Sauce, and two eggs. Dinner. As she began to mix everything together, her thin hands became glazed with raw meat and egg yolk. She kept her head bent to her task. "I haven't seen your father this way in a long time." Her voice was barely more than a hiss, and it seemed to emanate directly from her lungs, which years of smoking had made permanently thick with phlegm. She coughed once, and Sean almost expected something to come up and land in the bowl of meat.

"He's been quiet," Sean said. "Quieter than I thought—at least since Sunday night." She glanced up and he smiled, but she was having none of it. Usually a day or two after his father blew up, Sean and his mother could make light of it. But this time she wasn't willing to participate in their little conspiracy.

"What I want to know is when all this trouble's going to come to an end." She squeezed the meat so that it oozed from her fists.

Sean went to the refrigerator. "I need a beer if I'm going to watch this any longer."

"You think this is a joke, don't you?" she said.

"Ma, take it easy." He grabbed a can of Stroh's, shut the refrigerator door, and returned to his stool. "I don't get why I can't just pay for the headlight. I mean, it's a *headlight*."

"No, you just don't *get* it, do you, Sean?" She lifted the entire wad of gummy meat out of the bowl and laid it in the greased baking pan. He opened the can of beer and drank down a good half of it. "Know what I think?" She began to shape the meat into a loaf, pushing down with both hands as though she were trying to resuscitate a heart attack victim. "I *think*—that *you*—actually—en*joy this.*"

"Enjoy what?"

"*Trouble.*"

She stopped pumping. The effort seemed to have exhausted her. Turning, she rinsed her hands in the sink, then dried them with a towel.

"Come on," he said.

She lit a cigarette. "No, Sean. It's how you've been since you were small. You do something you shouldn't and if you get caught you show no shame. None."

"We're talking about a headlight! I had a couple of beers!"

"You show no shame," she repeated, inhaling her cigarette, her hand shaking noticeably. "And then—then what you do is you go and do something that makes it worse. Because you like it. *That's* why, Sean. You like the attention."

Sean got up off the stool, its legs scraping loudly on the linoleum floor. "The only reason this got any att*ent*ion is because my father's a cop. And I'm a cop—a summer part-timer, but still a cop. Any other guy—any college kid working here for the summer—and it wouldn't mean a *thing* to anybody."

"Well, *you* aren't just anybody—your *father* isn't just anybody."

Sean stepped backward and knocked the stool over, which clattered on the floor. "That's not *my* problem!"

She began yelling then. Her voice reached that frantic pitch that he couldn't stand. It got right into his nervous system somehow and seemed to alter the composition of his blood. He knew what she was saying without hearing the words. And he was yelling, too. All denials, all justifications. None of it ever worked. He opened the refrigerator, cold air pressing against his face and chest. She was screaming now, so he grabbed two beer cans with one hand, then slammed the door shut. Her voice chased him down the hall, down the basement stairs, until he was in his room, where he slammed that door with everything he had—and still her voice came down through the ceiling.

PART II

10

THE SECOND SATURDAY in June Hannah graduated from high school, and the following day she and Martin moved into the first floor of his house. They did so with her mother's blessing, which at first surprised Hannah. Her mother had met Martin, first over dinner at the Brownstone Inn out on Route 28, and then several times at her house, and saw that he was indeed unlike other boys who had taken an interest in Hannah. One night Suzanne explained her reasoning to Hannah. None of the boys Hannah's age who could be expected to remain in Whitefish Harbor had much sense of a future. In most cases they were kids like Arnie Frick who went into their father's business, usually a trade or the management of a shop. Some, of course, went to college. Hannah showed little inclination to do so, and Suzanne was somewhat relieved that she wouldn't have to figure out how to pay for college for the next four or five years. Even the state universities were no great bargain. But at the bottom of her acceptance was the fear that if Hannah left the U.P., she would never return. Suzanne had been born and raised here, and her husband had abandoned her with a baby when she was still a young woman. Over the years Suzanne became self-sufficient, durable, relentlessly practical. At the hospital she worked with an increasingly aging population, and just knowing that her daughter was still in Whitefish Harbor might be all the comfort she could expect in the coming years. So with her usual muted enthusiasm—she offered furniture, blankets, kitchenware, which they piled into the Mercedes and the back of Pearly's truck—she helped Hannah move into Martin's house.

Often when Martin and Pearly finished work for the day, they would go out to the shaded backyard, where Hannah had arranged the set of old wrought-iron lawn furniture she had bought at a yard sale. She had spray-painted the table and chairs white and washed the seat cushions. They drank beer and talked about the progress of the house. Pearly would stay for a beer or two, then drive home or, more likely, to some place like the Portage. Hannah always asked him to stay for dinner, but he seldom did. They were new at this and he could see they wanted to spend their evenings alone together.

Gracie took to the house and its yard, which was surrounded by woods, hunting for field mice, birds, and small snakes, which she proudly displayed on the back steps or sometimes in the bathtub. Many of the walls were still unpainted Sheetrock, with broad swaths of joint compound covering the seams. Hannah often sang to a CD or the radio. Sometimes while cooking she'd break into a little tap dance. She and Martin had made love so often, in the bedroom, in the living room, standing in the kitchen, that it was as though they were determined to establish territory through intimacy.

One night Martin finished his shower, and he pulled on a pair of shorts as he went into the kitchen. He got the pitcher of ice water out of the refrigerator and a glass from the sink. Looking up, he watched Hannah through the window screen. She was leaning back in her chair, with her long bare legs up on the table, crossed at the ankles. A faint imprint from the wrought-iron seat decorated the exposed underside of her tanned thigh. The newspaper was folded on her knees. Her hair hung down, so he couldn't see her face. She raised one hand, brushed her hair back over her shoulder, then began to gnaw on a thumbnail.

He said, "What is it?"

She looked up toward the window, startled. At first it seemed she wanted to conceal something, but she said, "I don't know, it's just . . . *this.*" She dropped the newspaper on the table.

HANNAH WENT INTO the kitchen to start dinner. Chicken, rice, and broccoli, with a salad. She was accustomed to cooking for two, but her mother had always wanted her food bland—no spices other than salt and pepper, and absolutely no garlic. Now Hannah used fresh garlic in almost everything. After the long days of working on the house, Martin ate two and three helpings. He had the metabolism of a twelve-year-old. Nothing stayed on him. From the sink she watched him sitting in the backyard. He wore only a pair of faded tan shorts; his ribs were clearly etched below his taut chest and shoulder muscles as he leaned over the new edition of the *Herald*. He didn't move as he read the article.

The front-page article was entitled "Police Hiring Under Scrutiny." The author of the article, Bettina Laakso, was the owner and editor of the newspaper, and she raised questions about Sean's early release from the army and how he had subsequently been hired by the police department. According to official documents quoted in the article, he had received an honorable discharge. However, Laakso also quoted several sources who said that Sean was sent home from his base in Italy as a result of some scandal—the article was not very specific—which the army may have tried to cover up. One source, a captain who had been stationed with Sean, said that there was more to Sean's early discharge than "meets the eye. Brass always protect themselves. They're just like everybody else. It's always, always CYA first, if you catch my drift." *Cover your ass.* The captain was currently stationed in Alaska. The other source was a fellow recruit from Duluth, Minnesota, Bobby Loomis, who had been discharged along with Sean. He was reluctant to speak on record but didn't refuse outright; it was clear he felt Sean was at least in part responsible for his own early discharge. The most specific thing he said was, "These women knew what they were getting into, and beyond that you're going to have to talk to my lawyer." There were also quotes from the chief of police, Buzz Gagnon, who said that Sean had been hired by the Whitefish Harbor police department based on his good military record and the fact that he had known this young man since he was a boy. Frank Colby refused to comment for the article. Sean, apparently, could not be reached at all. Charges against him of drunk and disorderly conduct and destruction of public property were pending in Marquette County District Court.

When Martin finished reading the article, he came into the kitchen. "Was Sean such a piece of work when you knew him?"

"It seems like a long time ago," she said. "Sean was a leader-of-the-pack kind of guy. I don't know how some kids establish that but he did. There were always other boys standing around him. I was very shy and nobody stood around me. I always felt alone in school—always. So I suppose that's what drew me to him at first." She turned the heat on under the pot of broccoli. "It didn't take long, though, for me to realize that there was, I don't know, this strange wrinkle in him. He needed others around him. What was he without them?" As an afterthought, she said almost to herself, "Not just a wrinkle, a twist. There's this twist to him I sensed but could never figure out. It's as though he was protecting it—you could never try to talk to him about it." She stared at the flame licking out from beneath the pot, then turned the heat down. "When I learned I was pregnant, Sean just disappeared on me. What do you call that?"

"An invertebrate," Martin said.

11

AFTER THE SECOND article came out in the *Herald,* Sean tended
to go out mostly at night. During the day he stayed in his room.
Because the house was on a slope, he could look out the sliding glass
door at the backyard, which was hemmed in by woods. The midday
sunlight was unbearable and he would draw the curtain across the
door. The light and heat that came through the glass reminded him
of Italy. Le Marche–Piceno U.S. Air Force Base was comprised primarily of air force personnel who maintained a fleet of fighters and
bombers. Technically, the army's role was to provide protection for
the air force, which as part of Operation Joint Endeavor was making
daily sorties across the Adriatic Sea to Kosovo. Sean's days were filled
with numbing routine.

When on leave, Sean, like most of the military, took the train to
one of the coastal towns. Some went to Venice, others to the resort
town of Rimini, which was popular with German tourists. Sean visited these places, as well as small medieval towns such as Macerata
and Recanati, tight stone labyrinths that had been perched on a hill-
top for centuries. But it was the seaport of Ancona that he continu-
ally returned to, once Bobby Loomis introduced him to Gregor.
Gregor had girls. He was Albanian and he usually could be found in
a bar called Mare Adriatico. The place was on a narrow street above
the harbor, and it reeked of tobacco. The regulars at Mare Adriatico

were mostly Eastern European. Though Bobby and Sean always wore their civvies, their haircuts were a dead giveaway that they were American military. They were treated well because it was assumed they had money.

Gregor's girls were young, some no more than fourteen or fifteen. The first time Sean didn't want anything to do with it, and he waited in the bar while Loomis went out back with one of the girls.

"Where do they come from?" Sean asked. It was their second visit.

Gregor was in his late twenties. His teeth were already rotten, but he had liquid brown eyes that had the sympathetic appeal of an injured animal. Sean knew he was pretending not to understand the question.

"The girls," Sean said. "Where do they come from? Albania, like you?"

"Ah, yes," Gregor said happily. "Many countries, many bad places."

"I read where girls are kidnapped and brought to Italy." Sean knew Loomis had turned his head to look at him, but he ignored him. "It was in a newspaper," Sean said. "*Il Resto del Carlino.* My Italian's getting to the point where I can figure out the newspaper."

"No, *no!*" Gregor said. When he spoke English his voice tended to explode in unexpected ways. He raised his hand, indicating to the waiter that they needed another round of *mistra.* "The girls want to escape and I *help* them. They want to come here. You have no idea what it's *like* there." Then he held his hands out in a gesture that commonly meant, *But what can I do?* "They have much difficulty finding work because they have not *had* school. So they do *this* because you have to eat, no? Look and see which one you like. I make *presentazione.*" From the inside pocket of his leather jacket he produced about a dozen small photographs of girls, which he spread out on the table.

Loomis studied each photo carefully, pausing over two. "God, will you look at this one?" he said. He'd already been out back once tonight, and Sean knew that after another drink he'd want to go again. Loomis looked forward to the trips to Ancona all week. It was all he could talk about; it was like being hooked on a drug. "I can't make up my mind."

Gregor smiled.

"He's ugly and he's from Minnesota," Sean explained. "They don't have many girls in Minnesota."

Gregor leaned forward and looked seriously at Sean's mouth. "*Nooo* girls?"

"Not like these," Sean said. "It's so cold—*freddo*—and you can never get them to take all their clothes off. Loomis never saw a naked woman before coming here."

Loomis had a long head with ears that stuck straight out sideways. Acne scars covered his neck and cheeks. "He's never even *been* to Minnesota," he said to Gregor. "So how would he know?"

Gregor reached into another pocket and removed a small notebook, which he laid on the table between their drinks. On each page was taped a photo of a girl. Some of them were bare breasted; some stared longingly at the camera as they sucked on their fingertips. Loomis flipped through the pages and stopped at a photo of a dark-haired girl. "Look at those tits," he whispered. Turning the page, he looked at a blonde. "Oh, Mama."

Gregor sipped his *mistra*. "You like two? I can get you two, *non c'e problema*."

IT WAS ON a Saturday night in November that Sean first saw her. Loomis had been gone nearly an hour with two girls. Mare Adriatico was not very crowded because of the rain, and there were a lot of girls sitting around, coming and going, looking bored. Sean first saw her back—something about her shoulders, the shape of her red hair—and then she leaned forward on her bar stool and turned. She had long legs. Her profile was somehow familiar. Her white blouse rose up from her black jeans enough to expose the arc of her hip. She leaned on the bar and lit a cigarette.

Sean got up from his table and walked toward the toilet; at the door he paused so that he could see her face in the mirror behind the bar. She had Hannah's cheekbones and mouth. The eyes were too made up and appeared large and startled. She caught his eye in the mirror and her stare was even, then abruptly she ignored him. He stepped into the bathroom and realized that he was sweating.

He arranged it with Gregor. Not in a car—cars in Italy were very small—but in an apartment. She said her name was Nikki and she seemed nervous. After a few minutes she said, "Why you look at me this way? What you want? You must tell me." They were sitting on a brown corduroy sofa with frayed armrests. The place smelled of cigarettes. When he didn't answer, she shrugged as she stood up. She went into the bedroom, undressed quickly, and lay down on her back on the bed. There was a poster on the wall above her of the medieval town of Ascoli Piceno. He only knew that Piceno was the name of an ancient people who had inhabited this part of Italy.

Finally, he got up off the sofa and sat on the bed. "You pay just to look?" She pushed out her lips and shrugged. It was a common gesture, which meant *This is strange but what can you do?* She was imitating it; she wasn't Italian. Her hair was the awful dyed red, but the roots were dark.

"Where are you from?" he asked.

"Why?"

"I want to know."

"No you don't."

"All right, I don't. You're here now." He reached out tentatively and touched her hair. "This isn't—" But he didn't finish.

"Isn't? Isn't *what*? I don't under*stand* you. What's *isn't*?"

"Nothing." He took his hand away from her hair and began to unbutton his shirt. "It isn't important." He unbuckled his pants. "You know what I want?" She watched his mouth, to make sure she understood him. "Guess," he said.

"Guess?"

"Yes, *sì*. You can figure it out."

———————

SEAN KEPT CLEAR of his father. He only went upstairs when he knew his father wasn't home. He'd lived in this basement room since he was six years old, listening to the floor creak overhead, and he used to imagine that it was giants roaming about in the kitchen. When he did something to upset his father, the door at the top of the stairs would be locked. Sean could still come and go through the sliding glass door that went out to the yard, but he was not permitted upstairs. At such times he used to think of himself as a prisoner in jail. He was doing time. Eventually his father would unlock the door and tell him to come upstairs so they could discuss what Sean had done wrong.

Once, when he was fourteen, he refused to come up the stairs when his father called. His father said, "You come up here now, mister, because if I come down there, you're not going to like it." Sean stayed put. When he heard his father coming down the stairs, he locked the door to his room, then sat on the bed. He was shaking. His father broke the door open with his shoulder—it was a cheap door that was hollow inside, and wood splinters sprayed all over the carpet. Once inside the bedroom, he removed his belt and used it on Sean's legs and fanny.

GREGOR ARRANGED FOR Nikki to be at Mare Adriatico whenever Sean and Loomis came into Ancona on leave. She would take Sean to the small apartment on the third floor of a building that had stucco walls the color of egg yolk. The wood shutters were always closed and they often rattled in the raw north wind that came off the sea in winter, called *bora*. On sunny days the shutters cast bars of light into the bedroom. Nikki had a cigarette lit almost constantly and the smoke drifted up through the bars of light above the bed. When they were finished they would take a shower together—she liked that—and then towel each other off. The tile floors were always cold.

After a month Sean asked her if she would change her hair.

They were sitting in Mare Adriatico with Gregor, Loomis, and a tall Russian girl named Zoya. Nikki was wearing the green-and-gold Packers T-shirt Sean had given her. "No," she said.

Gregor put both elbows on the table. "What *color*?" he asked Sean.

"I was thinking blond."

Nikki looked away.

Gregor tapped out one of his Chesterfields and lit it. "*Boh.* Make you think of girlfriend in *Stati Uniti*?"

"I'll pay for it," Sean said.

"But what if other men like red?" Gregor shrugged, pushed out his lips. His eyes suggested true pain. "What—red, blond, red, blond, red, blond?"

"Just blond," Sean said to Nikki. "Stay blond."

She got up and walked over to the bar and sat on a stool, keeping her back to their table. Gregor shrugged again, then he laughed. "See why I get paid for this trouble? I try to help, but it's always to be *trouble.*"

Loomis rarely went with the same girl twice, but he liked Zoya. He thought Sean was out of his mind not to try other girls. "You're not going to make Nikki into some girlfriend in friggin' Michigan, you know."

"You're so ugly you never got laid without paying for it."

Loomis only grinned. So did Gregor, though they had been speaking English so fast that he really couldn't keep up. Zoya looked bored as she lit another cigarette.

"You ever even get a date in Minnesota?" Sean asked.

"You need to lighten up," Loomis said.

"I hate this," Sean said. "Sometimes I think prison would be better than the army."

"It does suck—big time. But prisoners don't get to go on leave. Why don't you try that girl with the lips? I tell you, she can roll up your eyelids like a window shade."

The next weekend they went to Ancona, Nikki was blond and she'd had about two inches trimmed, which made her hair seem fuller. It curled around her ears much like Hannah's hair, though there were dark roots. Nikki wouldn't look back at Sean.

"Happy now?" Loomis said to Sean. "That ought to put rebar in your concrete."

"Shut up." Sean said to Gregor, "How much?"

"Hair salons, *allora!*" Gregor said. "Charge a lot, I can tell *you*. Lot of what they call *product.*" He sipped his *mistra.* "Think I will go into that business. You know, diversify."

At the apartment Sean saw the bruises on Nikki's ribs. "Gregor?"

She smoked her cigarette.

"I didn't want that to happen," he said.

She cut him a look as she inhaled.

"Why don't you get away from Gregor?"

Nikki sighed, exasperated.

"No," he said. "I mean it. Why don't you just leave Gregor?"

"Nobody just leave Gregor." She sat up and put her cigarette out on the nightstand. "He shot up a Hungarian last year and she OD. Found in—" She nodded her head in the direction of the harbor. "You think you be blond, you wear ugly Packer shirt, you look American, you be free?" She turned her head away. "*Boh.*"

"I could help you."

"Help me what? *Che?*"

"Get free."

She got up off the bed and walked to the bathroom door. The horizontal bars of light created an optical illusion; her body seemed to be comprised of a stack of illuminated disks. "Why don't you ask for other girls? That would get me free." She shut the door.

SEAN LISTENED TO his father's footsteps come down the basement stairs. It had to be in the nineties outside; even with the drape drawn across the sliding glass door, the heat invaded the room. His father stood outside the door for a long moment, and Sean almost expected him to break the door down. But then he knocked gently.

"It's open," Sean said.

His father came in with two cans of beer. "Awful dark in here."

"Stays cooler that way."

His father handed Sean one of the beers. He brought the desk chair over next to the bed and straddled it, propping his forearms on the backrest. After opening his beer, he sipped the foam that rose out of the top of the can. "Got a call from Dan Schofield." Dan Schofield was on every board or committee that had something to do with how Whitefish Harbor was run. He was a retired investment banker who played a lot of golf. Sean's father played three, maybe four times a year. When he did, it was usually with Schofield. Every time he came home from the golf course, he talked about how much he couldn't stand the game or Schofield. "He says the town commissioners have been working the phones real hard since that article came out." His father took another sip of beer. It was so dark Sean could barely see his father's face, but what little light came through the drapes lit up the sheen of sweat that coated his forehead and jaw. His father's voice was too even and it occurred to Sean that he was frightened. "Some of them think this could lead to a lawsuit against the town. Something to do with our hiring practices. Nepotism, Schofield said."

"I'm not even sure I know what that means," Sean said. "In this case, a father who gets his son hired?"

"That's about it."

"I have qualifications. A high-school degree. Military background. Christ, you've hired summer cops who have studied law enforcement in college for a couple of semesters."

"Uh-huh," his father said. "But they're not related."

"I could give you a list of people who are related that work for the town. On the road crew, in town hall, at the library."

"I know, I know. When I was young family mattered. It was the best qualification you could have. Not anymore, thanks to the Democrats." His father's patience was disconcerting. Sean really wanted his father to start shouting or something. "That's part of it, I gather. They start to look at how we came to hire you, and then they might ask why Anne Templeton works in the library and Dean Cooley drives a snowplow all winter. Because we all *know* a perfect *stranger* could do a better job."

"Fuck 'em." Sean waited, expecting there to be some reaction, some admonition.

But his father said, "People have been calling Schofield and the others on the commission, saying they have to get to the bottom of this."

"What do they want? I'm out of a job now. Go hire a stranger."

His father took a long pull on his beer. "What this is really about is not *your* job."

"What, then?"

"My job."

They were silent for a while. The cold beer can felt good in his hand and he finally remembered to take a sip. "So what do we do?"

"First, I need to know exactly what happened over there in Italy."

"I told you, we got into a little trouble with the local authorities. The brass thought it might be embarrassing to them, so they cut us loose and got us out of there. There are enough scandals in the military as it is."

"What kind of trouble exactly? You've never really been clear, and we've pretty much let it go, thinking you were young and what you got into over there didn't concern us."

"You mean 'couldn't hurt you.' " His father didn't answer. Sean dropped his head back against the cinder-block wall. He could feel the coolness of the concrete against his skin. "Jesus, this is all in the past, this is . . . history."

"And I want to know who else knows about this."

"You mean like Arnie? I haven't told him anything."

"I mean like who was involved over there. That bleeding-heart liberal who owns that fish wrap is already trying to track down people who knew what happened. Christ, she called some kid—what was his name?"

"Loomis. Billy Loomis."

"Yeah, way out in Minnesota." His father waited, and when Sean didn't say anything, he said, "I mean, was it girls? Or drugs, or what?"

After a moment, Sean said, "You could beat it out of me."

"I've thought about that, but you're too big now." His father was trying to make a joke, but he wasn't buying it himself.

"The only one who *really* knew anything was Loomis, and you don't have to worry about him. And the brass that sent us packing, they'll never say anything because then it'll come back on their heads. I can't believe this could mean your job. You've been there forever."

"What you don't realize is some people have wanted me out for a long time." His father tilted his head back and finished his beer. "You can't trust any of 'em. Schofield, Buzz, they're all politicians. They've been waiting for this chance." He looked at the can for a moment as though he didn't know how it got in his hand. "Listen," he said, his voice now—finally—angry, even threatening. "I want to know exactly what happened."

"No you don't," Sean said.

"You're going to bury me."

Sean lifted his head away from the concrete wall. "Eventually."

"All right." His father got up off the chair and went to the door. "Then I want you out of here. After tonight, this isn't your room anymore. Not free, at least. You want to stay here, you live by the rules, and you pay room and board." He went out and closed the door behind him.

ON A WARM night in March, Gregor wasn't at Mare Adriatico. The bartender told Sean that Nikki was at the apartment. He found her waiting down in the lobby. She had a bandage over her left eyebrow.

They went out into the street and walked up over the steep hill to the cliffs above the Adriatic, then took the path that wound down to the rocky shore. The pale stones underfoot were soft and brittle as sticks of chalk. They came to a long row of caves that fishermen had cut into the cliffs to store their boats. Each cave had a large wooden door, most painted bright colors. Nikki had a key to one of the caves. Inside she lit a gas lantern. There were tables and chairs, a sofa in back. The air in the cave was cool and smelled of fish and damp stone.

"How'd you get the key?" he asked.

"I live here. *Adesso*—now."

"Where's Gregor?"

Nikki sat next to him on the sofa. "Tonight you pay me."

"Gregor wouldn't like that."

"Gregor is gone."

"Where did he go?"

She shrugged.

He reached out and touched her forehead gently. "What happened here?"

She pulled her head back.

"Somebody hit you? Let me see."

Her eyes were large, worried, and for a moment he thought she might cry—they were often angry, even fierce, but he had never seen them like this. He'd never seen her frightened. "You can pay me tonight?" she said, pleading.

"You're going," he said. "You're hiding here and you're going free."

"*Sì*." She leaned forward until her face was close to his, and her hands rested on his thigh. "I am not me for you. I am somebody else. Blond."

"No, I'm here because of somebody else, but you are you."

"What is her name?"

"I'm sorry I started this. Loomis was right."

She shook her head. "*Suo nome?*"

"Hannah."

"*Haan-naah?*"

"Yes, I'm sure it sounds funny to you."

"What do you want? Anything I can do. *Haan-naah* love you."

Sitting in his bedroom in Whitefish Harbor, Sean remembered mostly the way their breathing echoed off the soft stone walls in the cave. And how the mist of the sea came in on the night air. But she didn't remind him of Hannah at all. She never had, not really. He kept wanting her to, but she didn't. Strange: For the first time it was all right.

When he paid her, he asked, "Where do you go now? Home?"

"Home?"

"Albania? Hungary? Wherever you're from."

"No." She counted the money. He had given her twice what he usually gave Gregor. She folded the bills, tucked them in the front pocket of her jeans, then leaned toward him and kissed his cheek. "*Nord.*"

"Where, north?"

"I must go. Meet Zoya."

"The tall Russian girl? Loomis will be sorry. He liked her enough to go with her more than once." Nikki didn't seem to understand what he meant or it wasn't important. She was looking toward the door of the cave. "I will go with you to meet Zoya," he said.

After a moment she nodded. "*Stazione.*"

"*Treno?*"

"*Sì.*"

They climbed back to the top of the cliff, then walked down to catch the bus for the train station above the harbor. They didn't speak, but Nikki held Sean's hand. He didn't know whether it was out of affection or fear. At the train station he got off with her. She put her hand on his chest as though to push him back, but he followed her through the station. She paused to read the schedule and then led him out to the platform and down through the tunnel that went under the tracks. They came upstairs at *Binario 3: Bologna.* There was a crowd waiting for the train, but no sign of Zoya.

Then it happened very fast. Sean looked up at the sign and saw the light flashing next to the word *Bologna,* which meant the train was about to arrive. Nikki said something he didn't understand, and looking across the tracks, he saw Zoya and Loomis coming out of the station. She carried a small suitcase, and from a distance she looked quite elegant in a long gray raincoat. They were both walking fast. Then Sean saw two men, both in leather jackets, sprinting through the waiting room inside the station. When they pushed through the glass doors, Zoya and Loomis broke into a run and disappeared down the stairs to the tunnel.

The train's headlight gleamed off the tracks as it approached, its horn blaring. Sean turned to Nikki, who was watching the men disappear down the stairs. Her eyes were glazed with tears and she was saying something in a language that was not Italian. Sean ran down the stairs back into the tunnel. As the train pulled in overhead, he heard shouts, a scream. At the bottom of the stairs he looked right and saw Loomis leaning with his back against the wall, and Zoya on her hands and knees, as though looking for something she had dropped. The two men were running back toward the stairs that led up to the station. As Sean ran down the tunnel, he saw Loomis kneel next to Zoya and try to hold her up, but she collapsed on the tiles, which Sean then realized were smeared with blood.

He was never sure exactly what they did then or how much time passed. The girl's throat had been cut and Loomis was trying to shout above the noise of the train overhead. Finally, Sean went to the stairs to get help. He climbed up to the platform and saw the *polizia* coming out of the station—there were three of them, and the shortest one took him firmly by the upper arm, while the others went down into the tunnel. The policeman spoke so rapidly, Sean couldn't understand a word. Sean kept saying *"Non lo so"* over and over. *I don't know, I don't know.* Then the train began to pull away from *Binario 3,* slowly at first. Sean watched the long line of cars pick up speed as they moved out into the darkness, and when the last car was gone, the platform was empty.

SEAN HEARD HIS father's van pull out of the driveway. He stayed in his room, listening to his mother overhead. Every twenty minutes or so he heard her go through the same routine: open the freezer door, fill her glass with ice cubes, close the freezer door, pour bourbon over the ice, put the bottle back on the kitchen counter. After a couple of hours, she walked out the front door and slammed it behind her. Quickly, he got off his bed, drew back the curtain, and opened the sliding glass door. He jogged around the side of the garage and watched his mother back her car out of the driveway at an angle. She was trying to steer by looking in the rearview mirror. Her glass of bourbon sat on the dashboard. When the right rear tire bumped over the curb, the fender hit the split-rail fence that was draped with roses. There was the sound of splintering wood. The drink slid off the dashboard.

Sean went down the driveway and looked in through the open window. "Going somewhere?"

Ice lay in his mother's lap. "*What?*"

"Why don't you come back in the house where it's cool?"

"*Why* are you doing *this*?"

"Doing what?"

"*This*," she said. "You're *ruining* us."

"Ma, you're hammered. And you just killed a bunch of roses it took you about ten years to grow. Every spring you look forward to seeing those roses bloom."

"No, I'm *not* hammered. But my pants're all wet." She threw open the door and tried to get out of the car. He took her by the arm but she yanked it away. "You're doing it, you know you are." She was leaning so far forward it looked as though she might fall over. "I don't know, maybe you think—I've *never* known what you think. I couldn't understand you when you're eight years old. I fed and clothed a *lit*-tle monster. Who *are* you?"

"You'll never know," he said. "You'll never get it."

"I don't get you *or* your goddamn father." She got to her feet, took an involuntary step sideways, and fell to the ground. "*Damn it,* help me get *up!*"

A mosquito flew into Sean's ear and he slapped the side of his head hard. The buzzing stopped. "No," he said. "I don't think so." He walked to his truck.

"You come *back* here."

Sean got in behind the wheel and started the truck, then backed around her car and out the end of the driveway. He left rubber in the street.

12

HANNAH STOPPED AT Superior Gas & Lube. Sean's pickup was parked beside the station. Arnie came out of the office and said, "He's been staying at my place upstairs." He leaned against the side of the Mercedes as the gas pump clicked along. "His dad chucked him out finally after that shit in the newspaper."

"How's he doing?" she asked.

Arnie played with the curved bill of his Red Wings cap for a moment. "Sleeps on the couch most nights, 'cept sometimes he wanders off, gets drunk, and I guess he sleeps on the beach. Some days he's got all these bug bites on his face and it looks pretty grim."

The gas pump shut off; he topped up the tank and screwed the cap back on, then jammed the nozzle back on the pump. She handed him a twenty. As he made change, peeling bills off the wad he kept in his pocket, Hannah heard a door shut. She squinted up through the windshield and saw Sean come out on the small landing at the top of the apartment stairs. He was barefoot and didn't have a shirt on, just a pair of faded jeans with a tear in one knee. Placing both hands on the railing, he stared down at the car. He looked so different it took her a moment to realize why: His head was shaved clean. It gleamed in the afternoon sun. *"Jesus,"* she whispered.

"Oh, yeah," Arnie said, handing her several worn bills. "Did that the other day. I can rib him about it and he can't pop me in the eye now 'cause he knows I'll throw him out, and then he'll be out of places to go."

Sean watched them for a moment longer, then abruptly went back into the apartment. Hannah started the car and said, "Thanks, Arnie." She started to pull away from the pumps but then turned and parked on the shady side of the garage. Getting out, she said, "Tell me, he alone up there?"

Arnie looked perplexed. "Sean's alone everywhere."

"I'm going to go up and talk to him."

"Ooo-kay." Arnie began walking back to the office door, scratching the back of his neck. "You don't come out of there in five minutes, I'll call in the militia."

"Deal."

Hannah climbed the wooden stairs up the side of the garage to the apartment. She rapped her knuckles on the door window. From inside, she heard footsteps, then the door, which stuck in the jamb due to the humidity, was pulled open. Sean stared out at her as though he had never seen her before. Without his hair, his face seemed beefy. No question he was his father's son. That jaw was oiled with a sheen of sweat.

"Hi," she said. "I thought maybe we could, you know, talk?"

"Talk?"

"Yes, Sean. Have a conversation?"

He gazed past her a moment. "What about?"

"Look, it's hot out here in the sun. Mind if I come in?"

He hesitated, then said, "Sure."

The door was low and she ducked her head as she entered a kitchenette. She'd never been up to Arnie's apartment before; all the ceilings were slanted, which made it seem tight and small. There were dirty dishes stacked in the sink, empty beer bottles on the counter. Flies buzzed against the windows.

Sean went into the living room and sat down on the couch. A sleeping bag was spread out beneath him, and there were magazines and more plates and empty bottles covering the coffee table.

Hannah's legs were shaking slightly and she wanted to sit down. There was a chair across the room, but she decided against it. "Listen, Sean, I just think we might try and clear the air."

"What's wrong with the air?" Without his shirt on she could see his shoulders and arms were still muscular but he'd put on at least ten pounds around his middle. He had bug bites on his face and scalp, and some looked as if they'd been gouged with fingernails until they'd bled.

Hannah waited. It wasn't easy. It was stifling in the apartment—worse than out in the afternoon sun—and the only sound was the buzzing of flies. Finally he raised his eyes, and she said, "There just doesn't seem to be any point in going on like this, is all. What happened can't be changed. I don't want to go on feeling this way every time I see you. You know?"

Something gave in his eyes. He seemed to have made some kind of decision. His whole head, she realized, was beaded with sweat. "I suppose you're right."

She went over to the chair and sat down. It was so hot it was difficult to breathe. "Do you suppose I could have a glass of water or something?"

He got up from the couch and went to the refrigerator in the kitchenette. "I guess I know what you mean. When you think about it, it's really dumb. We both are going to live here, we're both going to see each other. It only makes sense we get along." He took out a bottle of water, opened it, and brought it to her. Instead of going back to the couch, he sat on the edge of the coffee table and leaned forward with his elbows on his knees. One hand played idly with the tear in the denim.

Hannah took a long drink of cold water. "I'm sorry you're having this trouble with the police, and this court thing, and all that stuff in the newspaper—and now I guess your folks, too."

"It'll work out."

"I know it will." She took another drink and suddenly felt a bit light-headed. "It's really hot up here. I don't know how you can . . ." She drank more water.

"I know. Arnie's being really good about letting me crash here. Tell you the truth, I've been thinking about taking off, getting out of the U.P. entirely." He sounded almost hopeful and he never took his eyes off of her.

She didn't want to sound pleased, but she couldn't help saying, "You know, the summer people don't understand." He smiled. "They think Whitefish Harbor is always a sunny day in July. They don't see the *long* gray winters. It might be good to get away from it." She filled her mouth with water and swallowed with difficulty. "Where would you go?"

"Oh, I'm working on a few things, talking to some people, you know, down around Detroit. Or Chicago. Or maybe over to Minneapolis."

"You won't become a Twins fan?"

" 'Course not."

"God, this heat," she said. "Will you promise me something?"

"Sure."

"You'll let me know. You won't just disappear."

"No. I'll call or something."

She realized her hands were shaking and she was having a hard time holding the bottle. Her back was chilled. There were goose bumps on her arms and it was as though something icy were sliding beneath her skin. "I think . . ."

"You need to get out of this heat up here," he said, standing.

Hannah heard the plastic bottle hit the floor. She wasn't sure, but after that she might have fainted or blacked out for just a few moments, because suddenly she was walking down the outside stairs. The sun was so hot it seemed her hair would catch fire. She realized that Sean was holding her by the elbow and Arnie was standing at the bottom of the stairs.

"I'm all right," Hannah said. "I just had to get out of that heat."

"I could drive you," Arnie said.

"No, really—thanks. I'm feeling better already. I'll be fine once I get home." She stood up straighter and walked to the Mercedes. Arnie was at her side, one hand on her elbow, an oddly formal gesture. Before she got in the car, she looked back toward Sean. He gazed at her a moment, then climbed the stairs to the apartment.

WHEN HE REACHED the landing, it hit Sean: Hannah had said "home" differently. "Home" was no longer her mother's house, but that old place Martin Reed had bought. Hannah was now living there with him.

HANNAH OPENED HER EYES. Martin was sitting on the edge of their bed. She had slept for what seemed like days. She had no idea what time it was, only that it was dark outside. Martin had made hard-boiled eggs, which he'd peeled and chilled in a bowl of ice. Gracie was curled up asleep at the foot of the bed.

"He shaved his head clean," Hannah said. "On him it looks so . . . I don't know." She sat up and took one of the eggs from the bowl. "He's also put on weight, so he looks even more like his father." She began eating the egg. It had been awhile since something tasted so good to her.

"What do you think's happening with him? He's been thrown out of his parents' house. He's out of work. He's facing some kind of legal trouble that won't go away. . . ."

Hannah finished the first egg and took another from the bowl. "This afternoon, for a moment, I thought he and I were, you know, talking, getting through, and I said I wanted to make peace with him so in the future there wouldn't be all this . . . this *weight* whenever I saw him. I see him and it's like the air gets heavy all of a sudden. Maybe he wants to put it all behind him now, too. I don't know."

"Shaving his head, though. I know it's funny coming from me, but it sounds odd."

Reaching up, Hannah ran her fingers over Martin's skull, which had the slightest stubble. "It feels almost like fuzz," she said. "I like it. The first thing I noticed about you when we met here that day was this gleam, the way the light reflected off your head." She held the egg toward the lamp on the nightstand. "See?"

"Actually, it's time I shaved it."

"You know, I've never seen you shave your head." She took a bite out of the egg. "Can I?"

"Watch?"

"No, I want to do it."

"Now?"

She put the rest of the egg in her mouth and threw back the bedsheet.

They got his shaving kit and went into the kitchen. She told him to sit on a chair next to the sink. She shook the aerosol can and sprayed a large mound of cream into her hand, which she carefully spread over his skull. She put a new blade in his razor, and when she was about to begin she hesitated. "I don't want to cut you."

"Just go slow."

She positioned herself so that she was straddling his left leg, and her first pass over that side of his head was tentative. She rinsed the blade clean in the sink and made a second pass. The razor glided through the cream, rising and falling with the contours of his skull. When she had one side of his head done, she began to do the other side, working her way down to where she edged around the ears. Throughout it all, he held perfectly still.

"Are you enjoying this as much as I am?" she asked.

"I am. No one has ever done this before."

When she finished, she soaked a towel with warm water and washed off the remaining shaving cream. His head shone in the light; she ran her fingers over it, then leaned over and kissed his skin. At first he held perfectly still, but then he moved his head slowly so that her mouth and tongue glided over his skull. She wanted to kiss every part of it, and she took the back of his neck in her hands. He untied the sash and opened her bathrobe. His hand lifted her breast to his mouth, while the other hand slid between her legs. Her mouth and tongue moved over his skull, coating the skin with a thin membrane of saliva.

AFTER DARK SEAN had left the apartment and drove to the beach. Arnie was out with some girl. And again, he'd asked if Sean wanted to come along, because girls often work in pairs and this girl had a friend. But Sean didn't want to hear any of it. Pretty soon Arnie would start talking like Loomis, who was only happy with two girls at once. So Sean went down to the water because later Arnie and his girl would return to the apartment. If Sean slept on the couch, he'd have to listen to them go at it in the bedroom.

He walked the beach, his sleeping bag over his shoulder, a pint of tequila in his hip pocket. The air was still but the black flies weren't bad. He knew this was a dumb idea, coming to this particular stretch of beach, where he and Hannah had first done it. But there was a three-quarter moon, and the only sound was of waves running in from Frenchman's Channel. They'd gotten started in his mother's car. They did what they'd been doing for the past several weeks, making out, and she let him get his hands up beneath her blouse. But it was a warm night and it was her idea that they get out of the car and walk. He said there was a blanket in the trunk; he got it out and as they started along the beach she put her arm around his waist. There was that as much as anything else—her arm around his waist. She pulled him snug to her hip so that they had to walk in stride together along the sand. Her hair drifted across his face, his mouth, and she laughed when they fell out of step. He was conscious of how her fingers held the belt loop of his jeans. It was pure possession. When they got down to the beach, they spread the blanket, and she said, "It's all right now, Sean."

Now, lying there in the same spot, there were just fleeting images. He remembered that it sounded as if he was gently knocking the wind out of her, until a seagull glided overhead and landed near the blanket. They paused and looked at the bird, which turned its head mechanically, watching in every direction. The gull seemed both aware of their presence and oblivious to what they were doing. Finally, Sean moved a little, and Hannah drew in her breath.

After what seemed like an hour lying in his sleeping bag, Sean was still wide awake. He'd finished the tequila. Bugs had found him and kept diving for his ears. He slapped his head numerous times but they still attacked. Finally, he got out of the sleeping bag and walked crookedly back up to his truck, where there was another bottle under the driver's seat.

13

MARTIN WAS ABOUT to turn off the light over the kitchen sink when the phone rang.

"Hello?"

"Didn't wake you?" Pearly said.

"Where are you? It's after two in the morning."

"I'm a guest of the civil authorities."

"That's great. The police?"

Hannah came into the kitchen in her bathrobe. "Is that Pearly?"

Martin nodded. "Where are you?" he said to Pearly. "The police station? I'll be there in ten minutes."

"Not that simple this time." Pearly snorted. "I'm not sleeping it off on my bench. This time we made the *big* ride."

"They took you over to Marquette?"

"It's the only jail in the county," Pearly said. "Just wanted you to know I wouldn't be at work in the morning. My arraignment isn't until one-thirty in the afternoon."

"What exactly did you *do*?"

"*Nothing!*"

"Pearly."

"Why is it that I'm always considered the guilty party?" There was a pause. Finally, Pearly added, "The fact is I don't remember exactly what I did."

"You were drinking, obviously. Where? The Portage."

"Well, yeah."

"Stayed until closing?"

"That's a crime?"

"No."

"Last call—such a sad, lonesome moment it is," Pearly said. "But sometimes you get lucky. You know, they ring the bell and shout last call, and it's like everybody has ten minutes to finish their drinks and fall in love. I only succeeded in finishing my drink."

"What about your friend there, Sally?"

"Night off. Plus, she's taken up with a tourist. I think he drives a convertible. Don't worry, she'll get over it. Happens every summer. It's just a seasonal thing."

"So what happened after last call?"

"That's a very good question, Martin. It appears I'm guilty of falling asleep."

"Where did you fall asleep, Pearly?"

"In his car."

"In whose car?" Martin asked, but he already suspected the answer.

"Well, see, that's the problem," Pearly said. "I don't recall actually getting *in* the car. I think he found me asleep and placed me in the front seat."

"I'll come over," Martin said.

"Okay. I need two things. One, call Owen Nault—the younger one, not his old man—and tell him about my arraignment. And two, my truck is still parked on Ottawa Street. I don't get it off there, they'll have it towed and then I'll have to pay to get it back. You have the extra set of keys, don't you?"

"Yeah. We'll take care of it." After he hung up, Martin laughed and said to Hannah, "He's more concerned about his truck getting towed than spending the night in jail."

They got dressed quickly and drove into the village. Pearly's Datsun was parked a half-block down from the Hiawatha Diner. They decided that Martin would drive it over to Marquette.

"It's almost three in the morning," Hannah said. "What's the good of your going over there? He's probably sleeping it off now."

"I know," Martin said. "But I think I ought to be over there. I don't even know if they'll let me see him." She kissed him and he got out of the Mercedes. He leaned down to the open passenger-side window. "Don't forget the note."

"The note was my idea, Martin."

He smiled and walked to Pearly's truck. Hannah drove a block farther down the street. The Portage was on the corner, and two doors beyond that were the offices of Nault & Nault. Martin had wanted to call Owen Nault III right away, wake him up in the middle of the night, but Hannah said it would be better if he found a note when he got to the office first thing in the morning. She looked at the note she'd written:

Tuesday, June 18 (2 a.m.)

Mr. Owen Nault III,

Pearly's being held overnight in the county jail in Marquette. Don't know all the details but it's more than just drunk this time. His arraignment will be this afternoon at 1:30.

Thanks for your help,
Hannah LeClaire

She got out of the car, went up to the storm door, and stuck the note to the glass with Scotch tape. At first this all seemed exciting to her, a little adventure in the middle of the night. She realized that years from now they might laugh about this—the night when she put the note on the lawyer's door—but right now there was no humor about it. The folded slip of paper taped to the door seemed pathetic and forlorn.

SEAN HAD PARKED on the dirt two-track lane that was around the bend from Martin's house. He walked through the woods with the gas can from his truck. This time he'd be more thorough about it, burn that sucker to the ground. She thought he'd just up and run to some city? No, he was going to run *them* off.

The Mercedes wasn't there and the back of the house was dark.

Perfect.

In the driveway he unscrewed the gas cap and began to douse the clapboards. He was working his way along the wall when he heard a car—it was slowing down, then headlights began to swing in off the road. Sean ran across the driveway and crouched behind the bushes there.

The Mercedes pulled into the driveway and the headlights and motor were shut off. Only the driver's-side door opened. Hannah got out, walked a few steps, and then stopped. She looked around—she wasn't fifteen feet from Sean. He thought she was trying to see through the bush, but then he realized she was looking under the car. The only sound was a ticking in the engine. After a moment, she straightened up and went around to the backyard. He heard the screen door open on a dry hinge, then clap shut.

HANNAH WAS EXHAUSTED. It was warm in the bedroom and she took off her clothes, except her panties, and went right to bed. As soon as she turned out the light, Gracie jumped on the bed and curled up down by her feet.

At first she came up out of sleep, partially, in small stages, and then she drifted back down. She didn't know how much time had passed when she heard the back door open—she had left it unlocked because Martin didn't have a house key with him. She rolled onto her back as she heard him come through the living room and down the hall. She began to fall asleep again.

But then she was aware of a smell of gasoline. She realized she had noticed it out in the driveway, but now it was here in the bedroom with him. She was trying to wake up enough to tell him about the smell, to say that tomorrow they should check under the car to see if there was a leak. But she was confused and she wanted to say, *Don't you smell gas?* Suddenly her arms were held down by hands that tightly gripped her biceps—and his legs straddled her thighs. He lowered his face to her left breast and took her nipple in his mouth. When she tried to turn his tooth tore her skin. Then his mouth came down on hers hard—it wasn't really a kiss, but more like he was trying to force his face into hers. She could taste beer and tequila. It was worse than the smell of gasoline. She pursed her lips against his tongue until his head slid down next to hers, his stubble sanding her cheek.

"*Easy,*" Sean whispered against her ear. "*Easy!*"

Then she realized that he was already naked from the waist down. She could feel the hair on his legs and his hardness against her pelvis. His weight seemed to be pressing the air out of her and she was having trouble inhaling. When he let go of her left arm, his hand tugged at the elastic band until her panties ripped. She tried to roll to either side, but he was so heavy and his wet mouth kept kissing her cheek and ear as he whispered, "*Easy,*" over and over. It was as if he were talking to some animal, a young dog or perhaps a horse that needed training. His voice was both kind and loving, yet it threatened punishment if she continued to resist. She spoke his name many times. She said no over and over. She said, Stop it. But he only seemed more determined. He got one knee and then the other between her thighs and pushed her legs apart. Her panties were torn, but the fabric was crumpled between them. His hand was down there trying to guide him inside her, but she kept moving, trying to roll each way. Because his face was buried against her neck, she couldn't get at his eyes, with her hands. She thought she might have been yelling by then, she wasn't sure. His weight against her chest made her cough and gasp. He raised his head up away from hers and she could barely see his face in the dark. She pawed at his cheek, but felt so slow and weak. "*Wait*," he pleaded. "Just *wait*." And then he became still and his hand started to guide him inside her. She raised her left hip and he let go and then he came down on her, his body tense, his hips thrusting, as he came on her belly. Then, lowering her free arm to his back, she pulled him tightly to her, wanting to keep the hot spurts up on her stomach. As he finished his thrusts he whimpered, and she believed at that moment he thought she was embracing him, accepting him, and he was thankful. But her only thought was to keep it outside of her.

Then they were still except for their hoarse breathing. Hannah didn't know how long he lay on top of her. She felt as though she had run up a steep hill and could only think of getting air into her lungs. It was a surprise when his hands became affectionate. They stroked her face, her hair. He kissed her ear and whispered, "I'm *sorry*. I just couldn't—I just *couldn't . . .*"

And she pushed with her arms until he rolled off of her. She grabbed the bedsheet and rubbed her stomach. He sat up on the side of the bed, his back arched in the near-darkness. She got up and almost tripped on his pants, which lay on the floor. His belt buckle glinted next to her foot. She leaned over, the floor seeming to tilt, and pulled the buckle, drawing the belt out of the loops of his pants. As she gathered air into her lungs, she felt more alert, stronger. He was just sitting there on the edge of the bed, his back to her. She knelt on the mattress, and holding the ends of the belt in her hands, dropped it over his head, then pulled the ends together quickly. He made a loud noise as though he were trying to expel something caught in his throat. She pulled the belt tighter at the base of his skull and he fell back on the bed. His arms were moving, his legs kicking, but because she was kneeling behind him, he couldn't get at her. The more he struggled, the more tightly she held on. It seemed to last forever, his thrashing and her putting all of her effort into just keeping her hands tight on the belt. Then his legs and arms suddenly lost their spastic energy. They writhed weakly until they hardly moved at all. In her hands she could feel a tension in his neck, as though he were holding on tightly. It made her think of someone doing a chin-up, how the body becomes rigid as it dangles straight down while the hands and arms hoist the neck up to the bar. Then suddenly he let go. Everything about him turned soft and heavy. There was no tension, only weight.

She let go of the belt and he rolled off the bed, his bones seeming to knock hard on the wood floor. She was out of breath again and sat on the end of the bed for a moment. It was so dark she could barely see him curled up on the floor. Her torn panties were bunched around her left ankle and she kicked them off. Standing, she went down the hall to the bathroom, where she ran the faucet until hot water came out of the tap. She yanked a towel off the rack and soaked it with water until her hands couldn't take the heat, then wiped her stomach hard—hard, as though she could scrub off the top layer of skin.

She reached out and switched on the light above the mirror. A long scratch, beaded with tiny drops of blood, ran diagonally across her left breast, and her nipple was raw and puckered. The skin around her navel was wet and red. She remembered standing before mirrors when she was in her early teens, studying her breasts, her hips. For months they swelled and changed, and she grew pubic hair. Her skin then seemed so taut, so perfectly smooth. Now when she touched that skin it was sore as though she had been scalded. She was suddenly very tired but there was no place to lie down. She stared at the stained porcelain bathtub. Gracie was sitting in the corner by the tub, her eyes wide and alert.

Then the cat looked toward the bathroom door as a floorboard in the bedroom creaked. The sound seemed to transform Hannah's bare skin. It was a warm night, but she was immediately chilled, and she felt her flesh rise on her arms, her thighs. There was movement as he struggled to get to his feet. He began coughing, trying to clear his throat. Gasping for breath, he came out into the hall.

Hannah stood still in the bathroom. She saw the pair of scissors in the basket on top of the toilet tank and picked them up. Sean's footsteps were slow as they moved down the hall toward the living room. He went into the kitchen and let himself out the back door. She was holding the scissors so tightly that they hurt. She put them back in the basket. The scissors had left two deep circular impressions in her palm.

14

OWEN NAULT III showed up at the Marquette County Courthouse a little after noon. He and Pearly had known each other since they were kids. You could say that Owen first "represented" Pearly in high school, when he was elected president of the student council during their junior year. Since returning to the U.P. with a degree from Cooley Law down in Lansing, he had handled all of Pearly's legal matters and never billed him. The barter system still thrived in northern Michigan, and when his roof leaked, when his toilet didn't stop running, he called Pearly.

They were in the first-floor corridor of the county courthouse, awaiting Pearly's arraignment upstairs. "Attempted theft. Of a police vehicle?" Owen said. "Jesus, Pearly, this isn't going to be the usual program."

Marquette County Courthouse was an old sandstone building with a fine rotunda. Its interior was full of marble, which gave a resounding echo to even the slightest noise. In one of the offices a radio was playing "Peaceful Easy Feeling," to which a man with a baronial voice was humming totally off-key.

"What do you think you were *doing*?" Owen asked.

"I was sleeping is what I was doing."

Owen sighed for effect, to set the tone. "In Colby's squad car."

"That's what he says. But I really don't remember getting in. I remember that I left the Portage and went down to the beach by the harbor. I took a piss, then I sat down in the sand and, *boom*, that's the last I remember."

"You're saying Colby found you on the beach, picked you up and carried you up to his cruiser, and put you in the front seat. That's bullshit, Pearly."

"Well, obviously he had help."

"Oh, right: an accomplice."

"Exactly. I think I was set up. I think he found me down on the beach, fast asleep, and he got one, maybe even two of his pals—you know, they all drink coffee in the middle of the night over at the Hiawatha because it's the only place that stays open to serve breakfast after last call. I think he got them to carry me up to the cruiser and—"

"Now it's a conspiracy."

"It's *all* a conspiracy, Owen. Don't you *get* it?"

There was a sprinkling of dandruff on the shoulder of Owen's dark blue suit coat. Pearly reached over and brushed it off. To his credit, Owen bought decent suits, but he wore them to death. This one had been in play for at least five years. Standing this close to him, Pearly could see pulled threads, the pucker in a seam. To offset the fact that he wore suits all day, Owen had for years maintained his long brown ponytail. "Well," he said. "Let's consider another scenario, okay?"

"Why not, Owen? I have an open mind."

"You come out of the Portage utterly blasted, you stumble past the Hiawatha on the other side of the street, and you see Colby through the window at the counter having coffee—with or without his accomplices. His cruiser's parked right there in front of you and without thinking you try the door. Oh *look*, it's not locked. It's one A.M., the village is dead, and Colby wouldn't *dream* of anyone messing with his car. But you think, Why don't I just take it for a little *ride*? Leave it someplace. Just for laughs."

"Down by Petit Marais—yeah, that would work," Pearly said agreeably. "You know, you could get it good and stuck in the sand and they'd have to call Superior Gas and Lube to send out the tow truck."

"Harmless prank. *And* can't you just see the photo in the Fish Wrap?"

"You have to admit it's a good idea."

"True," Owen said. "But this time Colby's is better."

"Owen, I was *put* in the car."

Owen shook his head. "Driving over here, I talked on the phone with the prosecutor, Alice Hooper."

"Oh Christ. Why do I always have to get her?"

"She wants your body," Owen said. "Look, you have witnesses? *No?* Well, Colby does. He's going to claim that *two* guys came out of the Hiawatha with him and *saw* you lying across the front seat."

Now Pearly sighed for effect. "You're saying this is going to cost me more than usual."

Owen nodded. "I was thinking about remodeling that bathroom on the first floor."

"You know, if I were a truly honest man, I would defend myself."

"Bad idea, Pearly."

"If I don't have faith in democracy and our judicial system, then where am I?"

"Doing time."

"Dostoyevsky would be appalled."

"This is America, pal. Even Dostoyevsky would get a lawyer."

BECAUSE HE HADN'T gotten home until four, Martin slept late. He didn't climb out of bed until it was after eleven. Hannah was up and he could smell fresh paint. He dressed and went out to the kitchen, where she was rolling a nice muted yellow eggshell finish on the walls.

He said hi, she said hi, but she didn't look at him.

He knew right then something was wrong.

After getting the carton of orange juice from the refrigerator, he leaned against the doorjamb—everything was pushed to the middle of the room and there was no place to sit. He drank from the spout and watched her. She wore her bib overalls, and her hair was tied up under an old paint-spattered Tigers ball cap. Martin was trying to think about the night, if he had said or done something. When he finally returned from Marquette, Hannah had been asleep. Though it was warm in the bedroom, she had been wearing a pair of his sweatpants and a long-sleeved T-shirt.

"Pearly's going to be arraigned this afternoon," he said. "They wouldn't let me talk to him, but I hung around for a while, then came back."

"Uh-huh."

"How you feeling?" he said.

"Fine."

Gracie brushed against his leg. "I just thought you might be—I don't know . . ."

"Might be what?" Her voice was even, somehow protective.

"When I came home, you were sleeping in sweatpants. You coming down with something?"

"No." There was a moment when Hannah's arm paused and she held the roller high up on the wall. Then she continued to draw the wide swath of yellow down to within inches of the baseboard. "No, I'm fine," she said.

Martin took a last swallow of orange juice and closed the spout. He just didn't know where to go with this. Then he said, "What's the name of that paint? It's a good color."

Her arm paused again, and for a moment he thought she was going to tell him something he should have already figured out—something he should know instinctively. But then she said, "Ancient City."

"Great . . ." He took his weight off the doorjamb. The cat leaped up onto the kitchen table, which was covered with a drop cloth. She sat and stared through him. They were like a team this morning.

"Pearly called while you were asleep," Hannah said.

"He did?"

"He needs his truck so he can drive back after the arraignment this afternoon. So you'll have to take it back to Marquette." Her voice now was very flat, almost dismissive. He'd never heard it before. Never.

"Right." He put the carton back in the refrigerator. "Guess I better get going."

THE SCREEN DOOR clapped shut behind him.

Hannah usually loved that sound, but now it seemed like a rebuke.

She listened to Martin walk around to the side of the house and up the driveway, where he stopped suddenly. She put her roller down in the paint tray, picked up Gracie, and went to the open window. Through the screen she watched him, not twenty feet away, bend over next to his car. He seemed to be looking for something on the cracked asphalt. Then he knelt down and peered under the car. After a moment, he got back to his feet, turned, and leaned toward the house. He touched the clapboard wall with one hand, then raised his fingers to his nose. He continued along the wall, touching the wall, sniffing his fingers, until he was out of her sight.

Gasoline.

He came back into view as he stepped away from the house. He recognized the smell, too—she was sure of it.

Hannah shifted the cat to her right shoulder. She moved closer to the window, until the bill of her cap touched the screen. She wanted to tell him that yes, it was gasoline he smelled, and yes, it must have soaked into the bottom clapboards maybe all the way around the house, and yes, it meant that Sean had been there last night. But somehow the rusty screen was a barrier she couldn't overcome; it caused optical illusions, creating zigzags of light as she watched Martin climb into the Datsun pickup at the end of the driveway. The smell of fresh paint on the kitchen walls had caused her to forget about the gasoline from last night, but now she remembered it, and she knew that if she spoke, if she acknowledged it, she'd end up telling Martin everything.

Hannah listened to the truck back out of the driveway and head north toward the village. The engine was small and old and made a racket that took a long time to be absorbed into the distance. By the time the sound was gone, Hannah realized she could not hold it down. Gracie leaped from her shoulder as she crossed the kitchen and pushed open the screen door. She went down the steps and vomited in the uncut grass.

When she was finished she took the paint rag from her hip pocket, blew her nose, and wiped her mouth. Her legs were weak and she sat on the steps. There was a foul taste in her mouth and her sinuses burned so much her eyes wouldn't stop tearing. For a long time she just tried to breathe, to draw in each breath so that it didn't cause an aching shudder down in her lungs.

At one point finally, she seemed almost to laugh. Gazing up at the trees, she whispered, "Ancient City." The idea of fresh paint, of making this house, this life clean and honest now seemed absurd. There would always be fear. There would always be doubt. There would always be regret. Hannah wondered if she hadn't gone through with it, if she had decided to have the baby last year, would she be able to avoid this pain now? Perhaps this was all retribution. Maybe this was due to a guilt she could not cover over, no matter what you called the color, no matter how many coats you applied. Then she understood that she was afraid, that the nervous tension running through her—her hands trembled slightly—was caused by a fear that she'd never known before, and then immediately she knew this, too: It was a fear that had to be concealed.

Hannah sat on the step for a long time. Flies buzzed around the vomit matting the grass.

She got up and walked across the yard to the pile of rusted garden tools that they had found in the house. She picked up the shovel, its long handle cracked and weathered, returned to the vomit, and tried to scoop it up. But it could not be done—the grass was slick with it—so she began digging, using her foot to punch down through the grass and take up a tight, moist clump of earth. She did this twice, creating a small, shallow hole, with a slight mound of dirt next to it.

Hannah dropped the shovel, walked across the yard again, and brought the wheelbarrow back to the hole. For several minutes she worked steadily, digging up enough grass and dirt to fill the wheelbarrow. When she had a full load, she took it around to the back of the garage, where leaves had been piled for years. She emptied the wheelbarrow and returned to the hole.

All evidence of her vomit was gone. But it was not enough. She picked up the shovel again and, with her foot, drove the blade down through the grass. As she pulled back on the handle, a crackling of snapped roots was accompanied by the smell of fresh earth.

SEAN WAS HAVING TROUBLE SWALLOWING. He wondered if something had been damaged. When he was in boot camp there was a kid from Georgia who tried to hang himself. He was homesick, he missed his girlfriend, the DI scared the shit out of him, and the other recruits could tell he wasn't likely to make it. One day they came back from mess and found him hanging by a piece of oily rope in the showers. He was still twitching and they cut him down. He was taken away and they never saw him again. The only word that came back was that the kid had damaged his windpipe and required an operation. He might never be able to talk again.

Sean lay on Arnie's couch, staring at the slanted ceiling overhead.

Downstairs he could hear the radio in the garage, someone talking about last night's Cubs game.

Sean said, "Who gives a fuck."

Hardly anything came out. It sounded like it felt: a pair of hands clamped around his throat and squeezing tightly.

He thought of the word *windpipe*. He'd never considered this part of the body before, and now he envisioned something brittle, breakable, like PVC that was used in plumbing. He imagined his windpipe was cracked into several pieces, and every time he swallowed, it was so painful that he expected a sharp, jagged edge of PVC to break through the skin in his neck.

"Who gives a fuck," he said again, a mere croak, "about baseball."

He picked up the hand mirror from the coffee table. Some girl had left it in the bathroom. He looked at his neck in the mirror; the belt had left the skin blue. Another few seconds and he would have died. The last thing he remembered was his whole body convulsing, his feet kicking out, then he passed out. It was this swift, falling sensation, followed by nothing. He didn't know how long he'd been out. At first he was confused, didn't even know where he was, but once he got to his feet he realized he was alone in their bedroom. Hannah was gone, and he only knew he had to get away. Once outside the house, he staggered back through the woods and drove to Arnie's apartment.

She had tried to kill him and now he could barely talk. Burning the house to the ground wouldn't be enough. Not anymore. Somehow knowing this was comforting.

15

PEARLY'S PRELIMINARY EXAM in Marquette County Courthouse was on Monday, June 24. He met Owen at the top of the stairs outside the courtroom. One of Owen's hands nervously toyed with his ponytail, and he had the boyish enthusiasm of someone who gets to break bad news.

"What is it?" Pearly said.

"We got Emmett Anderson." He opened the door and led Pearly into the courtroom.

Where they waited and waited and waited, because otherwise it couldn't be justice. They sat in the back while another hearing, something to do with a property dispute in Big Bay, dragged on. Judge Emmett Anderson sat motionless up behind the bench as though he was aware of their disappointment and scorn. The man was well into his sixties and he had pork chops for earlobes. He was bald, and with one hand propping his chin, he sometimes appeared to be dozing. He was known for presiding over entire cases in this manner, then surprising the courtroom by suddenly asking a spate of pertinent questions.

When Bettina Laakso came into the courtroom she sat to the right of Pearly and Owen. She was a thin woman with silk-white hair, who owned the *Whitefish Harbor Herald*. She looked like she was anticipating a splendid night of opera. Worse, she did not acknowledge them. Pearly and Owen glanced at each other warily, then looked forward, remaining quiet like two kids who have been scolded before about misbehaving in church.

Laakso was there because Pearly was there, because Frank Colby would be there. And because Emmett Anderson was presiding. He was the kind of judge who occasionally got mentioned in the press for meting out "creative sentences." He had once required that a woman eat chicken for dinner every night for a month, and had ordered a father to sleep in the family doghouse for a week—the kind of thing that made for good short copy on the national news wires.

Pearly witnessed everything through the lingering effects of another raging hangover, which meant he was having difficulty keeping his eyes open. Though he could barely follow what was being said, he was convinced that he wasn't the only one with too much alcohol in his blood. Even Frank Colby, who arrived at the last minute, appeared to suspect something. Assistant Prosecuting Attorney Alice Hooper's speech was rapid, slurred, and periodically hysterical; her mountain of black hair was wild. At one point Owen leaned over and whispered in Pearly's ear, "She's been known to engage in a noontime quickie in an attempt to calm down."

Occasionally the judge interrupted the proceedings, asking Frank Colby questions about the "squad car in question"—the year, the model, the mileage, how often it was serviced. At one point he lectured the courtroom on the virtues of switching to heavier motor oil during the summer months and chastised the officer for using 10W-30 year-round.

Finally Pearly drifted off, and no one bothered to wake him, until Owen nudged his shoulder hard. It took Pearly a moment to remember where he was, and Owen made a desperate gesture with his hands. Apparently the judge had asked Pearly a question.

He got to his feet. "Excuse me, Judge, would you repeat the question?"

Owen leaned back in his chair and exhaled.

Emmett Anderson smiled. "You didn't get sufficient rest last night, Mr. Blankenship?"

Pearly wasn't sure if that was the first question, which he had missed, or the second. "No, Your Honor, I didn't."

"Tell me, before you were invited to avail yourself of our humble accommodations here in Marquette early in the morning last Tuesday, where did you sleep?"

Pearly suspected that this might be a trick question. He glanced down at Owen, but he was looking straight ahead, meaning Pearly was on his own. "Last Tuesday? I slept on the beach."

"The beach?" the judge said. He flipped through his notes. "There's been no previous mention of the beach." Looking up, he asked, "How was it, the beach?" This brought several snickers and a cough. The judge's eyes roamed his courtroom until there was silence.

"It was fine."

"How were the bugs?"

"Not bad, not bad at all, Your Honor."

"The beach more comfortable than the cot here in Marquette?"

"I believe so, Your Honor."

"Indeed," the judge said. "Indeed, I imagine it would be. It has been some time since I've slept on one of our beautiful Lake Superior beaches, but my recollection is that the sand has a rather uncanny way of shaping itself to the body." There was, to Pearly's right, some movement, and the judge looked sharply at Alice Hooper. "Counselor, were you going to say something?"

She ran a frantic hand up into her big hair, as though she had just realized that a small animal was nesting there, and said, "No, Your Honor."

The judge wasn't satisfied. "Perhaps you've never slept on one of our beaches?"

After a moment, she said, "Your Honor, I really don't see how my sleeping on a—"

He looked away from her, shutting her up. "Now, Mr. Blankenship," he said, "Officer Colby has stated that you were found in the front seat of his squad car, and that he suspects that you were in the act of hot-wiring the ignition. Were you stealing his car?"

"No, sir."

"Well, Mr. Blankenship, please tell the court how you managed to get from the beach to the front seat of the car. Perhaps you somnam-bulated?" He quickly scanned the room, waiting for someone to laugh or snicker, but there wasn't a sound.

"No, not to my knowledge," Pearly said. "I don't know how I got to the car." The judge seemed unsatisfied. Everything in Pearly's being said to leave it at that, but then he added, "I think I might have been carried, sir."

"*Carried?*"

"Yes, Your Honor."

"By whom?" When Pearly hesitated, the judge said, "You know that Officer Colby claims to have two witnesses who saw you in his squad car." Here he looked hard at Colby, who lowered his head. "I know both of these individuals, and neither seems present in this courtroom to testify." Leaning forward, he said, "How do you think you got from the beach to the car, Mr. Blankenship?"

Pearly stared back at the judge and said, "I don't know for cer-tain, sir."

"I suspect you're telling the truth," the judge said.

"Yes, sir."

"Because you're under oath."

"Yes, sir, I am under oath."

"Well, then, let me ask you another question, one of a historical nature." The judge paused to pour himself a glass of water, which he drank down without stopping. Looking at Pearly, he said, "Mr. Blankenship, have you ever put a fish on anyone's porch?"

"Your Honor," Owen said as he began to stand up.

With a wave of his hand, the judge said, "Sit down, Mr. Nault. I'm only curious here. You and I both know there's no law against placing a walleye on someone's front porch. Your client can't be fined or sent to jail for such an action. Besides, the statute of limitations on that walleye ran out years ago." He waited until Owen was seated again, then said, "Well, Mr. Blankenship?"

"Your Honor, I put that fish on your porch."

"Very good," the judge said. "Would you say, for the record, that that was the stupidest thing you've ever done?"

Pearly thought for a moment. "No, sir. For the record I would say it was this bet I won at the Portage years ago."

"What bet was that?" the judge asked.

"That I could eat the cork dartboard," Pearly said. "I won the bet, but with all the beer it bloated my stomach something awful for about a week."

"I imagine it would," Judge Anderson said.

"Excuse me, Your Honor," Owen said. "May I have a word with my client?"

"Of course."

Owen tugged Pearly's sleeve until he sat down. Cupping his hand in front of his mouth, he whispered into Pearly's ear, "Don't admit to the flagpole."

Pearly nodded, then stood up again. "Your Honor, were you going to ask me about a flagpole, too?"

"Was I? Do you mean the one that used to be in front of White-fish Harbor's town hall?" The judge poured himself more water and held the glass to his chest as if it were a cocktail. "Well, now that you mention it . . ."

"I'll plead the fifth on the flagpole," Pearly said.

The judge sipped his water. "You will, will you." He took another sip. "I suppose we've had enough truth here for one day. Please sit down, Mr. Blankenship. The charges against you are not sustainable."

Pearly wasn't sure he understood what the judge had said and stood there until Owen grabbed his sleeve and pulled him down into his chair. "That's it?" Pearly whispered.

Before Owen could respond, the judge said, "Now, Officer Colby."

Reluctantly, Colby pushed back his chair and got to his feet. Then Alice Hooper stood, too, as though they were about to hear punishment for a capital crime pronounced.

"Officer Colby, on the night in question, was there any evidence of tampering with your car?"

"As I said before, sir, he was found lying in the front seat and it appeared—"

"Were there signs of a break-in?" the judge asked. "Locks jimmied?"

After a moment, Colby said, "No, Your Honor."

The judge put his glass on the bench. "You left your squad car unlocked?"

"I had just stepped inside to get a cup of coffee. It was sitting at the curb right outside the window. I could see—"

Judge Anderson said, "Tell me, Officer Colby, do you *like* your squad car?"

There was one snicker from the back of the courtroom, which the judge ignored.

Finally, Colby's voice was very small. "Yes, Your Honor."

"Well, I've seen little evidence of it lately," the judge said. "Not long ago in this court a charge was brought against Sean Colby—he would be your son, wouldn't he?—for abusing this same squad car. I believe a headlight was broken with a bottle—a beer bottle, am I correct?"

Alice Hooper said, "Your Honor, that case is hardly relevant to—"

"Pipe *down*, Counselor." The judge leaned forward and folded his hands as if in prayer. "Officer Colby, if I were your superior I would take that squad car away from you before something really bad happens to it." Here, there was laughter echoing through the courtroom, and the judge waited patiently for it to subside. "What I'd do is have you walk your beat. You know, when I was a boy, growing up on the streets of Detroit, that was what our fine officers in blue did—they *walked* the neighborhoods, day and night. We talked with them—on the street corners, on front stoops, in shop doorways. They knew us. We knew them. I tell you it was the *greatest* deterrent to *crime* this country has *ever* had!" The judge stood up. "But right *now*, Officer Colby, I want you to walk out of this courtroom—consider doing so in honor of your predecessors, if you will—and don't come back here again with such lame accusations concerning your squad car." He tapped his gavel on the bench and said, "Case dismissed."

16

HANNAH HAD DUG UP a good portion of the backyard. With string and stakes, she had cordoned off a rectangle twenty-four by twelve feet, with a four-foot-wide path to the driveway, and another to the back steps. She was going down twenty-two inches—a lot of dirt, which she'd deposited in long rows behind the garage. Rocks she worried loose with a crowbar. Borrowing Pearly's truck, she brought in loads of pea stone, sand, and red bricks. Several times a day, Martin and Pearly would take a break from their work up on the second or third floors and look down from a window at her progress. She labored with the relentless obsession of a dog digging for a bone, yet she was tidy and methodical. For someone who never laid a brick patio before, she was doing one fine job.

Watching her, Martin was by turns curious and baffled. Pearly thought he might be angry, though it was hard to tell. He'd never seen his younger cousin get really angry, but he began to suspect that Martin actually had a fierce temper, which he was trying to control. For long periods Martin wouldn't say anything—about anything. Then he'd start in, complaining about Hannah, something he'd never done before. Each night, he said, she'd get in bed exhausted and read manuals on building patios. When he made suggestions about design and method, she'd listen but not respond. When asked if she wanted help, she'd say no. When he asked why she had decided to build a patio, she said she found it "therapeutic." What really bothered him was that she'd never asked him if he even wanted a patio.

And she'd left the paint job in the kitchen unfinished. The furniture was still pushed to the center of the room—the inconvenience this caused when they cooked didn't seem to bother her, while it gave rise to a smoldering resentment in Martin. Yet he refused to move the furniture back to where it belonged. Every time either one of them opened the refrigerator door, it banged against the corner of the kitchen table. It was clear that Martin couldn't comprehend what was happening between them. For Pearly, it was further proof that cohabitation was an unnatural state.

When Hannah finished digging the rectangle, pea stone was spread out, followed by sand, which was smoothed over with a twelve-foot two-by-four. One afternoon she said, "Isn't it ironic, we live in a place full of sand, but I have to drive halfway to Marquette to buy a truckload. If I just went down to the beach and took some, I'm sure I'd get arrested."

Pearly couldn't argue with her. Using his level, she made sure that the patio was gently sloped so that rainwater would run off away from the foundation of the house. When she began to lay the courses of brick, he often looked down to check her progress. She knelt as she placed each brick in the sand, then gently tamped it down with a wooden mallet. Her bib overalls stretched tightly across her hips. Sometimes when she'd sit back on her haunches, he'd get the briefest glimpse down the front of her shirt. There was a beautiful precision to her labor. Viewed from above, it appeared as though she were building a brick wall between herself and the earth.

ON WEDNESDAY HANNAH stopped working in mid-afternoon and went inside for another glass of ice water, which she took out on the front stoop, where there was cool shade. She collected the mail, two advertising flyers and the *Whitefish Harbor Herald,* and sat on the brick steps. Photographs of Frank and Sean Colby were on page one, the same two that had been in the paper two weeks earlier. She read the lead article.

TOWN COUNCIL TAKES JUDGE'S OPINION
TO HEART

by Bettina Laakso

In an unprecedented move, the Whitefish Harbor Town Council on Tuesday prohibited Officer Frank Colby from using his police car for one month.

The surprise disciplinary action, triggered by two incidents involving Colby and his car, follows the recommendation of Marquette County Judge Emmett Anderson, according to a letter from one town council member.

The letter, introduced at the meeting by Councilman Dan Schofield, outlined recent events that have led Schofield to recommend what the letter called "appropriate disciplinary action." In the letter Schofield described two recent legal cases that concern Officer Frank Colby's police cruiser.

The first incident resulted in the front left headlight being broken when a beer bottle was thrown at the vehicle. On May 19, Sean Colby, who had recently been hired as a summer-support police officer, was taken into custody by his father, Officer Frank Colby, and charged with drunk and disorderly conduct and the destruction of public property. At a preliminary exam, two witnesses, Lawrence and Mildred Eichhorn, testified before Judge Anderson that Sean Colby, 19, had thrown a quart beer bottle and broken the headlight on Officer Frank Colby's patrol car, a 1994 Chevrolet. Sean Colby's lawyer, Owen Nault II, asked for a continuance, which Judge Anderson granted, with the stipulation that Colby continue to be suspended from the police force without pay.

The second incident regarding Officer Frank Colby's car occurred on June 18. According to testimony by Officer Frank Colby in Marquette County Courthouse, Pearly Blankenship, 44, was found "at 1:37 A.M., lying across the front seat of the police car while it was parked on Ottawa Street." Officer Frank Colby contended that Blankenship was attempting to "hot-wire and steal the car."

Officer Frank Colby mentioned two witnesses, Lennie Morse, of Shelter Bay, and Jack Cluney, of Au Train. However, because neither appeared in court, Judge Anderson declared that charges against Blankenship be dropped due to insufficient evidence.

In his concluding remarks, Judge Anderson suggested that Officer Frank Colby be denied the use of a police car "before something really bad happens to it." The judge went on to say that "what I'd do is have you walk your beat."

In his letter, Schofield proposed that the town council follow Judge Anderson's advice and have "Officer Frank Colby patrol the Whitefish Harbor on foot for one month, starting immediately."

(Story continued on page 12, column 1)

Hannah had forgotten about her glass of ice water. She drank it down without stopping. Then she turned to page 12, the back page of the *Herald*. There she found a file photograph of Pearly, which had been taken in the mid-seventies—his hair was longer then and he had a full beard. Above the article was a photograph of a Whitefish Harbor police car.

TOWN COUNCIL CONSIDERS JUDGE'S OPINION
(From page 1, column 1)

——————

After Schofield's letter was introduced, several council members stated that the issue should be discussed in a closed session, as it was a personnel matter, but there was not enough support to shelve the subject and the meeting continued. "Our two patrol cars—like all of our police and fire equipment—are necessary to the security of Whitefish Harbor," Schofield said. "It is essential that our residents know where each member of the council stands on this important matter."

The town council went on to discuss Schofield's letter for over an hour. Councilwoman Marge MacLeod suggested that the cost of the replacement headlight come out of Officer Colby's pay. This idea, however, was tabled after Councilman Schofield said that contractually police officers could not be expected to pay for damages to equipment incurred while in the line of duty, unless it could be proved that they had been negligent or reckless.

Councilman Lyman Farr questioned the length of time that Officer Colby would be without the use of a police car. "If he has to walk his beat for a week, it would make the point."

There was considerable discussion over how such an action would affect the police force as a whole. Schofield stressed that a "strong message has to be sent," and he said he had already talked with Chief Buzz Gagnon, who said that if Officer Colby were to be limited to foot patrol for a period of time, it would be necessary to have the summer-support officer, Randy Lapointe, who had been hired as a replacement for Sean Colby, work more hours. "If that's what it takes," Schofield said, "that's what it takes. No halfway measures when it comes to our police force."

Councilman Walter L. Brock said his concerns went "beyond a broken headlight." Brock, who has sat on the council for 24 years, said he was "deeply troubled by how Sean Colby had been hired, particularly in light of information concerning the nature of his early discharge from the army." Brock suggested that Officer Frank Colby be denied use of his patrol car "until we have a full accounting of exactly how his son got hired on the police force. Convince me that this is not nepotism."

Finally, Councilman Whitaker Chase put forth a motion that the letter be accepted as written. Brock seconded the motion, and the town council voted unanimously to accept the letter introduced by Schofield, which recommended that Officer Frank Colby walk his beat for one month, effective immediately.

The council also agreed to meet next Tuesday, July 2, in a closed session.

Hannah folded up the paper and brought it, the advertising flyers, and her empty glass into the house. The muscles in her lower back ached. As she rinsed her glass in the kitchen, she stared out the window at her work. She loved the order of it, the smell of earth, the feel of the tools and bricks in her hands, which were becoming rough and callused. The patio was in sunlight now; in another twenty minutes or so the shade from the maple behind the garage would reach across the backyard. She went into the bedroom and lay down, thinking she would just close her eyes and rest until she could work in that cool late-afternoon shade.

It wasn't just the physical labor that exhausted her. Though she'd been going to bed early, she'd been having trouble sleeping. She would study the sections of Martin's books that described how to build patios until she became drowsy, then she'd fall asleep. The difficulty was when Martin came to bed. She always woke up but pretended to still be asleep. Lying next to him, she could feel his anxiety and frustration, which seemed to be greater each night. His hand would rest on her hip, her thigh, as he curled up behind her, but she could not respond. So often in the past, that was all it took for her to turn to him, but now she only remained still. For several nights, at first, he soon fell asleep. She knew he thought she was having her period; she wasn't, but she left the box of tampons out on the windowsill in the bathroom to reinforce the idea. What first began to bother him, she knew, was that she now slept clothed—sweatpants and a long-sleeved T-shirt, which she kept tucked in so he couldn't get his hands up onto her breasts. She knew he didn't understand her wearing clothes to bed, and the last few nights it had just gotten worse. Last night he got in bed reeking of beer and immediately turned so that he slept with his back to hers.

When Hannah was in the bathroom preparing to take a shower after working on the patio, she'd look at herself in the mirror. It had taken a day for the bruises to surface fully; she thought of it as a kind of blossoming—on her ribs, beneath her collarbone, and down on the inside of her left thigh. The worst of them turned a deep plum color, which then slowly diminished to an ugly brownish-yellow.

They would go away.

But the deep scratch across her breast had bled, leaving a long rough scab that often snagged on the fabric of her shirt while she worked. Anticipating the next snag was worse than the snag itself. Finally, the scab came off in the shower, but the scratch was still clearly evident, and she was afraid there might be a permanent scar. The new tender skin was a pink streak, trailing behind the comet of her nipple.

AFTER THE ARTICLE came out in the *Herald,* there was a lot of speculation about Frank Colby: He was hiding out in his house; he was, some believed, going to resign. But Friday morning he came out of the police station, which was in the town hall, and strode across the parking lot and down Ottawa Street. He was in full uniform. He moved with apparent ease, pausing to look in store windows or to converse with shopkeepers. He took his sweet time. The consensus was that Colby was okay with it. In fact, some believed that Judge Anderson's point about law enforcement was well taken, and a number of shopkeepers said they were considering asking the town council to require the police to walk their beat regularly during the summer months.

Sean learned about his father's activities through Arnie, who heard local gossip and opinion at the gas pump. There had been a number of small incidents—gestures—that indicated support. Ron

Deitz, who owned Deitz Hardware on Ottawa Street, met Frank Colby on the sidewalk and asked him his shoe size; then he took him into the store and, back in the work clothes section, fitted him with a good pair of black walking shoes. In addition, several of the restaurants in the village provided free lunches and cold beverages. Sean knew that walking the beat was his father's way of fighting back. He was certain that at night the man went home and seethed while his mother smoked menthols and worked through her nightly ration of bourbon. He could imagine them in the kitchen, his father silent, his mother talking in petulant bursts between drags. It had always been her contention that her husband was underappreciated by the town. She believed that Buzz Gagnon was chief simply because his father had been chief.

Tuesday afternoon Arnie came up to the apartment after work, got a beer from the fridge, and said, "Dan Schofield stopped by for a tank of premium." Sean was lying on the couch. "He and my dad go back to high school. Mentioned something about the town council meeting—the 'closed' meeting that's scheduled for tonight."

"Yeah," Sean said. "It's when they're probably going to talk about what to do about my father and me."

"Well, it's not," Arnie said.

"What's not?"

"On." Arnie went into the bathroom and began to take off his jeans and T-shirt. He always reeked of gasoline after work. "The meeting's been canceled. Don't ask me why." He shut the door and in a moment there was the sound of water running in the shower.

Sean knew why the town council meeting had been canceled: public opinion.

His father's strategy was working.

MARTIN HAD ASKED Hannah if she wanted to go out for something to eat and watch the Cubs game, but she said she was tired and told him to go ahead without her. He went to the Portage, which was crowded with locals and summer people. The Cubs were hosting the Dodgers. After a few innings he struck up a conversation with a girl at the bar. She had sun-bleached blond hair and an aqua-blue halter top. During the eighth inning Hannah walked into the bar. Martin didn't notice her at first but when he looked up, Hannah was already pushing her way through the crowd and out the door. He put his beer on the bar and stared at it for a moment. The girl in the halter top smiled and leaned a little closer. After a moment, he said, "I gotta go. Sorry."

When he arrived home and opened the screen door, he found Hannah sitting in the kitchen, crying. Her arms rested on the drop cloth that covered the table, and her forehead was red—she'd had her head on her arms before he'd come in.

"I'm sorry," he said. "I just don't know what's happening to us."

Hannah wiped her face with the back of her hand.

"What?" he said. "What is it?"

She stood up and put her arms around him. "It's not *you.*"

After that, they didn't say anything else. They undressed each other as they worked their way toward the bedroom, but they didn't make it, ending up on the rug in the living room. They went at it so hard that Hannah developed a small series of rug burns down her spine. Eventually, they awoke and moved into the bedroom, where they were slow and tender with each other.

Later, Martin ran his finger along the scar on Hannah's breast. He was nearly asleep but he asked, "How'd this happen?"

"While I was working a rock loose with the crowbar—it slipped in my hands."

There was something in her voice that he didn't recognize. For a moment he thought she might be lying to him, which he didn't think she'd ever done before. But why would she lie about a scratch? Closing his eyes, he said, "You've got to be careful with tools."

PEARLY STOPPED IN at the Portage for last call. Sally was working the bar and it was mostly locals left standing.

Bettina Laakso came in a few minutes later. "Cubs win?"

"Four-two, in ten," Sally said.

"My hangover's arriving ahead of schedule," Bettina said, "so I think I'll have a Bloody Mary for a nightcap."

"A woman who plans ahead," Pearly said.

Bettina removed her glasses, made a fist, and rubbed her left eye with her knuckles—so hard that when she took her hand away, the pupil was watery and bloodshot. When she put her glasses back on, the lenses made her eyes comically monstrous. A lot of people thought she was always trying to stir up trouble, and because she lived alone, there was speculation about whether she was not only the last of the pinko Commies but a lesbian as well. Pearly liked her.

"I consider the Portage at last call good research," Bettina said.

"Me, too," Pearly said. "Summer nights it's kinda Margaret Mead."

"Exactly. An anthropological study where you get an idea what people do at night and whom they do it with."

"I didn't know we had any 'whoms' this far north," Pearly said.

Sally placed the Bloody Mary on the bar. "Bettina, you're just a Peeping Tom."

"I prefer to call it journalism," Bettina said.

Pearly said, "Well, thanks for going easy on me in that piece on the Colbys."

Bettina sipped her drink. "You provide comic relief, Pearly. You're Falstaff."

"Somebody has to be the peasant."

A customer called Sally from the far end of the bar.

Bettina said quietly, "The Colby thing—it's about to get worse."

"That'll sell a few newspapers," Pearly said.

"You know how some people, particularly local merchants, have been supporting Frank Colby while he's been walking his beat?" she asked. "Well, this backlash has developed. People—people who live outside the village, in particular—have been calling in to the police station, asking for assistance." She leaned back and allowed Pearly to savor the implications. "Of course, Colby can't respond because he can't drive and it's making it tough on Buzz Gagnon. He's working this new summer kid he hired like he was a regular cop, which isn't making people happy, either. Let's face it, a cop walking a beat these days—it's an anachronism. So complaints have been made to members of the town council."

"And," Pearly said, "certain members of the town council will find this useful."

"Exactly." Bettina ate some of her celery stalk. "My guess is that some of the councilmen got this whole thing started. And then there's the kid, Sean. Something wrong with that boy." She drained the rest of her Bloody Mary. "But you'll have to wait until the next edition to read about *that*." She got off her bar stool. "You know, Pearly, the story I really want to write someday—sometime in the off-season, when there's not much going on—is the mystery of the stolen town hall flagpole. Everyone knows you cut down that old ship's mast and took it, but where'd you put it?"

"I took the fifth on that."

"My guess is you weren't alone. You had accomplices. Listen, nobody'll ever accuse you of ratting on your friends." She leaned over so she could whisper. "Trust me, Pearly, I could write it so that none of you would be incriminated."

"I'll keep that in mind."

As Bettina walked up the bar and out the front door, Pearly noticed that none of the men at the bar turned to watch. The fact that the woman held no sexual appeal was one factor, and the other was they were afraid of her.

As Sally came down the bar again, Pearly took some bills out of his pocket. "Anybody feeling anthropologically inclined tonight?" he asked.

She took the bills and fretted. " 'Fraid not, hon."

"Wrong season," he said. "That a convertible I saw you in the other day?"

" 'Fraid so."

17

SEAN RARELY LEFT the apartment above Superior Gas & Lube. Though it usually became stifling by noon, he had taken to wearing a turtleneck pullover to cover the welts on his neck. When Arnie asked what had happened to his voice, Sean whispered he didn't know, it was probably some kind of laryngitis.

He pretty much lived on the couch. He could operate the television with the remote control. He could listen to CDs on headphones. He could flip through the stack of porn magazines Arnie kept on the lower bookshelf next to the couch, page after glossy page of naked women and men: blowjobs, daisy chains, and gobs of come. Sean spent a good deal of his time jerking off. He often tried to remember what it had been like with Hannah. He'd concentrate on a particular time, a place, such as his mother's car, when a certain song was on the radio. It was disappointing how little clarity there was to his recollections, as though he'd only imagined that she'd willingly had sex with him. He tried to think of what she sounded like; he knew that she had moaned and whispered to him, but he couldn't hear it now. Retreating to the couch was not in his best interests. Sometimes it seemed that if he could only identify the root of the problem, the moment when his life took the essential wrong turn, he could go back to that moment and do something different that would change everything that followed. He didn't know what it was, but he knew it was defeating him, pushing him down, down into the cushions of that couch.

Wednesday afternoon Arnie came upstairs with the new edition of the *Herald* and said, "Hey asshole, you're still a local celebrity." He dropped the paper on the coffee table, then went into the kitchenette and made one of his liverwurst-and-onion sandwiches.

Sean picked up the newspaper and looked at the front page. There were two stories, one about his father, which was accompanied by a photograph of him walking down the sidewalk on Ottawa Street. The headline read COMPLAINTS MOUNT OVER FOOT PATROL. But it was the larger photograph on the right that stunned Sean.

Before he could begin to read either piece, Arnie came into the living room and, gesturing with the sandwich in his hand, said, "That's so weird. Where'd you find that girl? She's a *perfect* Hannah LeClaire—it's *un*believable."

"I hate the smell of liverwurst. How can you eat that stuff?" Sean looked down at the photograph of himself with Nikki at a table in the Mare Adriatico, and next to them was Loomis with Zoya sitting on his lap—the one whose throat got slashed at the Ancona train station. The headline read MILITARY DUTY?

HANNAH DECIDED TO take a bubble bath before going to bed. She was in the tub, reading the *Herald,* when Martin knocked on the door.

"Can I show you something?" he said.

"Well, sure . . ."

The door opened, and as he came into the bathroom, she slid down until the bubbles touched her chin. He had a gas can in his hand, an old one made of metal, with rust coming through the red paint around the base of the spout. "I found this in the bushes on the other side of the driveway. I think it means Sean's been here. Did you know he tried to burn the place down again?"

She shook her head. She was holding the folded newspaper above the bubbles and she didn't know what to do with it.

"What I don't understand," he said, "is why he stopped."

"What do you mean?" she asked.

"Gas—you can smell it out there in the driveway. I couldn't figure it out. At first I thought it was coming from the car, but it seemed to be on the house. He must have started to douse the walls, but why did he stop? Why did he leave this can in the bushes?"

"A warning?"

"No, he's past that."

Then she saw his face change as he focused on the newspaper in her hand. He put the can on the floor and reached out for the newspaper. She drew her arm back. Her muscles were sore from laying bricks in the patio, and she realized that her arm had begun to tremble.

"Please," he said.

She gave him the newspaper. He sat on the lid of the toilet seat, and as he looked at the photograph, his eyes became confused and alarmed. "It's incredible," he whispered. "It's *you*."

"It's pretty strange." She tried to giggle, to make it light, but it didn't work at all.

When he finished reading the article, he looked over the top of the newspaper at her. His eyes drifted down; he was not looking at her face, and she felt caught. "What's that?" he asked.

"What?" She didn't move.

He nodded; he meant her collarbone. Then he reached out but didn't touch her skin. When he withdrew his hand, his fingers glistened with small clusters of soap bubbles. "It must hurt."

She could only stare back at him.

"You do that working on the patio?"

She tried to will the tears away but it was too late. They came quickly and she could feel their weight building up on her lower lids.

He saw them, too. "Thank you for not lying to me," he said. "What happened?"

She couldn't speak. The tears were now streaming down her face, and she could see that her eyes were telling him what he wanted to know.

"He was here, in the house—with *you*?"

Her mouth trembled and she could only nod her head.

He glanced down the length of the tub full of bubbles. "Let me see," he said. "I need to see what he did to you."

"Please, Martin."

"You don't need to hide anything from me." Then his voice was pleading. "Don't you know that?"

So she stood up in the bathtub. The air was cool on her wet skin, but that wasn't why she was shaking. With his hand he wiped bubbles away from her ribs, her breasts, and his face became full of wonder and horror.

"Nothing happened," she said.

"Nothing? This isn't 'nothing.' You let him in?"

"No. I—I was asleep. It was the night Pearly was in jail."

"You were asleep and Sean came in the house?"

"I'd left the back door unlocked for you. It was so late. At first, in the dark—I thought it was you coming into the bedroom."

"And he did *this*?"

"He came—" She put her hand on her stomach. "He came *here*. And then—God, Martin—and then I strangled him. With his own belt. I thought he was dead, but he must have just passed out, I guess, because suddenly he got up and staggered out of the house. I was here, in the bathroom then, and when I heard him I thought he was coming for me again, so I picked up those scissors from the basket and I stood here waiting for him to come down the hall. But he didn't. He left."

Martin was still and something seemed to have been wiped clean from his eyes, his expression. And then he stood up. His bathrobe was hanging on the back of the door. He took it off the hook and draped it around her shoulders. He saw that she was shivering and his hand rubbed her back gently.

"He's gone," she said.

Martin withdrew his arm, leaned over, and picked up the gas can from the floor.

She pulled the robe tightly about her. "He's *gone* from the house."

"But he will come back." Martin opened the bathroom door and paused in the hallway. "You know he will, Hannah."

She sat on the edge of the tub and listened to his footsteps as he left the house.

SEAN WAS DOZING on the couch when he heard someone coming up the outside stairs. He thought it was Arnie, but then there was a knock on the door. Sean got up off the couch, his bare feet kicking over empty beer bottles on the floor. He could see Martin standing on the landing. He went to the door and opened it.

Martin said, "You're coming with me."

"I am?" Sean said hoarsely.

"You are."

Sean saw that he had the gas can—his gas can, which he had left in the bushes by Martin's driveway—in one hand, and quickly his arms came up in a pumping motion. Gasoline covered Sean's face, his chest, his arms, his legs. The smell, which was always faintly present in the apartment, was now so strong it made Sean gag as he staggered backward. Martin came into the kitchenette, extending his right arm. He flicked a lighter, a cheap pink plastic Bic, and held it within inches of Sean's face. "You drive," he said.

"All right."

Martin shut down the flame but continued to hold the lighter out toward him. He turned so that Sean could lead him outside and down the stairs. In the garage office Arnie had a ball game on the radio. There was no sign of Martin's car.

"Where's that Mercedes of yours?"

Martin didn't answer.

They walked to Sean's truck, parked near the back corner of the building.

"Where we going?" Sean asked.

"Shut up and get in."

WHEN HANNAH CALLED Pearly her voice quivered and she wasn't clear about what had happened, but he understood that she wanted him to go to Superior Gas & Lube, where she was sure Martin had gone to look for Sean.

"Martin found out," she said, "what he tried to do to me."

She didn't have to be any more specific. Pearly had seen the photo of her look-alike in the newspaper. He said, "I'm on my way," and hung up.

When Pearly reached the garage, it was nearly dark and he pulled up in front of the office. Arnie was sitting behind the desk, listening to the ball game. He came to the doorway, a can of beer in his hand, and said, "Hey, Pearly. I've shut down the pumps for the night, but if you need gas I can unlock them—"

"Where's Sean?"

"Think he just left a few minutes ago."

"Alone?"

"Dunno. I was in the garage—just heard his truck leave."

"Which way?"

Arnie nodded, indicating that Sean had driven toward Petit Marais.

Pearly pulled out of the station and headed south. He barely slowed down for corners and his toolboxes slid back and forth, slamming into the sides of the truck bed. It was nearly dark and the narrow road seemed to rush out of nowhere into his headlights. This was a stretch where there was a lot of roadkill, and several times a year somebody missed a curve. Often, trees arched over the road, so it felt like driving through a tube. Rounding a sharp bend, he came out of the trees, and the black water of Petit Marais spread out beyond the road.

He slowed down to check each of the turnouts overlooking Petit Marais but passed only a few parked cars. He picked up speed as he wound north again, doing seventy on the straightaways. It was dark when he reached Martin's house, and he saw there were no lights on in any of the windows. Pearly expected to see Sean's truck but there was nothing—until he noticed something in the driveway. He pulled in and in the headlight beams he could see a man in jeans and a sweatshirt, lying with his back toward the street. One arm was stretched out on the pavement at an odd angle. He didn't move.

Pearly got out of the truck, and as he walked up the driveway, he could see a pool of blood beneath the shaved skull.

AFTER SHE HAD CALLED PEARLY, Hannah lay down on the bed in Martin's bathrobe. There was nothing else she could do. She couldn't leave the house. She could only wait. She had been crying so hard in the bathroom, her ribs ached and she was exhausted. Suddenly, perhaps even thankfully, everything seemed to shut down and she lost consciousness.

Not sleep exactly; more a descent into a floating state. Occasionally she heard a car passing or a puff of wind coming through the open window. Gracie lept onto the bed and curled up against her legs.

At one point Hannah was aware of the sound of an engine, of a vehicle that seemed to slow down, perhaps even stop near the house. There was the grind of gears, and then the sound of the engine and tires grew faint and disappeared.

There came a loud noise and Gracie jumped off the bed. At first Hannah was confused, until she realized someone was knocking on the front door. People seldom came to the front door. She got up and walked out to the main hall in her bare feet, switching on lights as she went. Opening the door, she found Pearly on the stoop.

"It's Martin." He nodded toward the driveway. "We need to call—" And here he hesitated. "Someone," he said.

She came out on the stoop. "The police?" The absurdity of this—calling the police—struck her hard.

Pearly seemed to understand. "He needs medical attention more than anything."

She ran down the steps and across the yard to the driveway, which was still lit by the headlights of the Datsun. When she knelt beside him on the pavement, blood quickly soaked the bottom of her bathrobe. She kept saying Martin's name, but he didn't respond.

18

THERE WAS ONLY one time when Pearly considered the possibility that he might die.

It was 1974, the summer after his mother had been killed in her car accident. Since his father had drowned in Lake Superior when he was small, he'd always felt a great ambivalence toward water. But that summer, when he was twenty-two, he felt some need to deal with the lake. He bought a skiff at a yard sale. No outboard, just a fourteen-foot aluminum boat with oars that he could row out on the lake.

Almost every day after work he'd go down to the harbor and row out through the jetties and into the open lake. He didn't even pretend to fish; he'd just row and often drift. Sometimes he'd bring a few beers and sandwiches, which he'd take ashore on some uninhabited stretch of beach.

One hot night while rowing across Petit Marais, he slipped over the stern of the boat and found the cold water a relief. He swam alongside the skiff, or just floated, keeping one hand on the gunwale. After a while, he noticed something in the water, bobbing about fifteen yards from the boat. The water was calm and there was no wind. He swam toward the object. When he was halfway to it, he looked back and saw that the boat was standing broadside to him, and he continued on with an easy sidestroke. The object turned out to be a faded beach ball.

When he turned around the skiff was farther away than he expected. Now he realized that suddenly, just as the sun was setting, a breeze had begun to ruffle the water. He swam toward the boat, but he didn't seem to make any progress and he soon had to admit that the skiff was getting farther away. He looked around and figured that he was at least a half-mile from any part of the shore. He kept swimming toward the boat, trying to maintain a steady pace that wouldn't tire him out.

Shortly after the sun set, Pearly could barely see the boat, which he figured was at least seventy yards away. And he was getting tired. His arms and legs were so heavy, he had to stop and just float. Eventually, he was floating more than he was swimming, and then he lost sight of the boat in the darkness. He was very cold. He concentrated on moving his arms and legs, keeping his mouth above water.

PEARLY AND HANNAH called for an ambulance, which they followed to the hospital in Marquette, where they spent hours in the emergency waiting room. Hannah's mother met them there sometime around two A.M. and talked with the doctors. Martin's skull had suffered severe trauma. They had managed to stop the blood loss.

At dawn Hannah's mother sat in the waiting room and told her daughter there was no point in staying there any longer. She had to go on duty at seven and she would check on Martin's progress. Eventually Hannah agreed to go home and Pearly drove her back to Whitefish Harbor. They were both exhausted. When they reached Martin's house, they could see in the early-morning light a congealed pool of blood on the driveway. Hannah asked Pearly to stay. She gave him a blanket and pillow, then went into the bedroom and shut the door. He got on the couch and before he could untie his boot laces fell asleep.

———

LATE MORNING PEARLY was awakened by voices. He got up off the couch and went into the kitchen, where Hannah was talking to Buzz Gagnon and Frank Colby.

"Isn't this convenient," Buzz said pleasantly. "We went by your place looking for you." He was leaning against the kitchen counter, his arms folded over his perfectly round, smooth belly. He was in uniform; Colby was not.

"There any change in Martin's condition?" Pearly asked Gagnon.

"Not the last time I heard."

Hannah, who was in sweatpants and a T-shirt, said, "I'm going to go change."

Gagnon and Colby seemed relieved to see Pearly, as though his presence had confirmed a suspicion they both held. They stared at him as they listened to Hannah walk through the living room and down the hall to the bedroom, where she closed the door. The furniture was still crowded in the middle of the kitchen and much of it was covered by a drop cloth. Gracie was perched on the table, casually licking her paws. Buzz studied this arrangement as though it were modern art and he couldn't make up his mind what it meant.

"Why don't you tell us your version?" Colby said. He was wearing a god-awful Hawaiian shirt, complete with palm trees and sunsets. It was his way of saying, *Look, I'm off-duty, I'm relaxed*—which, of course, wasn't the case at all.

"My version?" Pearly said. "How many versions are there?"

"Right now we're only interested in hearing yours," Colby said.

Buzz had found a green apple on the kitchen counter. For a moment there was a look of doubt in his eyes, then he gave in and took a bite.

"My version is that Hannah called me last night and said that Martin had gone to Superior Gas and Lube to find Sean. She was upset and she was afraid of what was going to happen. I went by the garage and Arnie told me Sean had just left. I drove all the way around Shore Road looking for them—"

"Who?" Colby asked.

"Sean and Martin," Pearly said. "In Sean's truck."

Colby started to speak, but Buzz asked, "You find them?"

"No."

"You see Martin in Sean's truck?" Colby said.

"No."

"So," Buzz said, "you took this drive around. What exactly did you see?"

"Nothing, until I got back here," Pearly said, "and I found Martin in the driveway."

Buzz took another bite out of the apple. While he chewed, his eyes had the innocence of a child. Pearly could have been telling him a scary bedtime story.

"What about Sean?" Pearly asked. "You get his version yet?"

"Sean?" Colby said. "It hadn't occurred to us."

"Well, you should, and talk to Arnie, too," Pearly said.

"Look, Pearly," Buzz said. He stopped because they heard the bedroom door open. Hannah came back to the kitchen, wearing jeans and a man's white dress shirt with a frayed collar, which she often wore when she was working out in the yard. When Pearly looked back at Buzz, he realized that the police chief had put the half-eaten apple on the counter behind him. "The only *version* we have," Buzz said, "is that you knocked on the door here last night and Hannah went out and found Martin bleeding all over the driveway." He turned to Hannah. "You called Pearly earlier?"

"Yes," she said.

"You didn't mention that to us before," Colby said.

She wouldn't look at Colby, who was standing by the screen door, but said, "You didn't *ask*. You only asked how I found Martin in the driveway."

"Why did you call Pearly?" Buzz asked. He still had one hand behind him as he leaned against the counter. He was dying to get at the rest of that apple, but embarrassed to let Hannah know that he'd taken it without asking permission.

"*Why?*" she said. Her voice was high, nervous.

"She called me," Pearly said, "because she was worried about what might happen between Martin and Sean." Colby's expression didn't change. "There's been some bad blood between them," Pearly said. Hannah seemed on the verge of tears. "Since he's been back from the army," Pearly added, "he's been giving them a lot of trouble. You didn't know that?"

Colby seemed ready to come across the kitchen at him, and, sensing that, Buzz stepped in between them. "What're you talking about, Pearly?" Buzz asked.

"Frank doesn't know what his kid's been up to—not a clue."

Quickly, Colby stepped away from the screen door.

"*Frank,*" Buzz said. He seldom inspired confidence, not to mention fear, in anyone, but now the tone of his voice managed to stop Colby. "Whyn't you go on and wait out by the car now. I'll be right along."

Colby hesitated but then pushed open the screen door and left the house.

Buzz went back to the counter and picked up the apple. His ability to control his partner seemed to have helped him overcome his own embarrassment about eating the apple. "I hope you don't mind," he said to Hannah. She shook her head as she stroked Gracie's head. He took the last bite of the apple and, chewing, said, "Frank's got a lot on his mind right now." It wasn't an apology but merely an observation. "Well," he said finally, "I must say this has been interesting, and that was one delicious Granny Smith." He began to put the core by the sink but then looked apologetically at Hannah, who shrugged. The police chief put the apple on the counter and went out the screen door.

HANNAH MADE SOME COFFEE, then they went looking for Martin's car. In the village they saw mostly tourists. When they reached Superior Gas & Lube, Sean was out back washing his pickup truck.

"What do you think?" Pearly asked Hannah. "I want to talk to him, but . . ."

"Pull in," she said.

He turned into the gas station and parked in the side lot near a row of used vehicles for sale. "You sure about this?"

"I'm all right. Don't worry."

They got out and walked over to Sean, who was wearing a pair of baggy red trunks and wraparound sunglasses. He had a garden hose in one hand, a beer in the other, and he was as wet as his truck. "Gonna rain, guaranteed." He smiled as he tipped the beer bottle to his mouth.

"What happened last night?" Pearly said.

Sean hosed the front grill of the truck. "Last night?"

"Between you and Martin," Hannah said impatiently.

Sean shut the water off with the hand nozzle and turned his head until his sunglasses were aimed at her. "What?"

"Oh, *Christ*," she said. "Don't pull this—"

"Sean," Pearly said, "Martin came here last night to see you."

"He did? What he want?"

Hannah folded her arms.

"I followed you when you left," Pearly said.

"You did?"

"You drove all the way around Shore Road."

"Sounds like it's you who's got a problem, following people."

"You had Martin with you—"

"Who says? *You*, Pearly?" He waited. "You didn't *see* anything."

Hannah walked a small circle, trying to contain herself.

Sean pulled the nozzle trigger and sprayed the truck, then shut off the water.

Hannah started to walk toward him, but Pearly grabbed her by the elbow. "Wait in my truck," he said.

She shook her arm free. "This is— Sean, this is— You *can't*—"

"Hannah," Pearly said. He walked after her. "Please."

She stopped. They were all standing close together, their feet in the large pool of water that radiated out from under the truck. "And that girl in the newspaper . . ." But she didn't continue. She went back to Pearly's truck, got in, and slammed the door shut.

Sean took his sunglasses off and slid them on top of his shaved head. "Don't you love it when they get rattled?"

Pearly took a step closer to him. "In case you're wondering, you put Martin in the hospital and he's not in good shape at all."

"I'd say it looks pretty convenient for you, doesn't it?"

"*What?*"

"The guy's in the hospital? Pearly, I never thought of you as an opportunist. And you're what—at least twice her age? But that can work. I understand that can sometimes be a real turn-on."

Pearly made a fist and was about to take a swing at him, when Sean's expression changed and he stepped away. It was as though a kid had been caught tormenting a cat.

Pearly turned and saw that Frank Colby had pulled his van into the lot. He got out quickly and walked over to them.

"What's going on?"

"It's all right." Sean put on his sunglasses again, but didn't have a cocky grin now. "Just a little misunderstanding."

"You know why your father's here, Sean?" Pearly said. "He's going to ask you the same question we just did." Then he turned to Frank Colby. "Maybe you can get a straight answer out of him." He began to walk back to his truck.

"Don't you go anywhere yet," Frank Colby said.

"Fine. I'll be right over here." Pearly got in his truck.

Hannah stared straight out the windshield; her hands were in her lap, shaking. She whispered, "Thank you."

"Yeah, well." And he left it at that.

They watched father and son talk for several minutes. Body language can be everything, and in this case Sean was getting the third degree. For a moment Pearly thought that Frank was going to take a poke at his son. He leaned forward and into Sean, who was a couple of inches taller, but they had the same bulkiness. Frank was still wearing the Hawaiian shirt, and with their sunglasses they looked like a couple of aliens—a mutant tourist and his frat-boy son from the dark side. Several times Sean shook his head, until finally his father strode away in disgust.

Frank approached the Datsun, laid one arm on the cab roof, and leaned down to Pearly's open window. "You have a problem with my son, you come to me, understand?"

"You ask him where he was last night?"

"No. Why?"

"Why don't you ask him?" Pearly said. The muscles around Frank's mouth were bunching up, and for a moment it looked as if he was about to spit. "You can tell when your kid's lying, can't you?" For just a moment Frank's face revealed doubt. "Start with something simple, like 'Why are you washing your truck?' "

Frank tilted his head so he could look past Pearly at Hannah, and then he stepped back from the truck.

FOR YEARS PEARLY believed that he didn't drown that summer night out in the lake simply because his father had—that knowledge had kept his weary limbs moving just enough to stay afloat. For the longest time he could only see lights along the shore, but then he thought he saw something, a dark, angular form on the water. It came and went, but finally he was sure: It was the skiff. He realized that the wind had shifted, and that slowly they were now being drawn back toward land. The boat, more buoyant and graceful, was moving faster, and if he could just tread water a bit longer, it would catch up to him. Occasionally, he tried a feeble breaststroke toward the skiff. When the boat finally reached him, he managed to haul himself up over the transom.

19

TO SEAN, it was simple: Martin couldn't follow through.

Martin had shown up in a tight rage and doused Sean with gasoline. Obediently, Sean drove them down along the shore. Though Martin still held the Bic lighter close to his face, during that drive Sean came to realize he wouldn't use it.

When Sean asked where they were going, Martin seemed undecided. He said to just drive. Eventually, without being told, Sean pulled into an empty turnout overlooking Petit Marais.

"What're you doing?" Martin said.

"If you were going to burn me," Sean said as he opened his door, "I'd be a potato chip by now." He climbed out of his truck and went to the edge of the bluff. After a moment, Martin got out, too. He walked around to the front of the truck. When Sean turned Martin punched him in the stomach. It knocked Sean to the ground. He stayed there. Martin didn't even have it in him to kick Sean.

"You'll always know," Sean said, gasping for breath.

"Know what?"

"Who got there first. I'll always be there—in that fucking house." Sean managed to get to one knee, both hands still on the ground. "You'll never be alone." He stood up, and with the rock he'd felt under his hand on the ground he took a full swing at Martin. "*Never!*"

The first blow struck the left side of Martin's head. He staggered and then went down on all fours. Sean stood over him and beat him on the back of the head with the rock, which was about the size of a softball. It made a dull knocking sound against Martin's skull. He didn't stop even after Martin was motionless in the dirt. Sean's arm simply got tired and he quit. He hurled the rock out into the water, then went back and got into his truck. For several minutes he just sat there, the key in the ignition. He could leave Martin where he was, or he could roll him over the bluff and down to the beach. But instead he got out again, dragged Martin by the feet around to the back of the truck, and lifted him up into the bed. This was the hardest part. Martin was limp weight, and getting him into the truck was difficult, particularly because Sean's stomach muscles were sore from the punch he took. But he got him in, shut the tailgate, and went back for the gas can, which was lying on its side. It was empty. Sean got in the truck and continued along Shore Road. When he reached Martin's house, he backed the truck in and quickly rolled Martin out into the driveway.

As he pulled out into Shore Road and turned north toward the village, Sean was certain Martin was dead. He was only sorry that he couldn't be there when Hannah came out—first thing in the morning, he imagined—and found the body in the driveway. Sean's stomach was killing him, but driving through the empty village, he turned on the radio and sang along with the Led Zeppelin song "Stairway to Heaven."

WHEN HANNAH AND PEARLY got back to Martin's house, she spoke for a long time on the phone with her mother. Martin's condition hadn't changed. During the conversation, Hannah's face settled into an expression that is reserved for the besieged and weary. It was as though all her facial muscles had ceased to function; her lips barely moved when she spoke, and her gaze held that vague middle distance for long periods of time.

After she hung up she said she needed to sleep and picked up Gracie and went to the bedroom. Pearly stood in the kitchen for a while, considering what to do. To go back to his house seemed pointless, but then to remain there at Martin's house felt awkward, even intrusive. What was his role here? Moral support, guard dog, or both? Then he thought about the work Martin and he had left unfinished upstairs merely a day earlier. They had been re-hanging raised panel doors. He went up to the third floor and got busy. It felt good to run his block plane along the edge of a door, thin curls of wood piling up on the back of his hands.

Mid-afternoon Pearly heard a car pull into the driveway. He went to the window and looked down and watched Buzz Gagnon getting out of his cruiser. He was alone this time. Seeing Pearly, he said, "You don't expect me to climb all those stairs, do you?"

"Be right down."

They met on the front stoop, which was in the afternoon shade. Buzz stood with his hands on his hips. "We found the Mercedes."

"Where?"

"Why don't you tell me?"

"What?"

"She in?"

"Sleeping. She's wiped out. We both are."

"Ah." Buzz leaned back slightly. "I can imagine."

"When she wakes, we'll come pick it up."

"Will you now?"

"What're you saying, Buzz?"

"We're holding the car."

"I see."

"Lot of things in it. Tools with your initials. Lots of your things."

"So?"

"So we're going to hold the car and look it over good."

"You mean like fingerprints?"

"Sure. The crime lab in Marquette is sending a tech guy out."

"I get it. And blood, and hair, and anything else they can find to pin it on me."

Buzz seemed uncomfortable and he ran a hand along the side of his neck. "Like I said, Pearly, we're going to look it over."

"Jesus. Buzz. You really don't think—"

Buzz raised the hand off his neck and showed his palm as though he were directing traffic. "I'm just telling you where we're at with this thing, that's all." He had already started down the brick steps toward his car.

Pearly went back in the house and found Hannah standing at the far end of the front hallway. She was in her bathrobe and she still looked half asleep.

"You hear all that?" he asked.

"Enough," she said. "It's crazy. What are you going to do?"

"I don't know. Around here they're the law."

They stood a long time without speaking.

"I want to get back to the hospital," she said finally.

"I know. Take my truck."

"It's not just that. I don't know if I can stay here, alone."

"Why don't you go back to your mother's for now."

"What about you? Could you stay here?" She shook her head. "Guess that wouldn't look too good."

"I suppose not." Pearly started walking up the front stairs.

Hannah came down the hall and leaned against the large oak newel post. "Amazing, they got us worrying about how *we* look."

He stopped and ran his hand along the banister. "Call me from the hospital and let me know how he's doing. I'll stay here for now. I'm better off doing something that resembles work. Keeps me from thinking."

She smiled. "You look like shit."

"I know. People tell me that a lot. Believe me, I know."

"I must, too."

"No, you don't. You look like you just woke up. On you it looks real good, too."

She reached up and put her hand over his, squeezing tightly, then she let go and walked down the hall, closing the apartment door behind her.

It was like rising to the surface, drifting upward through water, until suddenly there's air.

There is absolute darkness.

Nothing is certain. Everything seems distant.

Sometimes there is awareness of breathing.

Sometimes there is pain.

Sometimes there are sounds. Footsteps on a linoleum floor. The sigh of a door closing. A telephone ringing.

There is no sense of time.

You drift up. You sink back down.

The state of suspension is so light you aren't even aware of your body until a hand touches your arm. Your bicep is wrapped in something cool that expands and tightens, then releases slowly, followed by the scratchy ripping sound.

Or your feet are hot and sweaty because they seem to be covered with something that compresses periodically, rhythmically, accompanied by psssh.

Or you are prodded. Sometimes a needle slipping into a vein. Sometimes a catheter.

One voice is familiar. Hers. But it recedes and you drift back down.

SEAN WAS TAKING a piss when he saw from the bathroom window his mother's car pull into the lot beside the garage. He went outside and down the wooden stairs. His mother was wearing her lime-green pantsuit and she was unsteady on her feet.

"What're you doing here?" he said.

Her hand floated up, found her sunglasses, which she began to remove; then she dropped her arm.

"You're blasted," he said.

"I am not."

"It's not quite five and you're well on your way. You haven't even reached your yardarm, whatever that means. I never knew what that meant."

"It's a nautical term." She took a little sidestep and caught her balance. "Has to do with the sun and the ship—don't know, don't ask me. I was thinking about dinner."

"Fine." He held out his hand. "If I drive."

She surrendered the keys, and as she made her way around to the passenger door, she kept one hand on the car at all times.

They went to the Harborview because in the summer his mother liked to go where the tourists dined, her logic being that if you lived in some berg the tourists flocked to for a few months in the summer, you might as well eat with the same view they do—plus, she had all winter to eat in restaurants frequented by locals. She ordered a vodka tonic; he got a white Russian, thinking the milk would settle his stomach. When she finally removed her sunglasses, he could see that she'd been crying.

"What?" he said.

"It's your father." Placing a fist under her chin, she took a moment to control the quiver in her mouth. "He got a call from Dan Schofield last night. It won't be official until after the next town council meeting, but they're going to suspend him. He has no real support on that council and they're going to suspend him and they're going to do everything they can to make sure he doesn't get his job back."

"All because they hired me."

"This has been a long time coming. It's—it's just politics, local politics—somebody always wanting to have a say, wield a little power." She took a long drink of her vodka tonic, which seemed to fuel her courage. "It's that bitch and her damn newspaper."

"Why don't they suspend Buzz Gagnon, too? He's chief. He does the hiring."

"*Oh* no. Buzz will never hang for this. He'll tell them that Frank deceived him, didn't tell him about any of this Italy business. No, Buzz will play this close, but in the end he really wants to see your father out. Be a lot better to bring in some new guy, someone green who isn't going to challenge him. This'll insure that Buzz stays captain for a long time, believe me."

"Where is Dad?"

"I don't know." She put on her sunglasses and turned her head toward the harbor. The lime color of her blouse was so summer-cheerful she might have passed for a tourist. Her hands fidgeted in her purse for her pack of cigarettes. "Before he blew out of the house, he was saying he'd quit before they suspended him." When she got her cigarette lit, she glared across the dining room and said, "You'd think we could get some service *here*."

Ever since he could remember, his mother turned regal—that's what his father called it—when they were in a restaurant. The service was either too slow, or the lettuce was limp, or the soup needed to be hotter. She often tried to use such flaws as leverage for a reduction of the bill.

"He can't afford to quit, can he?"

"Of *course* he can't." Her voice quavered and it caught the attention of their waitress. When she came to their table, his mother said, "Why don't you tell me about today's specials before they're tomorrow's leftovers."

HANNAH CALLED PEARLY from the hospital after ten. She didn't sound like a nineteen-year-old. Some hard realizations had begun to settle in. This would be her voice for years to come, a woman's voice, tender, soft, but weighted with worry. She wanted to stay the night in Martin's room, but her mother insisted that she come home. Pearly told her that was the best thing to do. He didn't need the truck; he could stay at Martin's house.

She said, "There's a lot—a lot of details to this. . . ."

"I know: hospital logistics."

"Keeps your mind off other stuff," she said. "Mom can follow me over there tomorrow morning so I can drop off your truck, okay? Then I'll ride to the hospital with her."

"That's fine," he said.

"You find enough to eat?" she said. "In the refrigerator there's—"

"Who do you think you're talking to? I found the beer," he said, which got her to laugh briefly. "And I made a meat-loaf sandwich, which was excellent, by the way."

"You think they'll release Martin's car tomorrow?"

"I don't know. I'm not counting on it."

"What do you think they're going to find?"

"Aside from some of my tools?" he said. "Hair. Actually, both yours and mine . . ."

"But they're really looking for blood, Martin's blood."

"Right."

After a moment, she said, "If they looked in Sean's truck—if you could *get* them to look—they might find it. But it's too late, now that he's washed it."

"Exactly," Pearly said. "Get some rest. I'll see you tomorrow."

After they hung up, he went out into the backyard. In July it stayed light until eleven—the U.P. is so far north, and Whitefish Harbor was near the western edge of the Eastern Time Zone. For several weeks in summer the long days seem just compensation for months of brutally short, dark winter days. Then, too, there was something about the quality of light, the way it lingered above Lake Superior. That broad plane of blue held the last light of day well after sunset. He stood at the edge of the woods, looking down through the trees until the horizon no longer separated lake and sky.

Darkness, he realized, was all Martin had right now.

Yet Pearly envied him.

20

HANNAH WAS BACK in Martin's hospital room by eight o'clock the next morning. He seemed not to have moved at all during the night, lying on his back, his eyes closed. She avoided looking at the tubes that ran from his arm to the machines. Down the hall she could hear televisions in other patients' rooms. She got up and shut the door, then pulled the chair up close to his bed. His head was wrapped in bandages. She leaned over him, bringing her face so close to his that she could hear and feel his shallow breathing, and she placed her hands on his cheeks. His skin was stubbled and cool; slowly it warmed until she could no longer feel the difference between her hands and his face.

For the first time last night, she'd tried some of her mother's Scotch. Her mother poured them, and Hannah winced at its flavor and heat. But when her mother got up after her second and said, "Tonight I'm going to have one more," Hannah held out her empty glass.

When her mother returned with fresh drinks, she said, "The fact is all these tests don't tell us anything for certain."

Hannah took a sip and nodded. "He'll come out of it."

"Let's hope so," her mother said, leaning back into her recliner. "There's brain activity. He's not in a coma, but it may take time for him to—look, sometimes they come in and out of it."

"If he stays like this, they wouldn't unplug him eventually?"

"No," her mother said. "He's not a vegetable. People these days make living wills, which usually say if it's a choice between being a vegetable and dead, they want you to pull the plug."

"If it were me, I would," Hannah said. But after a moment, and another sip of Scotch, she added, "But I don't know if I could make that decision for someone else—for Martin, or for you."

"Well, it wouldn't be your decision in Martin's case. You're not family yet, honey." Then she lowered her gaze from the ceiling. "I, on the other hand, am family, and I have it clearly written that you are to pull the plug under certain circumstances."

"You never told me."

"You never asked."

Hannah took another sip. "What now?"

"*That* is the question I ask myself every day," her mother said to the ceiling. "More tests. And we wait. That's all you can do."

ARNIE OPENED THE STATION at seven and he usually came up to the apartment around ten in the morning. Sean was just waking up when Arnie was making a sandwich. "You hear what they're doing to your old man?" he said from the kitchenette.

"Yeah."

"A couple guys stopped at the pumps this morning and wanted me to let you know that he didn't show for work today. Called in sick."

"He probably has about eight months of sick leave stored up."

"They're speculating he'll call in sick until the town council makes it official," Arnie said. "What do think?"

"I don't know. But it's killing my mother." Sean climbed out of the sleeping bag, went into the bathroom, and turned on the shower. "I got to see my lawyer today. Remember, I'm the guy who started all this by breaking a goddamned headlight."

"It sounds like it really started in Italy."

"If you want to go that route, then take it back to the first time I ever laid eyes on Hannah's ass."

Arnie came to the bathroom door. He was eating another one of his liverwurst-and-onion sandwiches. "Tell me something," he said. "That girl in Italy. How'd you find her? She just happen to look that way? Or you have her make herself look like Hannah?"

"Listen," Sean said, "you got to eat something else for lunch. The smell of that thing, it's an insult."

"You want an insult? Your mother cuts in line at the post office." Arnie took a big bite out of his sandwich and grinned as he chewed.

Sean closed the bathroom door.

THERE WEREN'T MANY successful businesses in Whitefish Harbor. Few retail stores other than Deitz Hardware, which sold a little bit of everything like a general store, remained open through the winter months. Larsen's Funeral Home, of course, did a steady year-round business. And Nault & Nault Law, but they didn't surround themselves with the usual trappings of the legal profession. No secretary, no tony waiting room full of large potted plants. Father and son shared one long room on the first floor of an old sandstone building two doors down from the Portage. Their desks were not twelve feet apart, and only a six-foot-high partition, which Pearly had built, gave their clients a sense of privacy.

When Pearly walked through the door, only Owen III's desk was visible in front of the partition.

"Funny, I was going to call you," Owen said. "We're thinking of putting a door through that wall between the den and living room."

Pearly sat in one of the two imitation-leather chairs in front of the desk.

A voice—Sean's—came from the other side of the partition. He said to Owen's father, "I still don't see why I can't just pay for the frigging headlight. I mean, we're talking about a twelve-dollar item down at NAPA."

Owen's father said, "Reimbursement isn't the point."

Pearly hesitated, but then said to Owen, "I think I might be getting arrested soon."

There was silence on the other side of the partition.

Owen's elbows were propped on the armrests of his chair as he fidgeted with the large silver ring on his right hand. "What, you're planning on going on a bender tonight? Maybe you want to abscond with another flagpole?" His eyebrows jumped playfully. "Are there any flagpoles *left* in Whitefish Harbor?"

"This is a little different." Pearly cleared his throat. "You hear about Martin Reed?"

"Yeah, at the Hiawatha they were saying something about him going to the hospital. What, he take a fall over at that Bob Vila Special you guys been working on?"

"Someone tried to beat his brains out. I'm going to get arrested for it."

"Jesus, Pearly, this *is* a little out of your league. Why you?"

"Because they're going over Martin's car for evidence."

Owen folded his hands on the desk.

"But I didn't do it," Pearly said. "Sean Colby did."

There was movement on the other side of the partition. Owen's father said to Sean, "*You* stay put." Then he came into view behind and to his son's left. His sport coat was powder blue. "Can you prove that?" he asked Pearly.

"Probably not, now that he's cleaned out his truck thoroughly."

There was the scrape of chair legs. Pearly turned and saw Sean behind him at the far end of the partition. "What're you talking about?" Sean said.

"Martin came to the gas station and you two went somewhere in your truck," Pearly said, getting to his feet. "What'd you use on his skull? He was nearly dead when you dumped him in the driveway at his house."

Owen's father began to speak, but it was too late. Sean rushed Pearly and they both landed on young Owen's desk. Pearly's arm felt numb from the impact, and Sean punched him in the face several times. Both Naults were shouting as Sean and Pearly rolled off the desk and onto the floor. Pearly landed on top and got to his knees. Sean took another swing at his head but missed. Pearly punched him once in the stomach, and he turned onto his side.

Pearly stood up and young Owen pushed him back around the desk. Both he and his father were shouting at each other.

"Get *that one* out of here!"

"No, *you* get *yours* out of here!"

Owen III kept shoving Pearly in the direction of the front door. Sean was sitting up, holding his stomach. The old man was pointing his finger at Pearly, still shouting.

Until that moment, Pearly never realized that he wore a toupee—it had come loose and slid down over his ear.

When they were outside, Owen III took Pearly's arm and guided him down the sidewalk. "*Jesus*, Pearly—what the *hell* was *that*?"

He opened the door to the Portage, ushered Pearly inside, and sat him down in the nearest booth. Everyone sitting along the bar turned and watched them with suspicion, curiosity, and, in some cases, amusement, then went back to their drinks and cigarettes.

When he opened his eyes, two women were staring down at him. The oblong of light above them in the ceiling hurt his eyes. They appeared to be mother and daughter, and the girl was crying and smiling at the same time. The mother wore a yellow blouse with little cats on it, and she was watching so carefully, he sensed he was in some kind of trouble.

The girl was holding his hand, which seemed odd but he didn't mind. She was pretty. She couldn't stop crying, and finally she leaned down and kissed him on the mouth. He could taste the salt of her tears.

Other people came into the room—two older women in uniforms like the mother's, followed by a man in a white smock, who shone a small flashlight in his eyes. The tag on the man's smock said Dr. V. J. Singh. He asked, "How do you feel, Martin?"

He wanted to answer. He tried to open his mouth. There seemed a great distance between what was in his mind and what he could do. Their faces changed. They all began to look somber, like the mother. The girl stopped crying and now she looked alarmed. The mother finally took her out the door.

Dr. Singh leaned down close to his face and said, "Martin. Martin, can you hear me? Can you say anything? Can you blink and give me some response so I know you understand me?" The doctor watched him for a long time, then said, "All right, let's try again later after you've rested." He and the other women left the room.

He wished someone would do something about the light in the ceiling. Turn it off. Take it away. Make it stop hurting his head. Finally, he closed his eyes and returned to the dark.

"I'M ALL RIGHT NOW," Hannah said.

Her mother sat across from her in the hospital cafeteria. "You were nearly hysterical. Take these. They'll help." She placed two pills next to Hannah's glass of apple juice.

"What's the matter with him? Do they know? Can they do anything?"

"It may be a temporary condition," her mother said. "It's not uncommon for people to not remember too much."

"When will you know if it's not temporary?"

"Take those, Hannah, please."

Hannah picked up the pills. "Will these put me to sleep?"

"No. Though when you go to sleep, they should help you stay asleep. I'm through with my shift in an hour and we'll drive home and get you to bed."

"I want to go back to our house, Martin's and my house."

Her mother dropped her chin that quarter-inch that said no. "I think it best you stay with me for the time being. Really."

FIRE POINT

AFTER A PHONE CONVERSATION with Hannah's mother, Pearly stayed another night at the house. Suzanne was accustomed to telling people just enough to let them fill in the blanks. She said there were complications; that Martin appeared to have suffered some memory loss. She said that Hannah was upset and she was going to stay with her for a while. On the phone Pearly felt as if he and Suzanne were forming an alliance. Clearly, it was difficult for her—Pearly could hear the tinkling of ice in a glass throughout the phone call—because this situation involved her daughter. He assured Suzanne that he would look after the house for as long as necessary. Suzanne appreciated that, thinking that it would help her convince Hannah to stay with her. Pearly didn't mention to Suzanne that in the morning he had to go to the police station for questioning. Buzz Gagnon had called and he suggested that he bring his lawyer too. That would just further upset Hannah.

He met Owen III outside town hall at nine Saturday morning. It was a small brick building, and when Pearly was young, he and other kids used to hang out in front of it because for them it was the center of the world. They would sometimes put one hand on the flagpole, close their eyes, and run around it as fast as possible, until they became dizzy and fell on top of one another, laughing, in the grass, or, for much of the year, in the snow. Lying on their backs, they'd stare up at the flag at the top of the pole, waiting for the dizziness to go away. There was a faint, not unpleasant nausea, much like you experience on a carnival ride. Above them, the red, white, and blue American flag appeared a bright rent in the sky, the pole seemed to be circling, teetering as though it might fall over at any moment, and, best of all, the earth beneath them seemed to be moving, spinning slowly. It was a remarkable sensation, and it was accompanied by the realization that they were on a planet called Earth, which was not stationary but hurtling through space. When the dizzy feeling began to subside, they'd get up, their steps still a little uncertain, place a hand on the pole, and circle it again, yelling with delight.

The cracked cement pad and the metal cylinder that used to support the flagpole were still in the ground. Owen and Pearly stood over the support. There was something shiny at the bottom of the collar, so Pearly reached two feet down inside the rusted cylinder and removed a Labatt Blue beer can.

Owen sang, "Oh, Can-a-da!"

Pearly dropped the can in the trash barrel by the front doors of town hall. Inside, they walked down the dark corridor, passed the city clerk's office, and entered the door of the police department. Buzz Gagnon was sitting on the corner of the desk behind the gate, and Frank Colby stood in the open side door, which led to the parking lot.

Buzz motioned for them to come through the gate and sit in the two straight-back wooden chairs in front of the desk. He was in uniform; Frank Colby was not—today he wore a white short-sleeve shirt. No palm trees or tropical sunsets.

Owen nodded toward Frank. "He here in an official capacity?"

Buzz folded his arms over his belly. "No. That a problem?"

"He shouldn't be here," Owen said.

Buzz sighed, and Frank took his weight off the doorjamb and walked outside.

"No," Pearly said to Owen. "He can stay."

Owen shrugged.

"Come on back, Frank," Buzz said. Frank returned and settled himself in the doorway.

"Okay," Buzz said. "Is everybody happy? Anybody need to use the bathroom before we start?"

"Knock it off," Owen said, "and get to it."

Buzz raised a hand to his face and felt the tip of his nose a moment. "Fine. Let's start with Pearly's story. You said you went to Superior Gas and Lube looking for Martin because he was looking for Sean."

"Right," Pearly said.

"How'd you know that?"

"Told you, Hannah called me."

"Hannah called you." Buzz stopped stroking his nose, as though to indicate that this was an important point.

"Right," Pearly said. "When I got to the station, Arnie was closing up. I asked him where Sean had gone. He said he'd just taken off in his truck. I drove all the way around Shore Road but didn't see anything, until I circled back up to Martin's house, where I found Martin lying in the driveway, his head bleeding badly."

"And where was Hannah?" Buzz asked.

"In the house," Pearly said. "Well, in the house until I knocked on the front door, and then she came out and saw him."

"What was she wearing? You remember what she was wearing?"

"A bathrobe," Pearly said. "She was wearing her bathrobe."

"Okay, then what?" Buzz asked.

"Then we called for the ambulance."

Buzz just sat there on the edge of his desk. Frank had turned so his back was against the doorjamb. He was gazing out at the parking lot as though he was expecting someone.

Owen said, "You have anything that contradicts that?"

Buzz picked up a sheet of paper from his desk. "We found Martin's car in the woods not far from the gas station." He paused as though this in itself was a significant point.

Finally, Owen said, "So? That's where Martin left it."

"I'm not so sure that Martin drove it there," Buzz said.

"Well, who did?" Owen asked.

"I'm not sure," Buzz said.

Owen started to get out of his chair, which creaked loudly. "When you're sure, let us know. This isn't—"

"I'm not sure whether Pearly drove Martin's car, or Hannah drove it."

Owen settled back in the chair. "*Ahhh.* You have a theory."

"I have a theory," Buzz said. "Want to hear it?"

Owen crossed his legs and made himself comfortable.

"I think Hannah or Pearly drove Martin's car over and left it in the woods by the gas station so it would appear that Martin had gone looking for Sean. My guess is that Hannah drove the car and Pearly followed her in his truck so he could take her back to the house. Also, because I called Arnie and he confirmed that Pearly did stop at the station in his truck, asking where Sean had gone." Buzz held up the sheet of paper as proof, then dropped it on his desk. "There's all sorts of evidence that both Hannah and Pearly had been in that Mercedes—"

"Christ, Buzz," Owen said, "nobody's denying that they'd ever been in that old car! I've seen both of them in it many times."

"As I said, it's a theory."

"So what's the rest of it?" Pearly asked. "What happened to Martin? What did *I* do?"

"You crushed Martin's skull. With some blunt object—I don't know what—which we'll probably never find. You did it right there in his driveway." Pearly was about to speak, but Buzz held up his hand. "Now, I don't know whether it was something you and Hannah planned in advance—frankly, I tend to think not. I think Martin found out about you two—"

"What *about* us two?" Pearly nearly shouted.

"—and you and he got into an argument right there outside the house. This is a matter of domestic discord, pure and simple, a crime of passion, as they say. You got in a fight over a girl. And we *know* she's a girl worth getting into a fight over." Buzz glanced toward Frank, who was still surveying the parking lot. "At some point," Buzz continued, "you hit Martin or he fell or something—but suddenly it went too far, and there he was, lying in a pool of blood in the driveway. Then you—you and Hannah—set it up so that it would look like Sean had done it."

"I'm forty-four," Pearly said. "She's—"

"I know what she is," Buzz said. "I got eyes, too."

"So that's it, we tried to frame Sean?" Pearly said.

Buzz nodded.

Owen nodded also. "I gotcha. No one saw Martin and Sean together that night."

"No one," Buzz said.

"So it *had* to be Pearly and Hannah," Owen said.

"You got a better theory?" Buzz asked.

Owen uncrossed his legs. "You have evidence? Enough to hold Pearly?"

Buzz placed a hand on the sheet of paper on his desk. "We got hair. Pearly's and Hannah's. We got fingerprints. We got some of Pearly's tools in the backseat and trunk."

"What you got is evidence that they'd been in the car *sometime*," Owen said.

Buzz nodded. "I hear you." He got up off his desk.

Owen was getting out of his chair, but Pearly couldn't move. "That's it?" he said.

"For now," Buzz said. He walked around his desk and sat in his swivel chair, which rocked back under his weight.

Pearly managed to stand up. He'd spent so many nights there in the police station that the idea that he was being let go made him uncertain, nervous—it made him feel guilty, more so than if they had walked him down the hall to the bench in the back room that he knew so well. Setting him free seemed the worst thing that could happen.

"There's one more thing." Buzz was staring at Pearly's feet.

"What?" Pearly asked.

"Mind if I have a look at those?"

"What, my boots?"

"The soles." Pearly began to lift one leg, but Buzz said, "I'd prefer it if you'd take them off."

Pearly sat down in the chair again. He untied his work boots slowly. He was waiting for Owen to object, but then he realized that would probably only make it worse. When he had both boots off his feet, he picked them up with one hand and looked at the soles. They were badly worn. There was a small nail embedded in one heel. There was a reddish-black stain on the right instep. He handed the boots to Buzz.

"There was blood in the driveway," Pearly said. "I'm surprised I didn't get more on these. You know, you try not to stand in a man's blood when it's on the ground, but it's not easy to do at night."

"I believe you," Buzz said.

Owen said, "It's just like the car, it still won't mean anything."

"You mind if I keep these?" Buzz asked.

"Nope," Pearly said. "Help yourself."

He got up and started for the side door. It felt odd, embarrassing, to be walking out of the police station in just his socks. Frank moved out of the doorway to let them pass. He wouldn't look at them.

When they were outside in the parking lot, they saw Hannah and her mother coming up the sidewalk toward the front entrance of town hall. Pearly took a step in their direction, but Owen caught his upper arm and said, "No you don't."

21

SEAN RECOGNIZED THE HORN. He went out the apartment door and stood in the sun on the landing. His father was sitting behind the wheel of his van.

"Come down here," he said. It was the same voice he used from the top of the basement stairs when he wanted to summon Sean up to the kitchen. "We're going for a ride."

Sean went down the stairs and got in the van. "Where?" There was a six-pack of Bush beer on the floor, and two empty cans rattled about his sneakers.

His father didn't say anything. He put the van in gear and pulled out into the street. They didn't speak all the way down Shore Road. The silence was working on Sean. The back of his T-shirt was sticky and clung to the seat. When Petit Marais came into view, his father parked in the first turnout.

"Bring those," his father said, opening his door.

Sean picked up the beer by its plastic ring and followed his father down a path that led to the water. At the foot of the bluff there was a narrow rock beach cluttered with driftwood. His father sat on a weathered tree trunk. "I want to know what happened."

His father opened a couple of the beers and handed one to Sean, who remained standing. It seemed as if anytime his father was buying the beer, it wasn't necessarily to celebrate.

"What *what* happened?" Sean kept his eyes on the water—a mistake.

"Don't . . ." His father waited until Sean faced him. "Don't think about it, just tell me what happened. You thought you could get away with it when you were way over there in Italy, but not this time, not here." He took a pull on his beer. "I want to hear it in your own words. You know Martin's in the hospital?"

"I know."

"You do it?"

Sean nodded.

His father scratched his chin. "With what?"

"A rock."

"A rock," his father said. "Why?"

"He threw gas on me, that's *why*."

"Gasoline? Why would he do that?"

"Because he's an asshole."

"Why would he do that—what did *you* do?" his father asked. "There's that fire at his house. But that can't be it—that was weeks ago. What else did you do?"

"Nothing, really." Sean took a long pull on his beer. It had been sitting in the van and could have been colder. The only thing to do was drink it fast before it got any warmer, so he drank it right down. He went over to the tree trunk, dropped the empty can in the sand, and took another beer from the plastic ring. "Nothing that I didn't do before," he said.

His father dug a hole with the heel of his shoe and toed the empty can into it. "That girl. Jesus, that's one dangerous girl. I hope she was worth all this trouble." Using the side of his shoe, he carefully buried the can with sand.

"Martin had it coming," Sean said. "I'm telling you, he threw gas in my face, on my clothes, and he pulled out his lighter, but he didn't have the nerve to light it. What, I'm going to let a guy walk away after that?"

His father didn't answer right away. "Where's the rock?"

Sean nodded toward the water.

"What about your clothes? And your truck—you took him back to his house, right?"

Sean almost smiled. Up until that moment he'd been tight with fear, but now he knew there was no need. "Clean. Don't worry, everything's clean."

His father was busy digging another hole in the sand with his shoe. He finished his beer and dropped the can in the hole and plowed sand over it until it disappeared. Then he stood up. "Buzz thinks he has it figured out, which is fine. If he can hang it on that girl and Pearly, nothing would be sweeter. Blankenship's been getting away with shit around here for years. I hear Martin can't remember squat. But he comes out of it, that changes everything."

"I could say I did it in self-defense," Sean offered.

His father looked directly at him. Despite the sun, he wasn't wearing his sunglasses, which was unusual. There was no question that he was disgusted by what he saw. "You don't say a word. To anybody. Understand? Not one fucking *word*."

He didn't wait for Sean to reply but started climbing the path up to the top of the bluff. Sean picked up the remaining cans of beer on the tree trunk and followed him.

PEARLY WAS JUST FALLING ASLEEP on the couch at Martin's house when the Mercedes pulled into the driveway. Through the open window he watched Hannah get out of the car. She walked around back and came into the kitchen, the screen door clapping behind her.

"You talked to Buzz Gagnon?" she said.

"Just before you."

"You know what they think?"

"It ain't pretty."

"It's bullshit. They can't prove it."

"Maybe not, but we can't prove what happened, either." Pearly sat up on the couch. "They kept my boots and they're sure to find Martin's blood on the soles. Besides, you know how it works: It's not a matter of what can be proved but of what people believe."

Hannah folded her arms. She was dressed as though she were going to church or to visit relatives. Pearly imagined her looking through her old clothes at her mother's house and coming up with this off-white silk blouse and a gray skirt. "I know," she whispered.

"They let you take Martin's car back, so you'll be staying here again."

"Right."

"I better go home and dig out another pair of boots."

"Sure," she said. "We don't want to fuel their suspicions, do we?"

"Too late. Did Buzz ask you about your bathrobe?"

She nodded slowly and Pearly knew she'd been thinking the same thing. "He did. Actually, it's Martin's robe that I was wearing."

"Did you tell them that?"

"No."

"Where is it?"

"In the hamper. I was going to wash it and bring it into the hospital."

"Can I see it?"

Hannah went down the hall to the bathroom and returned with the blue plaid bathrobe. She held out the bottom, which was stiff with dried blood. "I only knelt next to him in the driveway."

"Do you have a bathrobe of your own?"

"Yes."

"Then I should take this," Pearly said.

She handed him the robe. "Now we're acting as though *we* did it to him."

"I know."

"I feel like we're guilty of something."

"We're not, Hannah. You're not."

She sat on the armrest of the couch and put her hand over her mouth. "I wear his bathrobe, his shirts, his T-shirts all the time. I'm guilty of liking to wear my boyfriend's clothes."

"I'd better get going."

The pretty girl was back. Her hair was clasped behind her head, so he could see more of her face. He noticed when she came into the room that she was wearing a skirt, but he didn't get a chance to really see her legs. Her blouse was a fine material, and he was surprised when the word satin *came to mind. What was satin?*

She pulled the chair up so she could lean close to him. She laid her hand on his right hand, the one that didn't have tubes and bandages. He could smell her perfume. He watched her eyes closely. They were beautiful but they were worried.

"Listen to me," she whispered. "Listen to me, Martin. Your name is Martin. I know everything is confusing right now and you don't remember much, maybe anything. I don't know. So I'm going to tell you a few things at a time, all right? Not too much. If you can let me know you understand, it would be great, but don't worry if you can't." She waited. He wanted to speak, to squeeze her hand, but he couldn't do either. "It's all right," she said. "Just listen to me for now. My name is Hannah LeClaire and I'm your girlfriend. We live together in a house you bought, an old house, which you've been restoring with Pearly Blankenship, who's your cousin." She hesitated. "That's all I'm going to tell you for now. If any of that comes back to you, if you remember something, I know you'll let me know. Somehow you will." She leaned closer. "You look tired and I'm going to let you sleep. I'll be here, at the hospital, and I'll be back later." She came so close that he could feel the warmth of her breath on his face. "I want to kiss you, Martin." She waited, then smiled. "Well, since you haven't said no, I'm going to assume that it's okay." She leaned forward and kissed his mouth.

THERE WAS ONLY one way to go. Pearly couldn't go back, so he had to go forward, and by early evening he'd been in the Portage long enough to be thoroughly toasted. Someone sitting near him at the bar might have thought that occasionally he seemed to be talking to his feet—that he was swearing at his boots, which were very worn and a good five years old. When he finally left the Portage, his Datsun managed to get him home, with one quick stop at the IGA for a steak and a pint of potato salad. The old brick grill in his backyard was falling apart, but sometimes on a summer evening he liked to cook a piece of meat on it. He piled up the coals, doused them with lighter fluid, and had another beer while he watched the fire.

The fact was he was afraid. Burning the bathrobe seemed like an admission. Hannah was right: They both felt guilty, although they'd done nothing wrong. He couldn't grasp it, where it was coming from—he was standing out in his yard, preparing to cook a steak, and he felt the whole neighborhood was watching him. There were, in fact, three houses that had a view of what he was doing, all small cottages like his, which had been built back in the twenties, when a logging company set up its operation by the lake. He was convinced that if any of his neighbors looked out and saw him standing in front of the grill, they would see through the ruse: He wasn't making dinner; he was waiting until dark to burn evidence.

Once the coals were white, he put the steak on and cooked it till it was medium. He sat in an old folding lawn chair and ate steak and potato salad, then had another beer as the light faded to the west of the village. Throughout the neighborhood there were the sounds of kids, dogs, screen doors. Nobody seemed to notice him, except for Larry Bundt, who waved as he walked from his car to his back door with a pizza box cradled in his arm. When it was just about dark, Pearly went into the kitchen and poured himself a shot of Scotch and stuffed the bathrobe in the paper bag he'd left on the kitchen table. He took the bag and the glass of Scotch outside. The coals were fading embers now. The night air was cool, but the brick grill gave off a pleas-

ant heat. He tossed back the Scotch. He was so gone that all his movements seemed slow yet animated—this in itself would be nothing new
or extraordinary to his neighbors. He took the bathrobe out of the
paper bag, laid it on top of the coals, and waited. Like a magic trick,
the garment smoldered for several minutes until it suddenly burst
into flames, giving off a heat that made him step back from the grill.

It burned quickly. As Pearly watched the fire, he started to recognize the source of his guilt. He rarely envied someone, or so he told
himself, but he had to admit that there had been moments when he
would feel something close to envy toward Martin. The differences
between them were clear: Martin was making a life for himself, while
Pearly was simply living the one he had been given. That old house
was an achievement. Everyone knew that; they recognized that its
restoration—its very survival—was the result of Martin's labor. Yet
he was doing work that Pearly could do better. Pearly, who lived in his
mother's house. And then there was Hannah. Pearly needed to be
careful here, to make a fine and clear distinction. Few men could look
at her and not be stirred by desire, if not lust. But when you got to
know her, to know the kind of person she was, the nature of that
desire changed. She was someone a man could get lost in, and never
regret it. It had happened to Sean Colby, it had happened to Martin.
This had never happened to Pearly. Standing before the fire, watching
the flames die down, he had to admit there had been a few moments
when he wished that Hannah would look at him or touch him in a
way that meant she loved him. The fact that he was more than twenty
years older did nothing to diminish this desire. It seemed fitting that
his cousin should get the house and the girl. Not get, earn. For Pearly,
the man who had neither, the future seemed barren.

*He remembered the grass. It was June, the last week of school, and all
fifth and sixth graders got to take school buses into Wrigley Field. Their
seats at the ballpark were in the sun, well down the first-base line, and*

the late-afternoon sun had turned the grass a brilliant green, an unreal color, the green equivalent of fire. The Cubs were leading the Phillies, 5–3, in the seventh. He was sitting next to a boy named Teddy, who had a harelip. The vendor passed their hot dogs down the aisle. They were wrapped in aluminum foil, which kept them hot. When he peeled back the foil, the hot dog smell was so good it made his mouth water painfully. He ripped open the mustard packet and drew a thick yellow bead the length of the dog.

"No ketchup?" Teddy asked. "No relish?"

"Just mustard," he said.

"Then gimme your ketchup packet," Teddy said.

He handed the packet to Teddy and everyone jumped to their feet. Looking up, he saw that it was a high foul ball, arching toward them. It seemed to be falling right for him. He stood up, and as he raised both hands, he dropped the hot dog. He knew he should have brought his mitt. The ball came down toward him, getting bigger and bigger, until he could see the spinning red laces. Suddenly he was afraid—the ball might hit him right in the head—and he closed his eyes. He was bumped from behind as the ball hit the seat with a loud crack. Turning around, he saw several boys scrambling under the seats, screaming and pushing one another, until one boy stood, holding the ball high over his head like a trophy.

He looked down at the mustard streak on his T-shirt. The hot dog had rolled out of its bun and it lay on the dirty concrete by Teddy's sneaker.

"How are we feeling today?" the woman asked.

"I would like another hot dog," he said. "I dropped the first one."

"Did you?" She didn't seem angry. "Well, I think that can be arranged."

"Just mustard. Please."

PART III

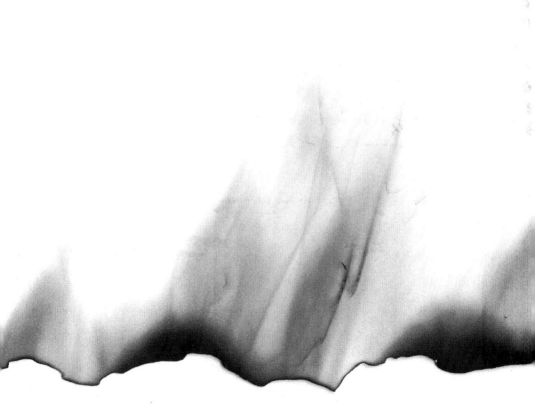

22

THE FIRST FEW TIMES Pearly went to Marquette General with Hannah, Martin was groggy and tired, and he often complained of a terrible headache. He remembered more every day, it seemed, including a lot from his childhood. He and Pearly talked about Aunt Jane, about years ago, when the entire clan would gather at her cabin during the summer. Martin would suddenly mention some obscure fact, something from sports or history. More recent events were less clear to him. He understood that he'd bought the old house and that they'd been restoring it. But he didn't remember the fire at all. When they were in his hospital room, he watched Hannah closely. He liked the attention she gave him, and the fact that she lived at the house with him, but he wasn't clear on how that had come about. She would describe the spring afternoons when he'd taught her to drive standard shift in his Mercedes. But they could see it in his eyes: He was trying hard to conjure up something, one image that he could see in his mind, but it wouldn't come. Then his eyes would lose focus, and at times they'd become confused and fearful. Sometimes when he was speaking he'd stop suddenly, and it was obvious he couldn't find the words to express what he wanted to say. More than once he became so frustrated he got teary-eyed. After a few days he seemed to level off—which was something the doctor had told them to expect: His vocabulary remained quite limited, and much of the time he didn't form complete sentences. Once he was asked to write his name, but he couldn't. He remembered nothing about how he was injured, and no one even mentioned Sean Colby to him.

When he was stronger physically, taking long walks in the halls and eating well, the doctor said that it would be okay for him to go home. He would have to keep quiet, but there was no point in staying in the hospital any longer. This was a relief for a number of reasons, one being the cost, because Martin had no health insurance. Pearly had called Aunt Jane in Florida and she said to have the hospital bills sent to her. So after nine days, which seemed an eternity, Martin was released from Marquette General and went home with Hannah.

Pearly knew how this was going down in Whitefish Harbor. People discussed all this with a muted enthusiasm that did not belie their keen interest. Martin—some still referred to him as the "Chicago boy"—had returned home. He was living again with that Hannah LeClaire. And Pearly Blankenship was over there at the house every day. What were those people up to in that old house?

Pearly could see it in people's eyes, when he entered a shop, a restaurant, a bar. Some stares clearly intended to tell him that they were certain of his innocence. Pearly Blankenship simply was not the sort who was capable of crushing another man's skull, for love, money, property, or whatever. But there were more averted stares, and these confirmed what Pearly suspected all along: Proof has nothing to do with anything; it's what people believe that matters. They believed that he was responsible for Martin's injury—his own cousin, which, when you thought about it, only strengthened the case for his guilt. It was, in part, a blood feud.

The other thing, the other point of interest, was the Colbys. The day after Martin returned home was Frank Colby's last day of active duty. Since the town council voted that he should be suspended from the police force, Frank had taken just the one sick day after he first learned of their unanimous decision. His final days on the force he was out there walking his beat. Some people admired him for putting a good face on things. His only act of defiance came on the last afternoon. He drove his cruiser through the village real slow so everybody could see him once more in full uniform. A few ardent supporters stopped on the sidewalks and applauded. He did not wave in acknowledgment, which seemed fitting, and his meaty bare forearm lay on the top of the car door like a reptile sleeping in the sun.

Sean suffered a less dignified demise. When he appeared before Emmett Anderson, the judge determined that he would have to pay for the replacement of the headlight he broke on his father's cruiser and, furthermore, he would be required to perform a hundred hours of public service at the town hall. "Odd jobs," the judge said as he raised his gavel, "performed during regular business hours—wash the police cars, clean the windows, the bathrooms, sweep the floors and front walk, trim the hedges." He tapped the gavel and said, "Dismissed."

BECAUSE MARTIN NEEDED rest and quiet, Pearly didn't do anything at the house that required hammering or power tools. Instead he taped and joined Sheetrock. Then he rolled primer on all the new walls. After a few days Martin began coming upstairs, first to watch, then, for short periods, to help. Downstairs, Hannah was finally completing the paint job in their kitchen.

But a hard realization was setting in: Martin did not seem to be coming back "in full." He approached some things with the wide-eyed innocence of a child, while at times he descended into a fathomless torpor indicated by a slack mouth and dull eyes. One afternoon while he was sleeping, Hannah said to Pearly, "I asked him to bring me a gallon of paint, and he looked at me and said, 'What's a gallon?' "

They became a family of sorts, resembling, say, a mother and an uncle who are extremely protective of a child. Pearly had never been a father figure to anyone and found it strange, but he liked it. Hannah seemed to accept the maternal nature of her role, but once Pearly found her cleaning paintbrushes at the kitchen sink, her face streaked with tears. There was nothing he could do or say, so he took the brushes out on the back steps and laid them out to dry.

One afternoon Martin went with Pearly into the village on errands. They parked in front of Deitz Hardware and Martin said he wanted to stay in the truck and listen to the oldies station on the radio. When Pearly came out of the hardware store twenty minutes later, Martin wasn't in the truck. The keys were still in the ignition and the radio was still on. Pearly walked a block south, looking in stores, but didn't find him. Then he saw him, standing in front of the town hall, talking to Sean, who was on a ladder, washing windows. Pearly crossed the street quickly.

"So this isn't your job?" Martin was asking.

"You fucking with me?" Sean looked around. "He's fucking with me, Pearly."

"No, he's not," Pearly said.

Sean put his squeegee and bottle of window cleaner down on the top of the stepladder and said patiently, "Okay. No, this isn't my job." Then he added, "You know why I'm doing this?"

"To make the windows clean," Martin said.

"Right," Sean said. "How am I doing?"

"Looks *good* to me!"

"I'll just bet they do." He came down the ladder and stepped up close to Martin. "You've had your fun, now get away from me." Then he asked Pearly, "It's not contagious, is it?"

"Sean, the question is, *how* did it happen?" Pearly took Martin by the arm and, as if he were a child, began to lead him back across the street toward the Datsun.

But Martin pulled himself free. "What's your name?" he asked Sean.

"*What?*"

"Do I know you?" Martin asked. "I remember . . ."

"I don't know what you're talking about." Sean put a foot on the bottom rung of the stepladder, but something made him hesitate.

"I've seen you before," Martin said. "In a bar. There were people, and a baseball game on TV. *Yes!* You were mad—what were you saying to me? And then . . ."

"Then what?" Sean said.

"Then—then someone hit you. Punched you. Because you were about to punch me. I remember that. It was Arnie! Arnie did it! Remember?"

Sean looked at Pearly for an explanation, for help even, but Pearly simply took hold of Martin's sleeve again, and this time he didn't resist. He seemed weary, and as they drove back to the house he fell asleep.

MARTIN LIKED GOING on errands and the following evening they were in the village again. Although the tank in the Datsun was more than half full, Pearly stopped at Superior Gas & Lube. Martin got out of the truck, walked around to the driver's side, and watched Arnie start the gas pump. At first Arnie didn't acknowledge Martin. He kept his head down, one hand on the gas nozzle. Finally, Arnie gazed back at him.

"What?" he said.

"Arnie?"

"Yeah?"

Martin wanted to speak. His mouth opened and closed, as though he was forming the words, but he remained silent. Pearly had seen this before, but it struck Arnie like a revelation. Then Martin went back around to the other side of the truck and got in the cab, holding both hands tightly between his knees.

After the tank was filled, Arnie came to the window and said quietly, "Jesus, Pearly, I've heard people talk, but . . ."

"Well, it's coming back slowly. But he remembers you fondly."

"He does?"

"You nailed Sean in a bar once, right?"

"Yeah, but I was pretty drunk."

"Martin remembers who his friends are. It's only a matter of time before he remembers the rest."

After a moment, Arnie said, "That's eight even."

Pearly gave him a ten. "Tell me something. You know what people are saying around town, that I had something to do with it. You believe it?"

Arnie peeled two ones off his wad of bills and handed them through the open window without looking at Pearly.

"You don't," Pearly said. "I know you don't. And you saw me that night, too. I came here looking for Sean."

"I can't help what people think. Officially, I don't have an opinion."

"*Officially*? Right." Pearly nodded toward Arnie's apartment. "He up there?"

"Yeah," Arnie said, sounding weary and fed up. "I'm afraid he is."

Pearly started the truck. "Well, you have a good one."

SEAN'S MOTHER CALLED the apartment around ten o'clock. She had that voice that sounded as if she'd run up and down the basement stairs repeatedly. "*Sean—*" Gasp. "*You—*" Gasp. "*Get—*" Gasp. "*Home—*" Gasp. "*Now.*"

Arnie was just coming up the stairs after closing the station for the night. He went straight to the refrigerator and got a can of beer.

Sean said to his mother, "I'll be right there," and hung up.

Arnie opened his beer. "Listen—"

"I need to get home," Sean said, opening the door.

"We gotta talk."

"About what?"

"About—about this living arrangement here." Arnie leaned

against the kitchen counter. "Look, this place is too small, Sean. When you moved in I thought it was just going to be this temporary thing, you know? Until you squared things with your folks, or you got a place of your own."

"Okay, we'll talk about it—later."

"I've been thinking about it a lot," Arnie said. "There's really nothing to talk about. I want this place—*my* place—to myself. So—"

"Fine. *Fine.*" Sean went outside, slamming the door behind him, and ran down the stairs to his truck. He made it to his parents' house in about five minutes, half the time it usually took. When he pulled into the driveway, he found his mother's car angled up onto the lawn and the front right tire was in her bed of roses. There were no lights on in the house.

He walked around the car and found his mother lying on her side on the lawn. He knelt beside her but she didn't move. Lowering his face to hers, he could feel the breath coming from her mouth, foul with the smell of menthol cigarettes and bourbon. It was too dark to see if she'd been hurt in any way. She seemed to have just passed out.

Sean walked up to the front door, which was slightly ajar; he pushed it open, went inside, and stood in the entryway to the living room. The light switch was on the wall to his right but he didn't turn it on. There was a smell that he couldn't identify. He walked across the living room—it was nearly pitch dark, but he knew exactly where the furniture was—to the kitchen. One of the stove coils was on, glowing red beneath a pot. Smoke stung his eyes. Something, some food—not meat, but some vegetable, he guessed—was burning in the pot, probably because the water had all boiled away. He went to the stove and shut off the heat.

He stood still and watched the coil lose its intense glow. The house was silent, but then he heard something, a faint knock coming from the basement. He walked carefully to the basement door, though he knew that if his father was downstairs, he would have already heard Sean overhead. That was the thing about living in the basement all those years—he always knew exactly where his parents were upstairs. Sean realized that maybe Arnie was right. He'd spent too much time living on that couch. He missed his old room, something he'd never thought possible.

He put his hand on the light switch but didn't turn it on. He waited, listening for another sound. Finally, he said, "Dad?" Then he flicked the switch, the bare bulb at the bottom of the stairs came on, and he could see the clothes dryer. As he went down the stairs, he said again, "Dad?" The other light, above the workbench, had not gone on, so the lone bulb above the bottom of the stairs cast long shadows down the length of the basement. To his right was the unfinished wall that closed off his bedroom. He went to the door.

"Dad, you there?" There was no sound from inside the room. Sean put his hand on the doorknob and turned it slowly, enough to know that it was locked from inside. He looked back toward the workbench again, to make sure his father wasn't somewhere in the shadows. Then he said, "Look, I know you're in there. Open the door."

There was a sound, a faint twang and groan, which Sean recognized as the box spring under his mattress.

"I'm coming in," he said. "You don't open this door, I'll kick it in like *you* did." He pounded his fist on the hollow door, but there was no response. He put his head very close to the wooden jamb and waited. "All *right*." Stepping back, he raised his right leg, kicked out hard, his foot hitting the door just below the knob. There was the sound of splintering wood as the jamb gave way on the other side of the door, and he heard movement in the room—footsteps. He shoved the door open with both hands and stepped into the dark, warm room.

He could barely see his father, standing by the sliding glass door. He'd drawn the drape back with one arm and his other hand was on the door latch.

"Listen, Mom called and—"

The door slid back on its aluminum track and his father went outside. The drapes billowed as cool night air filled the room. Sean went to the door and stepped out into the backyard. To his right, he heard running footsteps in the grass, but he couldn't see his father.

Suddenly he laughed. "Okay," he said loudly. "That's cool. You live out there awhile. Sleep on somebody's couch. See how you like it. This is *my* room!"

He went back inside and pulled the sliding door shut. When he switched on the desk lamp he saw his father's stuff. Clothes on the floor, draped over the chair. Empty beer cans everywhere, a plate of old food on the nightstand. The air smelled of sweat, unwashed clothes and sheets. On the floor by the bed were stacks of magazines, *American Police Beat, APB, Police Times.*

2 3

EVERYTHING WAS DIFFERENT NOW.

Hannah realized this one night after dinner. They had eaten out on the patio, which was now finished—Martin had helped lay the final courses of brick. He remained outside while she did the dishes. When she finished, she looked out the window above the sink and stopped wiping down the counter. For minutes she didn't move as she watched Martin, who sat perfectly still, gazing straight into the sun, which was setting down through the trees, as though he was trying to memorize it. The light was golden, and although it was only the second week of August, there was already a touch of fall in the air. He seldom blinked, and his face seemed burnished in the sunlight.

In high school Hannah had a history teacher, Mr. Byykkonen, who once talked about "the head in a vat," a phrase that made the class laugh. Mr. B., as he was called by the students, explained that there was one strain of philosophy that posited—he loved to use such words—that the world is nothing but the figment of your imagination. The desks they sat at, the cafeteria food they had eaten for lunch, boyfriends, girlfriends, pets, and parents—none of it was real. None of this, including this class period, or the quiz coming up in algebra, really existed. Mr. B was like that. Whereas most of the other teachers could drive you into a gray state of boredom with repetition and routine, Mr. B had the ability sometimes to yank your head around so that you could get outside yourself, could see things from a different perspective. Last year, when Hannah was recovering from the complications of the abortion, she sometimes reminded herself that this all might not be real, that it might just be in her head. She didn't believe it—the pain, the blood were all too real—but still it helped. It was as though for a moment she was allowed to drift up out of herself and look in all directions, so she could see everything around her with perfect clarity.

Sometimes when Martin stared at her now, it was as though he were imagining her. It was definitely not a blank stare. There was something about the intensity of his eyes as he watched her face. As though he was seeing her for the first time. Which could be disconcerting. Which could be a little frightening. Which she found very lonely. She knew now that she couldn't really talk to him the way she had before; to do so seemed false, trivial. It was harder now because she had to find new ways to speak to him. Words seldom worked the way she wanted them to, and even gestures and expressions often failed to gain a response. He would just continue to watch her.

The hardest part of each day was going to bed. Obediently, he'd change into the sweatpants and T-shirts that he used as pajamas. He'd always get into bed and lie on his back, staring at the ceiling. There were nights when she tried to sit up in bed and read, but it was too disconcerting just to have him lie there. A couple of times she read to him, but after a while he was either asleep or she could tell he wasn't listening.

Eventually she would have to turn the light out. Often he was already asleep. Several nights she would curl up against him, but he wouldn't move, wouldn't respond. But then two nights ago he began talking after she'd turned out the light. He remembered things—more things more often now. He'd told her about baseball games he'd gone to years ago in Chicago, about summers when he'd visited his aunt here in Whitefish Harbor. Little moments, little pinholes of memory shot through the darkness. But this night he remembered something they had done back in May, meeting at the movie theater over in Marquette. The theater was nearly empty; the movie was dull, but they didn't care. As he told her all this, he was lying on his back in bed; she lay against him, her left leg across his thighs, her hand creeping up under his T-shirt. She stroked his chest and stomach gently. She asked him if he remembered anything else about that night, anything they had done there in the theater. He didn't answer. This was common. If he couldn't recall something, he would just become silent. She had learned not to keep probing; it only made him anxious.

But as he lay there trying to remember anything else about their trip to the movies, Hannah unbuttoned her shirt—the old dress shirt of his she often wore to bed. Gently, she raised his T-shirt, then laid her bare breasts against his skin. He didn't move. She moved her breasts just slightly, her nipples swelling. She kissed his chest and teased his nipples. He lay there.

"Does that feel good?" she asked.

"It tickles."

"You want to touch me?"

He didn't answer.

She slid up, bringing her breasts to his face. "God, I think they're going to burst," she whispered as she brushed her nipples across his lips. His mouth responded, sucking and licking, though his hands remained at his side. He seemed to like it.

Then she drew herself on top of him so that her pelvis pressed against his. She knew that she shouldn't expect too much, and as she moved slowly against him, there was no hardness. But she couldn't stop, and she finally said, "I think I'm going to keep doing this."

"Okay."

She ground herself against him harder, and as she developed a rhythm, he slowly became firm. "Is that all right?" she asked.

"Yes."

"You want me to do anything else? Just tell me, it's all right."

After a moment, he said, "No."

She continued to move herself against him, and finally she couldn't help moving quicker. When they came they both cried out. Martin sounded startled, as though he'd been caught by surprise. As they fell asleep the clothing between them became warm and sticky.

Since then Hannah had looked for some sign from him, some recognition, some recollection. If he would just touch her, or say something that suggested he wanted her again. But he didn't. It was as though it hadn't happened, and she didn't know if it was because he didn't understand what had happened between them, or he simply didn't remember.

More and more she found herself getting lost in fantasies. While she'd been painting the kitchen she would imagine them fucking, standing with her hands braced against the counter, or kneeling on all fours on the drop cloth, or doing it so hard on the living-room carpet that she got new rug burns up her spine. But these thoughts only made her feel sad and even guilty.

Now, watching Martin stare at the sunset through the trees, she tried not to think about anything. He was seeing only the sun, the fading colors.

She tried to only see him as he sat there.

She tried to memorize him.

Errands.

He liked riding into the village in Pearly's truck. They went every day and saw the same people in Deitz Hardware, out back in the lumberyard, at the IGA. People were friendly and always smiled and said things like, "Hi, Martin! How are we doing today?"

When they were through with their errands, they sometimes went into the Portage. Sally served both Pearly's beer and his root beer in heavy glass mugs that were kept in the freezer. One day, while walking back to the truck, they passed the town hall across the street. He stopped to watch the man in the parking lot, washing a police car. He crossed the street and the man looked at him, but he didn't smile or ask how he was doing. There was a white pickup truck in the lot, too. He went over and looked in the windows.

The man said, "What're you looking for?"

"Nothing."

"Well, then, whyn't you just move away from there?"

He looked at Pearly, who said nothing.

So he moved away from the truck.

"Any word on your father, Sean?" Pearly asked.

"Like you care?"

"I'll tell you," Pearly said. "Your dad and I have a long history, you could say a 'professional relationship,' and there have been times when we certainly didn't see eye to eye. But I think he got a bum deal from the town council."

The man he called Sean turned off the hose and there was the sound of water dripping and running off the police car. "Well, it's too bad they didn't consult you, isn't it? Maybe you ought to run for town council?"

Pearly laughed, but Sean didn't seem to understand that he'd made a joke.

"Well," Pearly said, "the fact is a lot of people around here are worried about him." Sean looked at Pearly as though he hadn't heard him. "And your mother—"

"Leave my mother out of this," Sean said.

"Okay. Well, Martin, what do you say?" Pearly started to walk away.

"Gasoline," he said.

Pearly stopped and came back. "What?" he asked. He was looking at the water and suds on the pavement again, as though there was a problem, even some danger. "What about gasoline, Martin?"

"He smelled like gasoline. When we were driving," he said, looking across the lot toward the white pickup truck. He turned to the man named Sean. "It was nighttime and you smelled like gasoline."

For a moment no one said or did anything. Then Pearly said, "You see, Sean, it's coming back."

He started across the parking lot then and Pearly followed. The

water glistened in the sun as it ran down to the gutter beyond the side-
walk curb. It was interesting how water always ran downhill.

AFTER HIS FATHER DISAPPEARED, Sean had moved back into his basement bedroom. His mother was, more than ever, a complete nervous wreck. She smoked constantly as she watched one TV show after another. Only once did he dare mention the amount of bourbon she was drinking—this at lunchtime, after she placed a chicken salad sandwich before him on the kitchen table. He used to love her chicken salad, but she was getting sloppy and now he'd find tendons and small bones in it. He lifted the bread and examined the sandwich carefully. "You should make lunch before you start drinking."

"Don't you start," she said. Her glass, her pack of menthol cigarettes, and her lighter were arrayed before her on the kitchen table as though they were a line of defense.

Reluctantly, he picked up half of the sandwich. "Fine."

"You don't know what it's been like here."

"I don't even know what happened here," he said with his mouth full. "All I know is something burned on the stove."

"It was an artichoke. Your father hates them, but I don't care."

Sean grinned. "*Carciofi.*"

"Don't you use any of your . . . your Italian in this house."

"So you burned dinner, then what happened?"

"You don't need to know that."

"But something did happen—I found you lying out in the yard. I thought you were dead."

"Might as well have been."

"But you were only passed out."

"*Enough.*" She took a drag, her cheeks going hollow.

"All right. How long had he been sleeping down there in my room?"

"Awhile." She leaned over the table, across her little wall. "All I'll say is this: That man will *never* set foot in *this* house again."

"Jesus."

"*Never.*"

So he had only his imagination. What could his father have done to his mother at this point, after all these years? Sean assumed it was sexual, but right there his imagination began to short-circuit. The thought of his mother and father in bed—or anywhere—doing those things, Sean just couldn't stay with it. It was unknowable, unthinkable. What he did know was that he couldn't leave the house again. He had to remain there, living in the basement, as a form of protection for his mother, as necessary and reliable as her bourbon, her menthol cigarettes, and her mindless television programs.

And there were the rumors. His father had been seen, he had been spotted. His mother's friends would call and when she hung up she'd say, "We have another sighting." His father had been seen dancing at a powwow over at the Bay Mills Reservation. He was living in a motel on Route 41 outside Marquette. He'd been seen in bars in Sands, Harvey, and Grand Marais. In several instances he was reported to be in the company of an Indian woman. One of his mother's friends suggested he'd "gone native."

After Sean concluded his one hundred hours of public service, he had time to kill. He spent much of the day just driving around. He never stopped at Superior Gas & Lube anymore, but went all the way to Munising or Harvey to fill his tank. At some point after dark he always drove by Martin's house. Sometimes more than once. Martin had recognized his truck. He remembered the gasoline. Eventually he'd recall the rest. Once Martin put it all together, Sean was convinced they'd nail him good.

BUZZ GAGNON CALLED Pearly's house late one afternoon.

"You need to come in here, Pearly. I want to ask you some questions."

"When?"

"Right now, and you might want to get in touch with Owen, too."

Pearly called Owen and they met Buzz in the police station at five o'clock. Other town employees were closing up their offices, and their footsteps knocked loudly on the floor in the hallway as they left for the day. A tall blond kid named Randy, the summer cop who had replaced Sean, was also there, sitting on a folding chair in a corner by a fax machine.

"Just thought we'd have another little talk," Buzz said.

Owen said, "This is about Pearly's boots, right?"

"Boots from Whitefish Harbor aren't a top priority at the lab over in Marquette, but we finally got them back. There was Martin's blood on them, like I suspected."

"Like Pearly said!" Owen almost shouted. "He told you he was standing there in the driveway, which was covered with Martin's blood. It means nothing."

Pearly had never seen Buzz less jovial. "I just want you to know where we're at with this thing. See if you want to talk about it. It might be better in the long run."

"This office seems so empty." Pearly turned to Randy. " 'Course, now with Frank Colby gone, you're suddenly getting your feet wet."

"Never mind Frank Colby," Buzz said. He laid his beefy forearms on his desk. He appeared to be having second thoughts. "But I'll tell you something, Pearly. I think you know we're going to find something else soon, and it's going to be more substantial than some blood on the sole of your boot."

"So talk to us, then," Owen snapped. It seemed as if he was more fed up with his client than with the police chief. "In the meantime, my supper's waiting."

Buzz ignored Owen, which was unusual for him. "Actually, Pearly, Frank Colby is—well, how should I say this? You might be better off just taking care of business now. I think he's not gotten over the inference you made about his son in Hannah's kitchen. So it might be better for you to get it done for your own good. Know what I mean? Right here and now."

"What, you're offering me protection?" Pearly asked. "You going to take me out to the bench in the back room where I'll be safe?"

Buzz sat back in his chair and shrugged. It was meant to be a gesture of affirmation. "I'm just saying you might think about what's in your best interests here, that's all."

Owen stood up but Buzz didn't even look at him, and at that moment Pearly felt a respect for the captain he'd never known before—Gagnon was going beyond the law. He was doing the right thing: giving Pearly fair warning.

Pearly stood up, too, and leaned over the desk and offered Buzz his hand. Buzz took it, a bit surprised. "Thanks, Chief. I appreciate what you're doing here, but I'm fine."

"Your call," Buzz said. His handshake was firm and, Pearly thought, final.

"This mean I don't get my boots back, huh?"

The chief shook his head. " 'Fraid not."

Pearly followed Owen out into the hallway.

"What *crap*," Owen muttered. "Trying to *scare* you into a confession. Je-*sus*."

Outside the front doors Pearly stopped and said, "Know what I ought to do?"

Owen was still walking. "What's that?"

"Let you go."

Owen turned. His gray suit coat billowed behind him in the breeze. "Let me *go*?"

"Yeah." Pearly went over to the rusted flagpole stand and looked down into the dark hole. There was another beer can in there. He decided to leave it and began walking slowly around the stand, one hand out, touching the imaginary ship's mast, which was there when they were kids. "Yeah, I'll let you go, Owen, because this time I'm really free."

"To do *what*? Hire another lawyer?" He thrust his hands deep in his front pockets. Suddenly Pearly knew what was coming next. It was

Owen's greatest fear. "Wait a minute," he said. "You're not going over to my *father*?"

"Nothing like that, Owen." Pearly continued to circle the stand, walking faster. "Besides, he wouldn't take me anyway, you know that. He usually handles the winners. The rest of us, we just get you."

"Thanks," Owen said.

"Believe me, I've always been appreciative of your services."

"Right."

"But it's time." Pearly stopped walking, closed his eyes, and there it was—he felt the world tilt. He waited until the dizziness subsided, then opened his eyes. "I'm *free*—and it's just time, Owen. Can you understand that?"

Owen stood there for a moment, a little more than perplexed. Then he appeared to arrive at a viable solution. "Fine," he said, turning and starting down the sidewalk toward his car. "Fine, Pearly. I'm going home. See if you can understand this: I'm hungry."

24

THERE WASN'T A RESTAURANT in the U.P. that didn't have a fish-fry special every Friday night. The Portage was jammed as usual, but Hannah and Martin had managed to get one of the booths in back. Out the window they could look across the parking lot toward the lake, down between several shacks the commercial fishing boats used to store gear. It was late August and some trees down by the water had already begun to turn.

Pearly was at the bar, and when Hannah and Martin finished dinner, he joined them. He bought them both a root beer, and himself one more beer. They talked about the house. In a few weeks, the second- and third-floor apartments would be ready to rent. They were, in a sense, celebrating. Soon there would be tenants living upstairs and the place would pay for itself—a good thing, since Martin's money, which Hannah had been managing well, was running low.

It was nearly dark when they left, and as they walked across the parking lot, Sean arrived in his truck. Hannah was certain that he had timed it so he'd pull into the lot just as they were leaving. More than once she'd seen his truck pass by the house at night, but she'd never said anything to Pearly or Martin. You couldn't stop him from driving down the road.

Sean got out of his truck and walked toward them. Hannah

looked at Martin, who had the intensity of a bird dog. "What?" she said.

"The gasoline," Martin said. "It was his gas can. I found it out in the bushes by the driveway." He hesitated, then said, "He tried to burn our house down. He was going to do it again."

Hannah glanced at Pearly, then said, "Yeah, that's probably what he had in mind."

Martin turned to her. "Bruises. And you had bruises in the bathtub."

"You remember that, Martin?" she said.

"He came into the house while you were sleeping. I went after him."

"All right," she said carefully, as though telling him to go slow.

Sean was now about five yards from them. Martin walked over to him, and Hannah and Pearly followed.

"You knew I couldn't light the gas," Martin said to Sean.

"That right?" Sean looked at Hannah, then Pearly. "The fuck's he talking about?"

"What'd you use?" Martin asked. Sean tried to go around them but Martin stepped in his way. "I remember we went in your truck. Down to Petit Marais. One of the turnouts there. That's where you—you picked up a rock."

Sean placed both hands on Martin's chest and shoved him so that he fell back against the nearest parked car. Pearly took two steps toward Sean and punched him in the stomach, doubling him over. Sean put one hand on the car hood and took deep breaths.

"I told you it would come back to him," Pearly said.

"So the fuck *what*?" Sean gasped. "What're you going to do, go to the po*lice*?" He straightened up and grinned, though there was pain in his eyes. "A lot of good that'll do. Buzz Gagnon thinks you *two* did him. Just about everybody believes that. So you go right ahead." Sean turned and pointed toward the two picture windows in the back of the Portage. Both windows were full of people staring out at them.

"You tell *all* of them and see if they buy it." He started for the bar again, walking slowly with one hand on his stomach.

"We will," Hannah said. "Believe it, Sean, we will."

Sean took a couple more steps, then turned around. "I believe you, Hannah. I have always believed you." He walked up to the back door of the bar. People looking out the picture windows began to go back to their seats.

THE FOLLOWING MORNING it was raining hard when Pearly arrived at the house. Martin was still asleep. Hannah was sitting in the kitchen, drinking coffee. She was wearing a nightgown. He'd never seen her in one before. It was white and there was a tiny purple satin bow on the embroidered front that had been pressed flat.

"He was up late last night," she said. "He never has trouble falling asleep now."

Pearly sat down across the table from her. "What's he want to do about Sean?"

"He doesn't know. He's so confused. I hate to say this, but he's like a boy who's afraid to squeal on an adult." She got up and poured coffee into a second mug and handed it to Pearly. "Did you see that look on Sean's face?"

He nodded. The coffee was good and strong.

She stood by the table, looking out the window at the rain. "Do you know what it means?"

He didn't answer. He didn't have to.

"I could take Martin in to talk to Buzz Gagnon," she said.

"You could do that."

"But he'd just think we convinced Martin to lie for us."

"True," he said. "It'll only make us look really guilty." After a moment, he added, "I wish you'd sit down."

"You know Gagnon came by the other day?"

"No, I didn't."

"Know what he wanted?"

"The bathrobe," Pearly said.

She sipped her coffee. "So I gave it to him, but you know I felt guilty doing it—giving him the wrong bathrobe, *my* bathrobe, and I think he knew it. And I don't have *any*thing to feel guilty *about!*"

"I know."

"You burned Martin's robe, right?"

Pearly nodded.

"Jesus," she whispered. "I'm *so* tired. Martin finally settles down about three in the morning, and I'm still lying awake, waiting—waiting for *some*thing, I don't know what. It's like I don't know if Sean's going to try and burn the house down, or whether he's going to come through the door, a window, or what. But I know he's out there and he's coming. If not tonight, tomorrow night. And the work—everything we've done to this house, it's really coming together finally. You know, I always felt safe here with Martin. But now . . ."

"Now?" Pearly said. "How is it now?"

She ran a hand through her hair. She knew what he was really asking. "Now is now," she said. "I can live with it. I have to live with it. It won't be easy, but what can I do?" Then she surprised him. She put her hand on his. "You understand it, don't you? I couldn't leave him. Then I *would* be guilty." She squeezed his hand. "You don't know how much it's meant to me—to us—that you've been around, you've stayed around."

Pearly turned his head toward the window. The patio bricks were slick and bright in the rain. "He's all the family I have." He raised his head and saw that she was crying. "You both are. I never knew what I've been missing until now." He let go of her hand. "Listen, if you're going to sit here and bawl your eyes out, I've got to get out of here right this minute." She smiled as she wiped her cheeks. He drank the rest of his coffee and stood up. "Besides, it's a good day to finish that trimwork upstairs."

Hannah put her bare arms around Pearly's neck. After a moment he put his hands on her hips, her cotton nightgown as sheer as a veil under his fingers. She held him tightly and kissed him on the mouth. It was, he knew, a gift, just this once.

SEAN DROVE THE whole afternoon in the rain. There was no apparent logic to his route. It was like a dog trying to pick up a scent. His circle kept widening, eight miles east, six miles south, ten west. The connecting dots were bars and roadhouses. At a place called the Twelve Point Rack outside of Eben he found his father's van parked in back.

His father and a woman with long, straight black hair were sitting at a table beneath a dusty set of moose antlers. There were no other customers, just an old woman who sat on a stool at the end of the bar.

Sean went over to the table.

The woman with the black hair was Indian and she was just lighting a cigarette. The match flame illuminated her pockmarked cheeks. She could be thirty, she could be forty. Sean was only certain that she was older than he was, younger than his father. Somehow age didn't seem important. She and his father were both drinking shots and beer.

"Sean," his father said, "this is Mary Threefoot. Mary, this is my son, Sean."

"Hello, Sean," she said.

Sean didn't say anything.

She got up from the table and said to his father, "I'll wait outside."

Sean watched her go out the door. Through the window he could see her stand under the metal awning over the front door. Her gray sweatshirt was draped over large breasts. She smoked her cigarette and stared out at the rain.

The old woman sitting at the bar came over to the table. Whiskers grew out of a mole on her neck and she couldn't have been five feet tall. Sean's father said, "We'll have another round here, Hattie."

Sean sat down and unzipped his jacket. They didn't speak until Hattie brought two draft beers and two shots. She removed the empty glasses and bottles and went back to the bar.

"I'm not going back," his father said.

"Don't kid yourself. You *can't* go back. Mom doesn't want you around and she really means it. Whatever you do, don't go near the house." Sean waited for some reaction but there wasn't any. His father just downed his shot. "Where you been staying?"

"Around."

"Mom's friends have seen you with her." Sean nodded toward the window. His father didn't look like he believed it. "They call up and tell her."

His father hadn't shaved in a few days, something he never failed to do. He ran his hand over his jaw and his skin seemed to crackle. "She should be okay for money."

"She doesn't think so."

"The house, the car, the van—they're all paid for. The real difference between your mother and me is I pay as I go while she puts it all on a credit card. She can manage, provided she doesn't go shopping between drinks." Dim light from the window illuminated his left eye, which seemed hard and lifeless as a marble. "You look like you got a problem."

"I got a few."

"Name one."

Sean drank some beer, which was very cold. "Martin, he's starting to remember things now. When he puts it all together, I don't know— they might take him to Gagnon."

"You used a rock?"

"That's right."

His father seemed disappointed. "Sometimes it's better to finish what you start. I mean, if this girl still means that much to you."

Sean downed his shot, which was bar Scotch that burned his throat. He followed it with a long pull on the cold beer. "I don't think Buzz Gagnon would believe him."

"Who knows with Buzz, and who cares? All depends on what's good for Buzz. Right now he has me out of his way, which means he'll be chief until retirement a dozen years from now. Plus, if he could hang this Martin thing on a guy like Pearly and your old girlfriend, he'd look like he's actually doing his job. But I'm betting on Buzz doing what he does best, which is nothing. With Buzz, though, things can change real quick."

"You're saying I should have killed him."

"I'm saying you should have asked yourself what it was all about. What was it worth. You might have considered what you'd get out of it. What is it about, getting laid? You got laid in Italy. Or maybe it's about love? You tell me." His father drank some beer. "I'm just saying you got to know your business, and once you start something, you got to finish it. Right or wrong, you'll know you made up your mind and you did what you believed was necessary." He saw that Sean was about to speak and he waved a hand. He wasn't through. "I'm not talking about what other people think. About what friends say when they call on the phone. I'm not talking about committee decisions and local politics. I'm talking about what you know, what you can say to yourself. Only you can determine what you can live with."

"I don't know," Sean said. "I got to put a stop to it. This has really fucked me up. Sometimes I could murder somebody."

"A day never passes when the thought doesn't cross my mind."

"I want to kill him. I want to kill her. I'd like to throw Pearly into the deal, too. I want them and that fucking house to just go away." Sean drank down the rest of his shot, which went smoother this time, then followed it with another pull on his beer. "Tell me something," he said, looking out the window. The woman was still under the metal awning, just behind the stream of water that ran off the outer edge. When she took her cigarette out of her mouth, smoke drifted up into the damp air. "What'd you do to Mom?"

His father drained his glass and put it on the table. For a moment he watched the foam slide down the inside of the glass, then he said loudly, "We'll have a couple more here, Hattie."

The old woman poured two more shots and opened the bottles of beer. Sean tried to watch the rain, but his eyes kept drifting back to the Indian. She had never once turned and looked in the window at them, but just kept smoking her cigarette, lifting her head every time she exhaled.

His father didn't say anything while the old woman delivered the next round. After she went back to the bar, he said, "What'd your mother tell you?"

"She said you hated artichokes but she didn't care anymore, so she cooked one."

"That's all?"

"It was enough. She's the way she is because of you. So am I." There was a book of matches on the table, which Sean picked up. He struck one match and watched it burn down to his fingertips before waving it out and dropping it in the ashtray.

"Why'd you come looking for me?" his father said. Sean didn't answer. "You come to your father for advice? You picked a fine time. You want advice, I'll give it to you. Are you listening?" Sean nodded. "Don't do anything. Hear me? Don't tell your mother you found me." His father leaned forward and said softly, "And don't do anything."

Sean got up from the table suddenly. "Advice? You been telling me what to do my whole life." He put his hands in the pockets of his jacket.

"Somebody's got to."

"Not anymore."

"Listen," his father said, "just forget what I said earlier. Don't do anything."

"I'll tell you what I won't do. I won't tell Mom I saw you." He started to walk toward the door but stopped. "No, you were right earlier. It's the first good advice you've given me." His father watched him but then looked away. "That's right, you might regret it."

Sean went outside, where Mary Threefoot was trying to light another cigarette.

"Soggy matches," she said. "This rain."

He realized he had the book of matches in his pocket. He took it out and lit her cigarette for her. She lowered her eyes as she leaned toward him and drew on the cigarette.

"Thanks," she said.

"Sure. Need these?"

"No. I have matches."

For some reason he just stood there. Her gaze wouldn't let him go. Then he said, "Okay, then." He stepped out from under the awning, hunching his shoulders as cold water hit the back of his neck.

25

A WOMAN PEARLY did a job for years ago had asked him what he thought about while pounding all those nails into her deck. He didn't know how to answer. You pound a nail, you're thinking about hitting it square, you're thinking ahead to the next nail, the next measurement, the next board you need to cut. You think about your work. But it's work that requires repetition, which he'd come to appreciate. At certain times you get into the rhythm of the work and you forget you're doing it. And your mind wanders. He thought about things he'd read. He thought about things in the past. It all just comes up out of nowhere and sometimes his thoughts got in a comfortable groove. He liked it in there, his mind. Once, years ago, an old carpenter he worked with got up off his knees after spending a half hour nailing down subflooring, and he said, "Well, that was a good movie." Pearly knew exactly what he meant.

He spent the afternoon cutting and nailing the last of the trim in the second- and third-floor hallways, quarter-round molding, which was often called shoe. It was a final detail that was fussy and time-consuming. Nobody except a carpenter really noticed shoe, but if it wasn't there, everybody would know something was missing.

When he was putting the last piece in beneath the window at the top of the third-floor stairs, he heard tires out on the wet road. Raising his head, he looked over the windowsill and saw Sean's white truck pass the house—it slowed down briefly, then accelerated as it went into the curve. Pearly sat back on his haunches, listening to the rain beat against the glass. Hannah was right. He would come to this house again.

A door opened down on the first floor. "Pearly?" Martin called.

"Up here." He finished nailing the strip of shoe.

Martin climbed the stairs. Since he'd returned from the hospital, there was something plodding in his step, and by the time he reached the third floor, he was breathing heavily. He sat on the top of the stairs and caught his breath, watching Pearly sink the nails with a punch.

"See that truck, that white truck?" Martin asked.

"What about it?"

"It was Sean."

"I'm afraid it was."

Martin was running his fingers over a knot in a floorboard. "I remember everything." His voice sounded like it used to except it was deeper, slower. "I remember the whole thing now, Pearly. You know she's scared, really scared."

Pearly hesitated, then nodded.

"He's going to come back. She knows it, you know it, and I know it. She talked to me about going to the police."

"Is that what you want to do, go to Buzz Gagnon and tell him you remember?"

"No. That won't do anything." Martin took his hand off the floor. "I'm feeling better, I really am. I still get tired, and there's often the headache. But I'm okay now."

"That's good, Martin."

"We got to do something." He raised his head. His eyes were bright, alert.

"I'm afraid you're right." Pearly got to his feet.

Martin stood up, too. "What? What are we going to do?"

Pearly untied his nail pouch and put it on the windowsill with his hammer.

"What are we going to do, Pearly?"

"Well, I think it might help if I stayed here at night for a while." He knew Martin was staring at him, but he continued to look out at the rain as though what he had just said was of little consequence. "I have a roll-away cot I can sleep on. I'll go get it, grab a bite to eat, and be back here by nine. I won't set the cot up in your apartment, but near—over on the other side of the first floor."

"Then what do we do?" Martin asked.

"The only thing we can do. We just wait."

SALLY WAS WORKING the bar at the Portage that night. Pearly sat down at the far end under the wineglass rack, which he had built several winters ago, using some very nice bird's-eye maple that had been sitting in a guy's attic for decades. They had all-you-can-eat barbecue spare ribs on special, and he got his money's worth. It was a quiet night, late summer, the lull before Labor Day weekend. Over the next month Whitefish Harbor would shift into off-season, a subtle transition that takes years of observation to recognize, not to mention to fully appreciate. Sometime around mid-February, there are brutally cold days where absolutely nothing seems to happen except that snow accumulates, and it has a kind of perfection about it.

Sally brought another beer and they lit fresh cigarettes. She was keeping her glass of red wine under the bar down at this end and she sipped it as she checked the dozen or so customers spread around in the booths. Her hair was a light strawberry due to the sun, and the skin between collarbone and cleavage was pink and freckled.

Her son, Jason, came in, wearing his American Legion baseball uniform. He sat down at Pearly's end of the bar and drank a Coke quickly, then asked for his mother's car keys, saying he needed to give some of his teammates a ride home.

"How you do this afternoon?" Pearly asked.

"Split a doubleheader with Manistique." Jason was in a hurry, of course. He stood up, pure sinew and taut muscle. Even his tanned jaw seemed to flex. "Went five for nine."

"Sign him up," Pearly said.

Jason's glance suggested that he would not end up like Pearly, who was just another regular sitting in the bar where his mother worked. "I'll bet you played when you were young, right?" he said. "And you're dying to tell me something like you had a pretty good arm."

"Guess I don't have to bother now, eh?"

Jason nodded, almost gratefully. Sally handed him the keys and he asked what was really on his mind: "You need me to come back with the car?"

"No," she said. "I'm all set."

"Okay," he said, getting off his stool. "See ya, Pearly."

"Slugger."

They watched him walk up the length of the bar and out the door. "They get antsy by August," she said. She took a drag on her cigarette before crushing it out. "Maybe he's starting to wise up. He's not speaking to his father now. Refuses to go see him in Newberry."

She took another look toward the booths to be sure everyone was happy, then leaned her forearms on the bar. Her fingers toyed with Pearly's knuckles. "Could use a lift home after last call."

"This must mean summer's officially over."

"I guess so." She smiled as though the joke was on her. "No more convertibles."

"How 'bout I take a rain check?" he said.

"Got your own summer romance to wrap up before Labor Day?"

"Nothing like that, I'm afraid. Just a little obligation later tonight."

"I never thought of you as a guy with obligations, Pearly."

"It's based on friendship—Platonic love, at best."

"Maybe you could come over for dinner sometime this week?"

"I think that's the first time you've ever asked me to your place—for dinner."

"Could be it's time I did?" In the dim subterranean light of the bar her eyes were large, bright, and liquid. Her mouth seemed firm with conviction, or perhaps it was acceptance—it was hard to tell. "Haven't seen much of each other lately, not since that hot spell back in June."

"We rarely do during the summer," he said.

Her expression changed; it was neither conviction nor acceptance but something Pearly couldn't name. "I know," she said. "But there are only so many summers. Maybe next year things'll be different." For a moment she looked sad, as only a woman who is approaching a certain age can look. Pearly considered it an offering. "But anyway, we'll have dinner soon. You, me, and Slugger."

"Why not?" he said.

A couple got up out of a booth and came over to pay their bill. Sally hadn't let go of Pearly's fingers yet. She leaned across the bar and kissed him gently on the lips, and smiled as she withdrew.

He finished his beer and went out the back door to the parking lot, walking past his truck and down to the fishing shacks by the water. Sunset was earlier every night now. Out in the harbor he could hear the gentle lapping of water against the invisible hulls of moored boats. He watched the darkness and listened. The dark seemed complete and indifferent. It was better than nothing at all.

SEAN DECIDED ON a gun. He had the perfect gun in mind.

He went home after eight o'clock, when he was sure his mother would have left for her bridge game. His father kept his guns—three pistols, two rifles, and a shotgun—in a cabinet in the bedroom, but they were registered and the reinforced oak door was locked. Instead, Sean went to the shelves above the workbench in the basement, where there were several toolboxes, each marked with a piece of tape: *saw, saws-all, router, drill #1, drill #2.* They were all metal boxes except for the one wooden box, marked *saw.* He set it on the workbench and opened the lid. Years ago his mother had mistakenly backed her car over the original box—she had a long history of crushing things with the car—and his father had built this wooden box as a replacement. By chance Sean had discovered its other purpose.

He removed the Milwaukee circular saw, which fit into a false plywood floor with a wide slot for the blade. Then he put his hand down through the slot and pulled the plywood up out of the box. A handgun tucked in a white athletic sock lay in the bottom of the box. It was his father's throw-down, a Smith & Wesson 9mm. It was loaded. It was unregistered. He had no idea where his father got the gun, but he was certain it wasn't traceable. For years he knew that his father had kept it hidden in his patrol car. The logic was that as long as it was there, it wouldn't be necessary. His father had never needed to use it.

Sean put the gun in the pocket of his sweatshirt, which more than counterbalanced the pint of Scotch in the other pocket, and he went out to his truck. In the cab he reached into the pouch on the sun visor and removed the matchbook he had taken from the table in the bar. The cover read:

THE   NORTHERN   LIGHTS
MOTEL   &   EFFICIENCY   APARTMENTS
STEELHEAD   BAY,   ROUTE   28
DAILY - WEEKLY - MONTHLY   RATES

As he pulled out of the driveway, he wondered whether his father was paying by the week or the month.

The motel was almost to Marquette. Sean drove by the entrance and parked in the rest stop about a hundred yards down the road. He walked the beach back to the motel, the only cluster of lights on the dark road. A steady breeze came off Lake Superior and occasionally a wave would crack and thud, sending a little vibration through the sand. There were only a few vehicles parked in the back lot: several cars, pickups, and semis. It was the kind of place where construction crews holed up while on a job. His father's van was at the far end.

Sean kept to the dark beach along the edge of the parking lot until he stepped up onto the asphalt and stood near the back of the van.

Through a sliding glass door he could see the room, which had imitation-pine paneling and a kitchenette. The television was on, but it was angled toward the double bed, so he couldn't see the screen. Sean pulled the bottle of Scotch from the pocket of his sweatshirt and took a drink. He didn't like the idea of waiting, but he knew if he left, he might not come back.

He told himself it had to be now.

This had to be first and it had to be now.

He saw something move down by the water. After a moment he could see that it was a woman, walking out of the lake naked. She leaned over, picked up a bathrobe, and pulled it on. Then she lit a cigarette and walked up the beach toward him.

"He's not here," Mary Threefoot said.

"Oh."

It was his father's terry-cloth bathrobe and the sash was tied loosely, so that he could see an ample portion of her breasts sway with each step. She stopped and raised her head toward the sky. "Since the rain passed it's cleared. Stand back there and you can see the Milky Way." Sean looked up, too, but he couldn't see the sky because of the spotlight at the back of the lot. "Here." Her hand took hold of his forearm and gently she pulled him around the corner of the building. There was grass underfoot and it was very dark. Overhead was a wash of stars. "See?" she said. "That haze, it's all stars."

It was too dark to see her face clearly. "Where is he?"

She walked away from him and sat down on the grass, cross-legged. "Why?"

For a moment he was angry. He wanted to tell her it was none of her business. But then he walked over to her. "When's he coming back?"

"Who knows? He only left a little while ago. But then maybe he isn't planning on coming back at all."

"He made plans for years," Sean said. "Too many. This afternoon I got the sense that he's quit making plans."

"He learned that from me." She drew on her cigarette, the ash glowing. "Why don't you sit? You can see them better."

He sat on the grass, which was still damp after the rain.

She leaned toward him, an arm extended, and said, "Whatcha got there, huh?" Her hand felt his sweatshirt and slipped inside the pocket holding the pint of Scotch. She laughed as she removed the bottle. "Ah, you brought the firewater." She unscrewed the cap, took a drink, then held the bottle out to him.

His eyes had adjusted to the dark and he could see her better now. She looked younger than at the bar. He couldn't see the pockmarks, and her cheekbones were wide and high beneath large, sad eyes. Her voice was pleasantly reedy. He took the bottle and tipped it up to his mouth.

"Standing there by his van, you looked like you had a lot on your mind," she said.

"If his van's here, how did he—"

"He took my car," she said. "He does that sometimes. I didn't understand at first but then I figured it out. When he wants to go to Whitefish Harbor, he uses my car so he won't be recognized."

"What's he do?"

"Sneaks around without being noticed? My guess is he spies on your mother." She crushed her cigarette out in the grass and flicked it into the darkness. "But I think that tonight he might have gone to meet her."

"Who? My mother?"

"Maybe he has another girlfriend?" Mary laughed as she took the bottle back from him. "Yes, your mother." She said this as though it was obvious. "I got out of the shower and he had just hung up the phone. He said he had to see someone, and he took my keys and left."

"He was drunk."

"Isn't everyone?"

"My mother's at her bridge game."

Mary shrugged and took a drink. Handing the bottle back, she said, "Maybe."

"How old are you?" he asked.

"I'd say about halfway between you and your father. It surprise you, me and him?"

"I just don't think of him as a man with . . . with a girlfriend."

She laughed again. "Well, you are his son but you'll get over it. You want to know how often we have sex, that it? Not very. Not often at all. He just likes the company while he drinks. And of course I like that he buys the drinks."

"You're afraid he'll go back to my mother."

"Afraid? Why would I be afraid of the inevitable?"

"My mother said she never wants to see him in the house again."

"We *all* talk a good game. What are you afraid of, Sean?"

She unfolded her legs and lay back on the grass, her hands clasped behind her head. The bathrobe had opened, exposing her left breast, but she didn't seem to notice or care.

Sean realized the bottle was in his hand and he took a long pull. "I am not afraid."

"I see. But tell me, why'd you come here?"

"I made up my mind."

"Good for you."

He put the bottle in her hands. Her fingers held his for a moment, then she let go.

"And I bet I know what you decided," she said.

"You do?"

"I could tell this afternoon at the bar."

"How?"

"It was in your eyes as you left, when you lit my cigarette."

"What was?"

Her hand came up and touched his face. "Whatever it is that makes a son angry at his father. What were you going to do if he was here, kill him?"

He didn't answer.

"Poor dear," she whispered. She lowered her hand and took the bottle from him and drank. "I suppose killing him would prove something." Her voice was playful, teasing, but there was no ridicule in it. "Of course, if you really did it, your father would never understand, would he? He'd never know what it meant. Because he'd be dead. Ha!"

"But I would."

"And that's what's important, right?"

After a moment, he said, "That's what's important."

"But would it be enough, Sean?"

"Maybe. And there'd be others who knew—who it mattered to."

She thought about this for a moment, then said seriously, "It must be nice to have what you do matter to other people."

"Just certain people."

"I see." She offered him the bottle. "Last taste."

"You can finish it," he said.

"No, you."

He shook his head.

"All right," she said as she poured the rest of the Scotch out on the ground. "This is for the earth. For all of our ancestors." She flung the bottle out into the dark. They heard it land in the grass. "What did you and your father talk about in the bar this afternoon?"

"He gave me advice."

"Was it good?"

"He said don't do anything."

"He's a wiser man than I thought."

She got to her knees unsteadily, and she placed a hand on his shoulder as she rose to her feet. "He said you had a problem." She laughed briefly. "Which of course means a girl." She began walking back toward the building and Sean followed. "After you left the bar he said you had a problem and he'd take care of it."

"He did?"

"Which I guess is why he advised you not to do anything. Hombre, I think you're both in a heap of shit, and have been for a long time. Neither of you can see the solution, even if it's right there before your eyes."

"You're probably right."

"Probably? Ha!"

They reached the sliding glass door of the efficiency apartment. She turned and leaned against him, her head on his shoulder. Her hair smelled of the lake. He slid back the door and with his arm around her shoulder guided her into the room. The television was on but the sound was muted.

"But I know what he's going to take care of," Sean said.

"The girl?"

"It sure isn't my mother."

Mary seemed perplexed as she stared up at him. "Listen to me, Sean. You don't have to go. You don't have to go there—wherever you think you're headed. You won't see the stars from there, you won't be satisfied, no matter what happens, no matter what you do." She stepped away from him and lay down on the bed. Her hands untied the bathrobe and drew it open. The blue light from the television flickered over her breasts, hips, the large triangle of hair. "Your father was right," she whispered. "You don't have to do anything."

"I'm afraid I don't have any choice."

"But you do." Her voice was resigned. "You really do." She closed her eyes and shook her head. "And you told me you weren't afraid."

Sean went out the door and walked back down to the beach.

26

PEARLY LAY ON HIS cot in the dark. He had set it up in what would be the living room of the other apartment on the first floor so he would be right across the hall from Hannah and Martin. The problem was he couldn't sleep, which he attributed to being sober.

Sometime after midnight, he got up and went quietly out the front door and locked it behind him. He walked down the driveway to the backyard. The doors and windows were all locked, but he was glad to be doing something, even if it was just walking around the house.

First Pearly heard the sound of branches breaking in the woods to his right. The man who stepped out into the yard moved something like Sean, but it was too dark to be certain. One thing was certain: He was drunk. He angled toward the back of the house. Pearly followed quietly, but not quietly enough, because when he reached the patio, the man turned around and Pearly stood still.

It was not Sean.

"Frank?" he said.

Frank Colby raised his arm and Pearly could see that he was holding a gun. "Frank, it's just me, Pearly. What's going on? Out here kind of late."

"I am taking care of it." Frank's arm began to sink, but then he straightened up and took careful aim. "Told him to do nothing. So I'm going to take care of it. Let it be on my head."

"Well, if he's doing nothing, then everybody's happy."

"That boy would screw up anything."

"What exactly is on your mind, Frank?"

"You shouldn't be here."

"I expected you. Not you, but the idea, if you catch my drift."

"The idea."

"I thought we'd discuss it, you know?"

"Ideas. We're way beyond that now."

"You sure, Frank?"

"Yeah, I think we're moving on to execution. Execution of the idea." Frank went up the back stoop and opened the screen door, but the inside door was locked. Turning, he said, "You got a key, right?" When Pearly hesitated, he said impatiently, "Am I going to have to shoot you for the damn key?"

"I don't have a key to the back door," Pearly said.

"Okay, then."

Frank came down off the stoop and waved his gun, indicating that he wanted Pearly to lead him around to the front of the house. They walked up the driveway and climbed the brick steps to the front door, which was wide open. Pearly could have sworn he had locked the door when he went out, but now he wasn't so certain. The front hall was dark.

"You want me to turn a light on for you, Frank?"

This seemed to perturb Colby, but after a moment he said, "Yeah. And don't fuck around. Just show me where they are."

"Right." Pearly switched on the light and tried the knob of the door to Martin and Hannah's apartment, which, to his surprise, opened. He was certain now that Hannah and Martin had heard them talking in the backyard. Maybe they left the house. He just wasn't sure.

He pushed the door open and led Frank into the living room, which was only lit by the light coming from the hall. Without asking, Pearly turned on a lamp next to the couch. Frank walked through the living room to the kitchen and back again. "Somehow I didn't think she'd be so tidy," he said with genuine surprise.

"What you expect?" Pearly asked.

"Sean's a pig. Most of them are at that age."

"You want my opinion, Frank?"

"No." But Frank looked at him anyway.

"You misjudged Hannah from the start. Sean would have been better off if the two of them hadn't been yanked apart. They should have been given a chance to work it out. My guess is some of Hannah's tidy would have rubbed off on Sean's pig."

"That so?"

"Yeah, and now Sean's been out of control for a long time."

Frank didn't deny it. In fact, he nodded his head slightly. It was clear with the lights on that he'd been drinking for a long time. The skin around his eyes was dark and had lost its elasticity. Even his stubbled jaw, which for years had been a firm complement to his pressed uniform, was pale and fleshy.

"I happen to know that there's some good, strong coffee already made in the kitchen," Pearly said. "How 'bout if I heat it up?"

Frank became more alert, though the gun now hung at his side. "How 'bout if you show me what's down this hall?"

"All right, Frank." Pearly went down the hall and stopped at the first door. "Bedroom," he said. He reached in and turned on the wall switch. The bedsheets looked as if they had been thrown aside in haste.

He started down the hall, but Frank said, "Wait a sec." He went into the bedroom. The closet door was ajar and he opened it with his free hand. There was nothing but clothing on hangers, boxes stacked up on the shelf. Turning, he said, "What else?"

"Just the bathroom, down here."

Pearly led him to the end of the hall and switched on the light in the bathroom, which was empty. Without being asked, Pearly pulled back the shower curtain. "You always want to check the tub."

"I said don't fuck with me."

"Frank, you got to evaluate this thing. They're gone. They heard us coming and they did the sensible thing and ran."

Frank raised his head and gazed at the ceiling. "It's a big house."

"They're gone, don't you get it? You're not going to solve anything this way," Pearly said. "They're gone and you need to sober up. You *know* I know what I'm talking about. Look, if you don't want coffee, let me drive you down to the Hiawatha. Get some eggs into you. Protein always helps."

"Who said anything about solving anything?" Frank said. He turned on the cold-water spigot, leaned over, and cupping his hand beneath the faucet, drank water from his palm. Straightening up, his chin dripping, he said, "Besides, I got you, don't I?"

HANNAH HADN'T RUN much since her abortion and soon her ribs ached. So she slowed to a fast walk, which she could maintain. The next house was at least a half-mile up the road, a family named Cryzinski, but there was no one home. She had pounded on the front door, but the house—one of those prefabs that were delivered in halves—remained dark and silent. The only vehicle in the yard was their flatbed truck, which had *Cryzinski Well and Septic Service* written on the doors. So she continued up Shore Road, where the next house was perhaps another quarter of a mile away.

It had happened so quickly, and now she was sorry and quite panicky about running away from the house. But Martin had insisted. Something had changed in him just the past two days. He was clearer, and at times he was more like his old self. When she was awakened by voices in the backyard, Martin was already getting out of bed. She followed him into the living room, where they heard someone try the back doorknob. Then a voice—she thought it might be Frank Colby's but she wasn't sure—said, "Am I going to have to shoot you for the damn key?"

Martin pushed her with both hands, indicating that he wanted her to go out into the front hall. She resisted at first—she was only in sweatpants and T-shirt, with nothing on her feet—but he was very insistent. When they were in the hall, he whispered, "You go," and she said, "Go? Go *where*?" They argued briefly. He wanted her to run up the road to the next house and call the police. When she started to say that that wouldn't do a lot of good, he pushed her again, once toward the front door, which he opened, then again until she was standing on the stoop. He whispered, "Don't worry, I'll be all right. You just got to get somebody. Anybody." When she heard footsteps coming down the driveway, she jumped off the front steps and ran.

It was hard walking barefoot on the pavement. Pebbles became embedded in the soles of her feet, and she'd have to pause to brush them off with the palm of her hand. She was doing this, awkwardly bending over and slapping at her foot, when a pair of headlights came around the bend. She looked up into the glare as the vehicle slowed down and pulled over in front of her. Raising a hand to shield her eyes, she saw a man get out of a truck.

"Well, here we are," Sean said.

She stood upright. He remained beside the car, difficult for her to see. Then she turned and ran, her feet slapping on the pavement. He called to her again and then began to run after her. Her side ached but her wind was good. He wasn't gaining on her—it sounded as though he was favoring one leg slightly.

She saw an opening in the trees to her right, one of the many two-tracks that laced the woods. There was no time to consider which was best, the road or the woods, so she turned up into the two-track, where at least she was out of the glare of the truck's headlights. She could barely see the track she was on, and then the faint, pale line ahead curved and disappeared. She slowed down, but it was too late as her legs crashed through branches, and then her forehead hit something hard.

MARTIN COULD HEAR *them downstairs. Pearly was talking a lot, as though he was trying to keep Martin informed of their movements. Frank Colby—whom Martin remembered was Sean's father and on the police force—was with him. At first Martin wondered if he had come looking for his son. He apparently had a gun, and he was obviously pissed off and drunk.*

They were coming up the stairs. Pearly had tried to convince Frank that there was no point in searching the rest of the house, but Frank wasn't buying it. Standing in the dark stairwell on the third floor, Martin leaned out over the banister and looked down at the two men as they climbed to the second floor. Frank raised his head and Martin pulled back into the dark. When they reached the second floor, Pearly switched on the hall light, and Martin listened to them walk through the rooms.

He went down the hall toward the back of the house. The only light came up from the second floor. In the shadows he found the sconce on the wall and unscrewed the lightbulb. Entering the room on his right, he knew there was only one bare bulb there, hanging by the wire from the middle of the ceiling, and he removed that one too. He stood still and he could hear that they were directly below him. By the groan of dry hinges, it was clear that Frank insisted on opening every door. Martin moved quietly through the other rooms on the third floor, removing lightbulbs as he went, cradling five in his arms like eggs. Setting them on a windowsill, he nearly dropped one. Their footsteps came into the second-floor hall and began to climb the stairs.

He looked across the room and saw Pearly's tools in the corner. Walking carefully, he went and knelt down in front of the boxes and buckets.

RUNNING, Sean's feet still hurt and he couldn't catch up to Hannah. His shadow, cast by the lights of the truck, was long, and up ahead she was difficult to see—only her T-shirt seemed a faint smudge against the dark trees, and then it disappeared.

He knew there was a two-track nearby, and when he reached it he stopped and listened. All he could hear was his own breathing and the wind rustling the treetops. He could see the faint parallel tracks and he began following them into the woods, where it was even darker than out on the road.

He'd walked perhaps thirty yards—it was getting more and more difficult to see the two-track—when he paused and looked up. The gap in the trees was filled with stars. He tried to remember what Mary had said about the stars, about not being able to see them where he was going. He saw again the blue television light flickering over her skin. He wondered why he left her, her invitation. Something extraordinary seemed to have happened back there and he had to admit that it frightened him. And she had said something about that, too, fear, which he couldn't remember. Maybe he was trying to deny that anything had happened at all. The whole thing seemed so bizarre, sitting on the damp grass beneath the stars, sharing the bottle of Scotch with her, the way her breasts seemed to emerge from his father's bathrobe as though beckoning to him. As he drove back to Whitefish Harbor, his sense of purpose had become more and more confused, uncertain. Something had been jarred loose.

To his left he heard movement in the bushes, followed by a groan. He could barely make out the T-shirt. After wading through branches, he knelt down on one knee. Hannah was lying next to a tree trunk. When she saw him, she tried to get up, pleading, *"Leave me alone! Don't touch me!"*

He caught her arms and said calmly, "Take it easy." Though he held her tightly, she began to relax. He helped her sit up. "I guess you ran into that tree."

It was too dark to see if she was cut, but he carefully touched her forehead and scalp with his fingers. Her skin was rough, as though scraped, and he could feel what he thought were bits of bark in her hair. "You got a good whack on the head, but no blood," he said. "Think you can stand up?"

Slowly, she got to her feet. He could feel the tension in her arms, but she didn't actually resist his help. They pushed through the brush until they were out in the two-track.

"What are you doing here?" She sounded sleepy.

"That's a good question," he said. With one hand on her elbow now, he guided her along the path toward the road. "I'm looking for my father."

"He's at the house." She became more alert and insisted on walking without his help. "He's drunk," she said, "and he's got a gun."

"I know," he said.

"You do?"

They reached the road and stopped. "Listen," he said. "Earlier tonight I thought I was ready to kill people. Start with him, and see who else I could take down. Maybe myself, too. I was that bad. But now it's . . ." He paused. "Now I don't know. Where is he?"

"He's back there at the house with Pearly and Martin. I was going for help."

"And you found me." Sean laughed. The headlights were at least fifty yards away, but he could see her face, her stunned eyes. The bruise on her forehead had already begun to swell up. "Come on," he said. "Unless you want to run back there barefoot." He turned but she didn't move. "All right, fine." He began to walk toward the truck. After a few steps he heard her feet slap the pavement as she came up beside him.

PEARLY THOUGHT HIS MIND was playing tricks on him. When they reached the top of the stairs, he had switched on the third-floor light, but nothing happened—they were still in near darkness. First the front door, now the hall light. He was sure the light had worked that afternoon.

"Awful dark up here, Frank."

"Keep going."

Pearly went into the first room on his left, felt along the wall until his hand found the light switch—but it remained dark. He knew now.

"Somebody messing around here." Frank paused for a moment,

long enough that he might have been having some doubt. But then he said, "Let's go through there. What's that?"

"Kitchen."

"Okay."

Pearly went through the door, found the wall plate, but again no light came on. Frank placed one hand on the counter and walked down past the stove to the refrigerator. "All new," he said. "Let's see here." He yanked open the refrigerator door and the interior light came on. Its harsh white light illuminated an oblong of the floor in the living room. Frank said, "In there."

Pearly walked into the room and he saw them on the windowsill, the light gleaming off their rounded surfaces. They looked like large pearls. Frank saw them, too. He went over and picked up one of the bulbs.

"All right, put it in and let's see what we got here. You know we're not alone."

Pearly took the bulb, felt around in the air in the center of the room for the electrical wire, but then he heard feet, the scuffling of shoes. Frank's gun fired, the flash from the barrel imposing a silhouette image on Pearly's vision, two men entwined. They slammed against the wall, and then there was one long, painful gasp.

There was stillness and only the sound of their breathing. Pearly found the electrical socket above his head, screwed the bulb in, then walked over to the door to the kitchen and felt around for the light switch.

SEAN TURNED OFF his truck and saw a light come on in the third floor of the house. Hannah got out, ran up to the front door and into the hall. Sean went after her, and as she reached the staircase, he caught her by the elbow. "Why don't you just wait down here?"

"What are you going to do?"

"I really don't know anymore," he said. "Except I'm going up there." Sean put his other hand into the pocket in his sweatshirt and took out the 9mm Smith & Wesson. "See, he's not the only one who came prepared."

She leaned back against the banister as he passed, and when he was almost to the landing, she said, "I should call for help."

On the landing he paused and smiled down at her. "Good. You call Buzz Gagnon. He'd enjoy this."

Sean continued up the stairs to the second floor, which was dark, but as he turned up the flight to the third floor, each step took him into the light, which angled through a doorway above him. He could hear a voice—it was his father whispering.

He reached the top floor and entered a room where a bare light-bulb swung on a cord from the middle of the ceiling. Pearly stood above Sean's father, who was sitting on the floor, his back against the wall. Martin knelt in the corner near several toolboxes. Their shadows swayed beneath them, making the room pitch and yaw as though they were in a rocking boat. At first Sean was baffled by the shadow in the center of the floor—it wasn't attached to any of them, and it spread slowly, running along the seams between boards, filling knots and nail holes.

"He's bleeding bad," Pearly said.

"Who did it?" Sean asked.

Martin tried to get up but remained on one knee. He didn't look afraid, but resigned. "I didn't know it was him. We were expecting you."

"And now I'm here." Sean realized that Martin was holding his leg with one hand and that he had a utility knife in the other. "You shot?"

"Strangest thing," Martin said, his voice oddly high and curious now, as he slit his pajama pants open, from the knee down. Peeling back the fabric, he exposed a long splinter of wood that had been driven at an angle clean through his calf. There was hardly any blood, just a trickle that ran down over his heel.

Pearly said, "The bullet must've broken off a piece of the floorboard. I don't know if pulling it out will make it better or worse." As Pearly spoke, the shadow of his nose swung like a pendulum over his mouth. "The bleeding could get worse."

"Hannah's calling the station," Sean said. He put his gun in the pocket of his sweatshirt and walked toward his father, but he avoided stepping in the blood. He could see that it was coming from beneath his father's hand, which he held over his left side. A curved wood handle protruded from his fingers. "What is that?"

"Keyhole saw," Pearly said. "The kind used for cutting holes in Sheetrock. Sharp point, rough teeth. Might do more damage to pull it out."

"You're not supposed to be here," his father said hoarsely.

"More advice?" Sean said.

"I was taking care of this."

"You did that all right."

"I'll finish it." His father winced as he leaned over and extended his right arm out toward his gun, the .357 revolver he'd used on duty for years, which lay on the floor.

Pearly kicked the gun across the floor and it hit the baseboard.

Looking up at Sean, his father whispered, "I said I'll take care of it."

"You always have," Sean said. "I guess we think too much alike."

Pearly nodded. "You could see that."

"Could you?" Sean said. "And I always thought we were, I don't know, so different."

"Right." Pearly went over to Martin and helped him lie down on his side, arranging his legs so the splinter wouldn't touch anything. "All we got to do now," he said, "is wait till Buzz comes."

"We could." Sean squatted down in front of his father and again said, "We could."

"The hell," his father said.

"Maybe we've done enough?"

His father turned his head away. "You'll never understand."

"But I do," Sean said. "You should have listened to Mary. She gave you good advice. She gave me good advice."

"What advice did she give you?"

"Do nothing," Sean said.

"How would you know about her advice?"

"How do you think I knew you were here? Listen, you can't go back there to Northern Lights, and you sure as hell can't go to Mom. Your problem is where you going to be?"

"*My* problem?"

"Maybe you should find your own place."

"Now you're giving *me* advice."

"Let's call it an opinion."

Something changed in his father's eyes and Sean realized he was being shut out.

There were footsteps on the stairs and Sean knelt on the floor and turned around.

ALL FOUR MEN looked at Hannah when she entered the room. For years men had looked at her, but never like this. The bare light hanging in the middle of the room was harsh, forcing her to squint. She saw the blood in the middle of the floor, which was coming from a wound in Frank Colby's side. In the corner Martin was lying on his side, in pain. There appeared to be a piece of wood sticking out of his calf.

Pearly started across the room. "It's not as bad as it looks," he said to her.

She said, "Buzz Gagnon is on his way." She was surprised by the calm neutrality of her voice, as though she were making a public announcement, one which would not favor anyone in particular.

Sean knelt in front of his father, whose face was as white as the freshly painted wall behind his head. His stare was hard enough to make Hannah take an involuntary step back into the doorway. She had seen that stare the night Frank and June Colby came to her mother's house. He wrote out a check at the kitchen table, tore it off—the sound of the paper separating along the perforation seeming as cruel and final as the procedure the money was intended to pay for—and then he gazed up at Hannah, who was standing behind her mother's chair. Suddenly she turned and walked out of the kitchen, through the living room, and down to her bedroom, where she slammed the door shut. But now, with her hands clenching both doorjambs, Hannah refused to retreat any further, and she stared back into Frank Colby's hatred until he lowered his eyes.

Everything was sideways.

Lying on his side, Martin's view of Hannah was partially blocked by Pearly as he walked toward her.

Martin watched Frank Colby lower his head and take his hand off the wound in his side. There was a moment, a pause, when Colby seemed to make a decision. Then he reached out toward his son and yanked something from the pocket of his sweatshirt, causing Sean to lose his balance and fall forward so that he knelt with his hands in the pool of blood.

Frank Colby aimed a gun—another gun—at Hannah.

She didn't move but stared defiantly across the room.

Pearly took another step, then turned. "Frank," he said. His voice was not unfriendly, perhaps a little disappointed. "Come on, Frank."

"Step out of my way," Frank Colby said.

"Frank," Pearly said. Behind him, Hannah remained in the doorway.

"Last time," Frank said.

"No, Frank."

Martin tried to get up, but the splinter through his calf caused pain to surge up his leg into his haunch. He rolled onto his back and closed his eyes just as a shot was fired. Hannah yelled, and when Martin opened his eyes, Pearly was sprawled on the floor at her feet. His arms and legs strained as though he was trying to climb the floor, then he simply stopped moving.

Hannah crouched over him, screaming. Her arms stretched out to

Pearly, but it was as though she couldn't quite reach him. Her hands came within inches of his shoulder, his head, his face, but she couldn't actually touch him.

SEAN WAS ON his hands and knees. Blood covered his hands. He turned around and sat back on his haunches, rubbing his palms on the front of his jeans. His father still held the gun, both arms extended, but he was weakening and his hands shook. He was trying to aim at Hannah, but as Martin began to crawl across the floor toward Pearly, he turned the gun on him.

"Enough," Sean whispered.

His father seemed to be having trouble seeing. "It's never enough."

"Dad." Then Sean said louder, "Frank, let it go."

His father was suddenly alert and genuinely curious, and with effort he aimed the gun at Sean's chest. "Why?" he asked.

Sean stopped wiping his hands on his thighs. "Listen to me. This afternoon you said something about what you know, what you can say to yourself. That's what's most important. You can say *enough.*"

Behind him Hannah was moaning as she knelt over Pearly's body, and Martin was gasping as he tried to crawl across the floor. Though the gun was still pointed at Sean, he felt oddly cleansed. What seemed so urgent and important wasn't anymore. He was calm, as though this weren't happening. His father stared hard at him, confused, perhaps threatened. Finally, Sean made his own decision and slowly turned his head away.

He waited and he kept telling himself it was all right. Or perhaps in the confusion and noise he was saying it—he wasn't sure. When the second shot was fired, it sounded different, muted. Sean looked back at his father, who was slumped forward now, blood and bone and hair coating the wall above his head.

27

NOTHING LIKE THIS had ever happened before in Whitefish Harbor. Suicides, occasionally. But murder-suicides were something that occurred out there—or, to be more accurate, down there, in the world below the Mackinac Bridge. For several days the town was taken by a kind of possession. Newspaper reporters came from Detroit, Chicago, and Milwaukee, and more than one TV camera crew was seen filming a news segment with the harbor or Ottawa Street as a backdrop. Business was good at the Hiawatha Diner.

St. Luke's Episcopal Church was packed for Frank Colby's funeral. Hannah sat in the last pew with her mother. People spoke about Frank's devotion to his family, to serving the community, to his military service. The actual events surrounding his death were never referred to directly, as though there was no need to name the vile disease that had needlessly taken another victim. It could have been the funeral for anyone but the man who had died. To acknowledge what had happened to Frank Colby might almost suggest that there was some flaw in the fabric of the town itself. No one spoke to Hannah before, during, or after the service. Her mother had said she didn't have to attend, but Hannah was insistent. To not go would have been worse, far worse.

———

THERE WAS NO memorial service for Pearly. No church could claim him. Instead, the day after Frank Colby's funeral, about a hundred people gathered on the beach while Peter DeJohn rowed out into the harbor and poured the bag of ashes into Lake Superior. Afterward they walked up to the Portage.

Around two in the morning, Peter and Michael DeJohn went down to their fishing boat, the *Elizabeth Ann,* accompanied by Hannah, Martin, Sally, and her son, Jason. They cruised into Petit Marais and dropped anchor about fifty yards off a small wooded point. Peter donned his wet suit and scuba gear and went into the water with a flashlight. He found the mast exactly where they had left it on the silt bottom in 1975, perfectly preserved in twenty feet of cold water. He fastened the winch hook and Michael raised the mast up to the boat.

The following morning when the first cars started to pass through the village, some slowed down and others even stopped in front of the town hall. Somehow, overnight, the mast had been erected in the flagpole stand, which is really a measure of how quiet it can get in Whitefish Harbor. Carved into the base of the mast was *Pearly 1952–1996.*

HANNAH COULDN'T GET Pearly out of her mind. Several times she went into the Portage. She sat at the end of the bar where she could look at the photograph of Pearly that had been in the *Herald* in the early seventies. Even though it was before she was born, she knew—everybody knew—about how he had put the walleye on Judge Anderson's porch. In the photo Pearly was in his twenties. His hair was darker, longer, thicker, and his cheeks hadn't yet collapsed. He was fiercely handsome and the look in his eye suggested that he could take on anything that came at him.

The Pearly she knew was more chiseled away, more tempered. He possessed a dogged restraint and was mildly disappointed in everything. Except her. When she looked into his eyes, when she spoke to him, he was always right there. The last morning when they sat together at the kitchen table with the rain outside the window, he had said she and Martin were the only family he had, but she understood that he was avoiding the truth, that he loved her both like a lover and a daughter. She felt it when he put his arms around her, his hands gentle on her hips. She couldn't help but kiss him on the mouth that one time. It was for both of them. She would keep it for the rest of her life.

One afternoon she found Martin sitting in the Datsun parked in the driveway. His aunt Jane had called from Florida several times. She said that Pearly's house had been sold, but Martin should keep his truck and tools.

Hannah got in the passenger side. Martin's hands gripped the steering wheel.

"You like the truck?" she said.

"What do you think we should do with it?" He stared out the windshield as though he was pretending to drive. He hadn't driven since being released from the hospital.

"You know what Pearly would say—keep the truck or sell it. But keep the tools. You'll need them for the house."

"Nobody'd buy this truck," he said.

"Even Arnie couldn't sell it."

After a moment, they both laughed.

"I say we keep the truck." Martin seemed pleased at his own decisiveness. "We can sell my car instead—but we shouldn't keep the money. We could donate the money to something in Pearly's name."

"Okay," she said. "What could we donate it to?"

"Something to do with keeping the lake clean."

"Pearly would like that."

"See what people think about that. I know how they look at you. They think we're both somehow responsible, don't they? But it doesn't matter." He took his right hand off the steering wheel and laid it along the back of the seat.

"Let them think what they want." Hannah slid over and leaned against him.

"Pearly didn't give a shit what they thought. Why should we? You know, he's still here. I believe that. This is really his house, and now it's our job to take care of it."

"I believe that, too."

"What do you say when somebody dies?" he asked. "When somebody decides to die for someone else? Someone they love?"

"I don't think you need to say much. You go on living."

"It's a gift," he said. "You treat it as a gift."

Hannah raised her hand and touched his cheek. "Do you remember the day we met, here in this house?"

He looked her right in the eye and shook his head. "What did we talk about?"

"Dead cats."

"Dead cats?"

"And I was in love with you before you even got out the back door."

"I know what people think, I know what they say about me—I see it in their eyes. The fact is I can't remember not being in love with you."

She reached for the door handle. "Now come into the house with me."

THE SECOND TIME Buzz Gagnon talked with Sean was more informal. There were no state detectives present. It was mid-afternoon and he had stopped out at the house, ostensibly to pay his respects to June. She sat at the kitchen table with her drink and cigarettes, and she wouldn't look directly at either of them. After a few awkward minutes, Buzz asked Sean if he could see where his father had kept the unregistered gun.

Sean led the chief to the workbench in the basement.

Buzz said, "I just want to go over it again, why there were two guns there."

"Sure." Sean put the wooden box on the workbench, lifted out the Milwaukee circular saw, and removed the slotted plywood floor. "Dad kept the throw-down in here, when he didn't have it with him in his cruiser."

"He's got the gun cabinet in the house," Buzz said. "You couldn't take any of those because it was locked?"

"Right."

They went outside and walked around to the garage. Since yesterday, when the house had been full of friends and relatives, Sean had been looking for something to do, something that, as he told his mother, would make him useful. Before Buzz arrived, he had been cleaning out the garage, and there were three bulging plastic bags full of refuse piled out in the driveway.

"So you saw your father that afternoon and somehow you just knew he was going to go to Martin's house that night—with his gun, his registered gun." Buzz squinted at the bags as though he could see their contents. "And then you followed him over there with the unregistered gun he kept in that box—the one he used on Pearly and himself."

"That's about it."

"He must have said something at the bar, something that revealed his intentions."

"He had been drunk for a while," Sean said. "I knew what was on his mind."

"What about the woman?"

"What woman?"

"The Indian that was in the bar." Buzz seemed rather pleased with himself. "I talked to Hattie, who runs the place, and she said he had an Indian with him."

"When I arrived, she went outside."

"What's her name?"

"I don't know."

"You didn't mention her when you talked to me and the staties."

"No, I didn't," Sean said. "My mother—I didn't want to bring that up."

"I see." Buzz folded his arms over his stomach. "So you had a hunch that your father was going over to Martin's armed, you got this gun here, and went over to protect Martin and your old girlfriend."

"I had an idea," Sean said. "I had no clear intentions."

"You think you might have to shoot your father?"

Sean didn't answer.

"Take him down like a rabid dog?"

"I told you, I just had an idea. I thought it would be better to be armed."

"Something's missing here, Sean. You know it and I know it." He dug his car keys out of his front pocket. "But the staties seem satisfied with it. They kept saying how it could have been worse. A situation like that, more people often get shot. A man decides to take himself out these days, he often takes everyone else in sight with him." Buzz shook his head. "Didn't used to be that way. That was someone who's crazy. But now—now it can be your neighbor, or someone you worked with for more than twenty years."

"I guess," Sean said. "In the land of the free, anybody can go postal."

Buzz walked down the driveway but stopped when he reached the garbage bags. "Funny you throwing this stuff out now."

"Something to do," Sean said. "You think there's clues in there, have a look."

Buzz pondered this long enough that Sean expected the chief to decide to load the bags into his cruiser. When he shifted his weight, Sean knew that he had decided to let it go.

"You know where your father was staying?" He glanced toward the house. "With this Indian?"

Sean just stared out at Buzz Gagnon.

"Place called the Northern Lights. But they don't know her name, either."

Sean looked down and saw a stiff paintbrush on the concrete floor, which must have fallen out of one of the bags. He picked it up and said, "So you haven't talked to her?"

"Can't find her."

Sean ran a finger along the bristles, which were hard as the wood handle. "Think she'd help?"

"Doubt it. They tend to come and go on you."

Gagnon walked down the driveway, passed Sean's father's van, his mother's car, his pickup truck, and got in the cruiser, which was parked at the curb. Sean didn't watch him leave, but went back into the garage, where it was cooler in the shade.

"EVENTUALLY YOU HAVE to accept that there aren't clear answers," Hannah's mother said. Suzanne had called and suggested they meet for breakfast at the Hiawatha Diner. The best way to get people to stop staring was to make yourself visible. She seemed relieved that Martin hadn't come with Hannah. "We could take him back to the doctor's, but they'll only order more tests."

"What are you trying to say, Mother?"

"I'm saying the doctors don't really know what's going on inside that boy's head and they may never know."

"He's doing better," Hannah said. She leaned forward slightly as if to meet her mother's skeptical gaze. "Sometimes he's still quiet and solitary, and I know when he's talking to himself he's talking to Pearly. But actually since this *thing* happened he's—I don't know if *better* is even the right word, but he's more himself. He's still not like he was before, but he's coping with it."

"You know, you don't have any real obligation here." Suzanne hesitated and ate some home fries. "It's not like you're married. It's . . . it's *your* life. He could go on like this for a long time. He may never be—"

"I under*stand* that," Hannah said. "You think I don't know what this means?"

"I don't think you know what the years can do to you."

"You're talking about *me.* You're talking about raising me, aren't you?"

"No, that's—it's different. You're my daughter. I love you, you know that. It's just that, that doing something like this on your own is going to take its toll."

"And if I don't? Then what?" Her mother didn't answer. "Then what happens to him? I'll tell you one thing, if it had been me—say, in an accident—I *know* he wouldn't walk away from me."

Her mother cut into one of her eggs over easy. Once they bled she never stopped. When she had sopped up the last of the yolk with her toast, she put her fork down. She'd come to some decision. "He's a good boy, he really is. All right, listen to me. You should expect it to go on like this. He's going to have his good days, and he's going to have days where it's difficult, for both of you." Hannah was surprised that her mother was close to crying. The only other time she'd heard such resignation in her voice was when she explained in medical terms what happened during an abortion. "I don't know what kind of a future that's going to be for you."

"I've been thinking about that," Hannah said. "I was talking to Arnie Frick at the station yesterday. He's going to start taking classes at Northern. Airplane maintenance. Maybe I could take some courses this fall. I could ride over with him."

"What would you study?"

"I was thinking nursing, starting winter term. If I can get in. I hear it's tough."

Suzanne looked away. After a moment Hannah offered her paper napkin.

WHEN THE PHONE rang now, Sean's mother seldom answered it. Sometimes Sean let it ring, but this time he picked up in the kitchen.

"I want to see you," Mary Threefoot said.

"Where?"

"That bar, the Twelve Point." She hung up.

"Who was that?" his mother asked from the living room.

"Some guy," Sean said.

"What?"

"Turn the TV down. It's a guy interested in buying the van."

His mother put the TV on mute. The silence was worse than the game shows. He stayed in the kitchen where he couldn't see her.

"We haven't told anyone we wanted to sell it," she said.

This was true. They'd only discussed putting an ad in the news-paper. "Arnie must have mentioned it to the guy." She didn't answer, and there was the sound of ice cubes rattling in her glass. She didn't know that he hadn't spoken to Arnie since moving back into the house. "I'm going to take it down to show it to the guy."

He heard his mother get up off the couch and walk across the car-pet until her shoes clicked on the linoleum floor in the kitchen. "When?" she asked.

He took the van keys off the hook by the garage door. She reached the counter where she kept the bourbon. He watched her pour the drink. Her hands seemed to have aged in days. "I'm going now," he said.

"You be back soon?"

"Sure."

"Well, on the way back, stop by the liquor store for me. You need money?"

"No." He went out the garage door.

He drove the van to Eben. Pulling in to the Twelve Point parking lot, he found Mary sitting in her car, a beat-up Chevrolet. He under-stood that she was reluctant to enter the bar by herself. They went inside and sat at the table by the window. There were only a few men in the place, and this time a heavy young woman with stringy blond hair was working the bar.

Sean ordered shots and beer while Mary lit a cigarette.

"The police were looking for you," he said.

"They're always looking for people like me." She waited until the girl set their drinks on the table and returned to the bar. "How was the funeral?" Before he could answer, she said, "I hope you're not disappointed that I didn't attend." Then she sort of laughed. "That would have been something, eh? I can see the headline in the paper: 'Indian Massacred at Funeral.' "

"Or," Sean said, " 'Indian Massacred by Women's Bridge Group.' "

They both laughed enough that the men at the bar looked to see what was going on. Out of disgust, they turned back to their drinks. It was the first time Sean had laughed since this had all started.

Mary put her hand on his knee under the table. "How you doing?"

He tipped his head. "You?"

She removed her hand and sat back. "I don't know."

"You look tired."

"I am." Mary drank her shot, then chased it with beer. "Mostly I've been thinking about things."

"What things?"

"Can you guess?" she asked.

"I'm not good at guessing."

"Try, Sean. Tell me what things you've been thinking about."

"Who says I've been thinking at all?"

"I know you have. Tell me." She smiled. "Honestly."

Out the window the sun was setting beyond the pine trees. It was a few days before Labor Day and the humid air made the sun deep red. It seemed to melt into the evergreens.

"Honestly, I've been thinking about you," he said. "About you lying there on that bed in the blue light from the TV. If I hadn't left, if I had done what you said—nothing—and stayed, none of this would have happened. Well, at least not the *way* it happened."

She wouldn't take her eyes off him. "What else?"

"And I've been thinking about leaving," he said.

After a moment she put her cigarette out in the tin ashtray. "Me, too," she said. "I've been thinking about leaving. Going over to Canada. In fact, that's why I called you."

"To say good-bye."

"To say I have lots of family in Ontario."

"Where?"

"From the Soo north to Wawa. And I see us both up there. That's what I think about." She exhaled slowly. "I'm leaving. Soon. Want to settle in before winter."

"I need some time."

"I know."

"How can I get in touch with you?"

She picked up the matchbook that lay on top of her pack of cigarettes and placed it next to his glass of beer. It was from the Northern Lights. He flipped it open and saw a phone number written on the inside.

"You think this is crazy?" she asked.

"Yes. But so what?"

Mary lit a cigarette and her eyes shone in the flame.

He walks until his leg tires and the ground seems to beckon to him. He has favorite places. One is along a deer path that's always strewn with fresh pellets. He follows the path up to a small knoll, where there are soft depressions in the grass. He lies down in the flattened tall grass and it doesn't feel like he has any bones left. He curls up and dozes but never really sleeps. He can smell the lake. What he likes is how sometimes things will just come to him. He talks to Pearly often, tells him things like how he once read that there is enough water in Lake Superior to cover North America, Central America, and South America with a foot of water. When he gets up off the ground, he walks with haste and purpose in broad shafts of light streaming down through the trees. The lake wind is at his back, pushing him gently.

IT WAS THE LAST WEEK of September, the foliage was at its peak, but it felt like they could get the first snow of the year. Hannah was sweeping the hall floor, working her way down toward the open front door. Now that tenants had moved into the second floor of the house, there was always something to do, something to clean. There was a retired couple interested in the third-floor apartment and they were coming to look at it this evening. Hannah had been worried that people wouldn't want to live on the top floor, but it didn't seem to matter once things had been cleaned up and repainted. People just had to see the house to realize it had a lot of history, a history long and deep enough that one incident, no matter how terrible, could not change the character of the place.

At the sound of an engine out in the street, she raised her head and watched Sean pull his truck up to the curb. He got out and walked into the front yard. It was the first time she'd seen him since his father's funeral. He was letting his hair grow out—it was about an inch long and spiky in places. The way the gray sweater hung from his shoulders, it appeared that he'd lost some weight, too.

"Wonder if I could talk to you," he said.

But something else had gone out of him. Seeing him didn't strike her with the jolt of fear she'd expected—dreaded, even—when she saw him again. She left the dustpan, which was largely full of Gracie's hairs, on the floor, then came out on the front steps and stood with the broom in her right hand. Her posture, she realized, probably appeared defensive, even militant. That was fine.

Yet he moved closer, stopping on the front walk a few feet from the brick steps. "I came to say good-bye." His voice was oddly formal and she understood that he was nervous.

"Where're you going?"

"Canada."

Hannah's mother said she had heard about Sean and the Indian woman his father had been going around with; Hannah thought it was just gossip, but now she realized it was true. "You're not going alone," she said.

His shoulders appeared to lose some of their tension and he shoved his hands deeper into the front pockets of his jeans. "I suppose everybody's heard about me and Mary," he said. "My mother wasn't happy about it, but you know, now that I've decided to go, I think she's okay with it. I think all of this is harder for her with me around."

Hannah was tempted to say something about her own mother, but that would be a kind of trade-off. Across the street the maples were red and yellow, incredibly bright against the overcast sky. "What about work?" she asked.

"Mary has a cousin who has a construction company. Says he'll take me on." His eyes scanned the front of the house. "It came out all right, this place. You got tenants now?"

"We'll be full up soon."

He nodded, looking for the next thing to say. "Saw Arnie last night."

"Did you?"

"Yeah, I couldn't leave that be, either. He says you've gone back to school, too. That sometimes you drive into Marquette with him."

"I'm going part-time for now."

"That's good," he said.

"I hope to get through winter semester, then I'll have to stop for a while."

Sean stared at her, but she wouldn't go any further. She could see that she didn't have to. "This time it's for real," he said. "Well, good luck with that." Then he tried to see beyond her into the front hall. "Don't suppose Martin's around."

She knew Martin was out in the woods or down on the beach. "No. The doctor said walking was the best thing for his leg."

Sean appeared relieved. "Will you tell him I came by?"

"I will."

Neither of them spoke for a while, and then Hannah realized that a few snowflakes had angled past her face.

"Here it comes," she said.

Sean raised his eyes to the sky. He put one foot up on the bottom step, but didn't try to come any closer. "I better be going."

He lowered his head and started to turn away, but then he extended his arm and took a light hold of her free hand. She didn't move. He was about to let go, when she turned her hand and allowed his fingers to embrace hers.

When he let go he didn't look at her before walking back to his truck. The snow was coming in now, large wet flakes that tapped on the leaves that already covered the front yard. Hannah stepped back up on the threshold where she was more protected from the damp wind. She watched the truck go around the bend and out of sight, knowing that the last thing he would see in his mirror was her standing in the doorway.